Shadow's EDGE

WHITE HAVEN HUNTERS BOOK TWO

TJ GREEN

Shadow's Edge
Mountolive Publishing
©2021 TJ Green
All rights reserved
ISBN 978-1-99-004722-0

Cover Design by Fiona Jayde Media
Editing by Missed Period Editing

*S*hadow looked at the house that blazed with light and the driveway filled with cars that spilled onto the road, and then stared at Harlan.

"Are you serious? They're having a party!"

"I did say they were!"

"I presumed it was a small dinner party, not a huge one with hundreds of guests!"

Harlan shifted uncomfortably in the driver's seat, having the grace to look sheepish. "I know this looks difficult, but it's actually easier for you to break in this way. And besides, you're exaggerating. There aren't hundreds!"

"But there are a lot! I could get in trouble with Maggie Milne—again!"

"Of course you won't! You're fey, right? Which means you won't get caught by anyone."

Shadow narrowed her eyes and resisted the urge to wipe the smirk off Harlan's face. She hated it when her own words were used against her. "I like to plan my own methods of breaking and entering, thank you. Methods that involve a little more stealth. I'm not invisible!"

Harlan gave her his most charming smile. "But you are very skilful."

"And you are pushing your luck!"

"But not yours."

Shadow took a deep breath and exhaled slowly, reminding herself that she liked Harlan—most of the time. It was Sunday night, and they were sitting in his rental car on a leafy road on the outskirts of Hope Cove in Devon. His own car was outside the farmhouse in White Haven, because it was so recognisable he hadn't wanted to risk being spotted.

Harlan continued, "It might look like an ordinary house, but as I told you it has a very sophisticated alarm system. It would be a nightmare to disable. This way, we don't have to."

"We?" Shadow turned in her seat to stare at him. "And what are you going to do?"

"I'll wait a little further down the street."

"How nice for you."

"You mean you want me to come with you?" Harlan angled himself towards her, but in the dark confines of the car, all Shadow could see was the hard line of his jaw and his lips curving into a smile.

"Absolutely not. Now remind me, where am I going?"

Harlan had picked her up from White Haven a couple of hours before, and they had talked about the night's plan, as well as the more interesting matter of JD Mortlake, but with the house looking so full, she wanted to make sure she had got things right. She was prepared to fight her way out if necessary, but it would be so much easier not to.

"You need to enter through the back door, next to the kitchen, and if I know Henri, he'll have brought in catering staff. The rear stairs are to the right of the door as you walk in, and they bring you out close to the library that overlooks the garden. The Map is rolled up and stored on a shelf with several other maps, but it will be obvious. He keeps it in a red leather tube-shaped case."

Shadow nodded and gazed back at the house. The well-manicured gravel drive was edged with shrubs, trees, and low lighting, but close to the boundary wall, it was dark. "And you say I should keep to the left?"

"Yes. There's a gate in the wall that leads around to the back of the house."

"Any dogs?"

"A Pekinese called Walter."

"Walter?"

"Henri is a fan of Sir Walter Raleigh. A big fan." Harlan's teeth flashed white in the darkness as he laughed. "At least you won't have to worry about being attacked."

"Great. It will just yap a lot and make me want to throw it over the hedge."

"Walter leads a very cosseted life. I'm sure he will be inside on such a cold night."

"Good." She patted her pockets to make sure she had her tools at hand, and then opened the door, allowing cold air to rush inside. "I should be out within the hour."

"I'll be just down the lane. Good luck."

Halfway out of the car, Shadow paused and asked, "What if the unthinkable happens and I do get caught?"

"You're on your own. I know him, so I can't afford to get involved. Or get The Orphic Guild dragged into it. But you won't. I trust you."

Resisting the urge to say something scathing, she shut the door softly, raced across the road, vaulted over the low wall, and ran beneath the trees. The sound of laughter and music reached the end of the drive, getting louder as she approached the house.

This was their first major job since they had met JD a few

3

weeks before. Since then, Gabe had seen him a couple of times at his Mortlake Estate, telling her that he'd been questioned for hours about his life before the flood, and so far wasn't sure what to make of him. Shadow had spent her time reading up on JD's history. Harlan was right. He was a very famous historical figure with a colourful past, and Shadow didn't know what to make of him, either.

Tonight she was retrieving an old map from a member of the Order of the Midnight Sun, but as yet, she had no idea why because Harlan had been so deliberately cagey. As she drew closer to the house, she saw the catering van that Harlan had predicted, but the driveway was devoid of people, and it was impossible to see into the house, as the curtains were drawn. She felt her way along the wall that provided security between the front and back garden, and quickly found the gate. She depressed the latch and came upon her first problem. The gate was locked.

Shadow stepped back and looked up. The top of the wall was several feet above her head, but it was rustic enough for her to get hand and footholds, so she scrambled up and peered over it, seeing an unlit path running alongside the house. She swung over and dropped to the path. Immediately, a security light went on, and she dived into the borders on the left, flattening herself under shrubs.

Heart hammering in her chest, Shadow waited, feeling the damp, cold earth beneath her, and the tickle of leaves against her cheek. It was early May, and although the days were warmer, the nights were still cold. After several seconds of waiting, no one came running out, so keeping to the boundary wall again, Shadow headed deeper into the garden until she could see the entire back of the house.

At the far side there was a large, paved patio area filled with tables and chairs, and thanks to some outside mood lighting, and the light from the room behind, she saw a few hardy people smoking and chatting, their voices only a low murmur. But this end of the house was quiet. Half a dozen people moved around in what looked to be the kitchen; the back door was a short distance from it, and above it was another security light.

Shadow contemplated her options and decided the best way to enter was to round the corner of the house as if she were part of the catering staff. If anyone looked over from the patio area, they wouldn't question it. She edged back to the house, stepped onto the path that lit up straight away, walked confidently around the corner, and opened the back door without hesitating. She slipped inside and shut it softly behind her.

She found herself in a broad passageway in nearly total darkness. A chink of light escaped through the partially open kitchen door to her left, allowing her to see a line of outdoor shoes, boots, and coats hanging on the wall in front of her. A hallway ran deeper into the house, but to her right was the staircase. Shadow ran up it, pausing halfway to listen for any voices, but it was silent, except for the distant thump of music and laughter, and she continued, only stopping when she reached the landing.

The hall was dim, lit by a lamp on a small table placed under a narrow side window. To her left the passage ran a short distance before turning right into the centre of the house. She followed it past an open doorway, the room beyond in complete darkness. She pushed the door open further, letting her eyes adjust to the light. It was a spare bedroom by the look of it. A bag was on the floor, and the bed was made, so maybe a guest was staying here.

Remembering Harlan's instructions, she hurried onwards, following the corridor until she reached a doorway on her left, and she peered inside the lamp-lit room. Bingo. The study was lined with shelves that were packed with books and files, and a desk sat under a long window that was covered in thick curtains. Shadow shut the door behind her and turned slowly, shaking her head.

The room reminded her of William Chadwick's house. It was stuffed with occult curiosities, a variety of astrolabes, a huge globe of the world, and things she quite honestly didn't recognise. Henri was a member of the Order of the Midnight Sun, so she presumed he'd be some kind of lover of alchemy, science, math, or astronomy—or all of them. But now was not the time to linger.

She scanned the bookshelves looking for the red leather case, but although there were plenty of rolled up scrolls, there was nothing of that description. *Damn Herne's hairy balls, and damn Harlan.* There were a few cupboards and glass cabinets and she searched them too, again finding nothing, and she turned back to the desk, just spotting the case peeking out from under a jumble of paperwork. Excellent. That must be it. She had just placed her hand on it when she heard the unmistakable sound of the handle turning and the door opening. There was only one place to hide—behind the thick velvet curtains.

Shadow squashed behind them, her back pressed to the cold window, and heard the pad of footsteps across the floor. She peered through a narrow gap in the curtains, seeing a young, petite woman with short, spiky black hair and wearing a catering jacket look around the room. She walked quickly to the table, picked up the red leather case that Shadow had just exposed, and slid the map out to examine it. Seemingly satisfied, she rolled it back up and slid it into a cardboard tube, similar to the one Shadow had strung across her back.

Shadow had a moment of indecision. Should she step out

now, overpower the thief, and claim the map, or follow her? She was pretty sure she would win in a fight, but she'd give herself away. And any noise would attract attention. She needed to be patient, and clenching her hands, she waited.

The woman headed to the door again, paused to listen, and then left. Within seconds, Shadow darted after her, following her silently, before coming to a sudden halt partway down the stairs. This time there was no easy exit. The catering staff were packing up their equipment and chatting loudly, and a stack of plastic boxes sat by the open back door. The thief placed the map onto the top of one of the large containers, picked it up, and shouted as she headed outside, "I'll start packing the van."

For a moment Shadow hung back at the bottom of the steps, and when it was clear no one was about to follow her, she cloaked herself in her fey magic and sprinted into the shrubbery. She worked her way to the drive, just in time to see the woman put the box into the back of the van. She froze, back to the wall, relieved to see the mystery woman return to the house, the security light illuminating her short, slim figure. Who are you?

Barely waiting for her to be out of sight, Shadow wrenched the back door of the van open and clambered in, fumbling through the jumble of objects until her fingers closed on the cardboard tube. She grabbed it, swapping it for her own empty one, and then leapt out, just as she heard the front door open and the sound of voices approaching. Shadow didn't hesitate. She ran to the boundary wall and retreated the way she had come, only pausing when she was safely sheltered in the dark corner of the garden next to the footpath.

Harlan was nowhere in sight, but she trusted the fact that he'd be alongside the road somewhere. Taking one last look behind her, she vaulted the wall, and spotting the car idling further along, sauntered to it as if she hadn't got a care in the world.

When she slid inside, the warm air wrapped around her, and Harlan looked at her expectantly. "Got it?"

"Eventually. Go—*now*."

2

*H*arlan focussed on driving down the twisting country lanes, checking his rear view mirror frequently, but no one was pursuing them, and the roads were quiet around the sleepy Devon seaside town.

Shadow looked composed as she leaned back in the passenger seat, the map on her lap. She was dressed in black and her long, slim legs were stretched out into the foot well. Even a close run-in with other thieves didn't faze her, and Harlan rolled his shoulders as he allowed himself to relax. "Are you sure they didn't see you?"

"Positive." A smile played at the corner of her lips. "I was tempted to fight her for it, but I decided stealth was the best option. Have you any idea who she is?"

Harlan grimaced, running through a few options. "Not really. There are several groups that steal for the black market, and a couple are more prominent than most. I know a few of them, but I don't recognise her description. But of course, I don't know them all. They aren't groups we generally associate with." Shadow sniggered next to him, and Harlan gave her a sharp stare. "What?"

"You sound so morally upright, and yet you sent me in there to steal a map from a man you know!" She shook her head with a mocking glance. "Harlan, Harlan, Harlan! I think you're in denial."

Harlan shifted in his seat and clenched the wheel. "Tonight's activity isn't something we do regularly, and for the record, I like Henri and feel very guilty about stealing it. But it's necessary."

"Necessary for what? I've indulged you tonight. I didn't ask questions about this map or why it's important, but someone else wants it—*right now*! Coincidence? I think not." Her voice was teasing and mischievous. "What's going on, Harlan?"

"Nothing."

"Bullshit."

"You've picked up some very interesting vocabulary."

"I know. It's so that I fit in. And I like swearing. Now, stop changing the subject and tell me what prompted the theft." She crossed her legs and reached for the bottle of water in the drink holder. "We have a *long* journey back to White Haven, after all."

Harlan fell silent for a moment as he considered how much to tell her. He had deliberately held back information before the theft in case anything went wrong, but now, well, Shadow and the Nephilim were going to get more involved with this, and he had a feeling this was going to get complicated—especially as it seemed others were interested. He gave her a sidelong glance. "Okay, but this is between you, me, and the Nephilim. Don't go running off to the witches with this!"

"How dare you!"

"Dare you my ass. Promise?"

Shadow snorted. "All right."

"The map you have stolen tonight is called The Map of the Seeker. It was made in 1432 and indicates a place in England that allows the worthy a way to talk to angels. But it has long been thought to be fantasy and therefore although beautiful, was considered essentially art and not fact."

"I presume it's been investigated, then?"

"Sure," Harlan nodded. "Extensively at one point, and then it was kind of forgotten, because the actual place was never found, and it was thought to be a hoax perpetrated by the mapmaker himself, Phineas Hammond. I mean, not surprising, right? A place to talk to *angels*? Henri bought it for its beauty. It's not particularly worth a lot."

"So, what's happened to change that?"

Harlan negotiated the turn onto the main road and sighed. "Phineas was a low-order magician and scryer who could talk to spirits, and he said an angel had contacted him and told him where a worthy man could talk to them directly. But of course it wasn't that simple. The place was in an obscure and hidden temple. There was a ritual to follow to enable the doorway—or whatever you want to call it—to open, and there was also a key that was needed. The final piece. Collectively they are called The Trinity of the Seeker. All the written accounts of it, especially in the fifteenth century, said Phineas had finished making the trinity, but had decided they were too dangerous to keep together, so he separated them."

"If he thought they were that dangerous, why even make it in the first place?" Shadow asked, incredulous.

"I don't think he had much choice—he was compelled by the angel to do it. If I recall correctly, it sent him mad, and he had just enough about to him to break the trinity apart before he died."

"It killed him?"

"Sort of. He kept a diary and records, which by the end were a rambling mess. We must have a copy somewhere," he said thoughtfully.

"And the key? Did he make it, or was he given it?"

Harlan laughed dryly. "No one really knows. Anyway, a few weeks ago, a rare book collector was employed to appraise a private library. The owner had died and the family wanted it catalogued, ready for sale. It was quite the treasure trove, apparently. But he found a document that had been wrongly catalogued for years." He glanced at Shadow, who was watching him with narrowed eyes. "That's not uncommon, by the way. There are probably thousands of documents long thought lost just shoved in a drawer somewhere in the basement of a library or museum. After doing some work on it, the appraiser realised what he'd found. It was The Path of the Seeker."

"Wow. Part of the trinity."

"Yep. It's coming up for auction this week—but no one should know, at the moment. My contact gave me a head's up a few days ago. JD wants it, and he wants the map."

"But obviously someone else knows, too."

Harlan nodded, distracted, his mind once again whirling through the possibilities. "It seems so."

"And JD wants it because of the angel connection."

"Yep."

"Are you saying he actually *spoke* to angels?" Shadow's voice was dripping with scepticism.

"JD or Phineas?"

"Both."

"You know, many people claim to do just that."

"But they don't exist."

"Even though the Nephilim are sons of angels?" he replied, equally scathingly.

Once again he felt Shadow turn to stare at him and he glanced at her, her face brindled with lights from the road. "They are some kind of fey. Not heavenly creatures. Are you seriously telling me you believe in God? Just one! The big guy with the beard in the sky?"

Harlan squirmed. "Not particularly. But there are many Gods and Goddesses and entities we really don't understand. Look at the Empusa! She was Hecate's enforcer in the Underworld. I think what we're arguing about is semantics. You're objecting to me calling them angels, because you want to call them fey. But in the end, we're not denying they exist. Fey or angels? What does it matter what their name is?"

"Because to call them angels suggests they have some kind of heavenly message and righteous role, while fey suggest something far more earthbound—although admittedly Otherworldly."

Harlan's head was already starting to ache, and he wasn't really in the mood for theological or philosophical discussions. "But the Nephilim are something, aren't they?"

"We're all *something*, Harlan! Yes. I agree, there are many Gods and Goddesses—we all remember the mess that ensued at Beltane." She shrugged at his startled glance. "Anyway. Did Phineas *speak* with an angel, or whatever we want to call it?"

"According to him, yes, through a vision! I have no idea of the angel's name, however."

Shadow groaned. "It sounds too pat. I mean, why tell him? Why wasn't JD told when he talked to angels?"

"I have no idea, Shadow! Do I look like an oracle?"

Shadow drank some water and then asked, "Why does JD care? He speaks to angels already, right? In his Enochian language. What does it matter to him?"

"Ah, that! It turns out JD hasn't spoken to them in years. He was never able to scry effectively, and that's why he had a partner. A man called Kelley who died years ago. Since then, he's had to rely on other mediums, but they've never been as effective—and of course JD hasn't wanted to reveal who he truly is. He thinks the trinity is his way back to them."

"But why? What do they give him? What's the point?"

"Knowledge, Shadow. Haven't you got that yet? That's all that matters to these men. Knowledge and the power it gives them. The key to life itself."

"He found immortality. Hasn't he solved that one?"

Harlan shook his head and laughed softly. "Immortality is just one part of it. It's an addiction—seeking something that is forever just past their fingertips. And to every one of them, knowledge is something slightly different. It's intangible, nebulous, and all the more attractive for it."

"It's a wonder he hasn't gone mad over the years."

"Who? JD? I think he might have, on occasion, and dragged himself back from the brink. Have you been reading about him?"

Shadow nodded. "I have. He's an interesting character."

"That's one way of putting it."

"The map is for JD, then?"

"Yes." Harlan glanced at her. "He wants to find this place —desperately."

"Right," Shadow said, almost audibly rolling her eyes. "And the catering thief? Who is she and who is she stealing it for?"

"Well, those are the million-dollar questions."

***

Gabe was waiting in the lamp-lit living room at the farmhouse for Shadow to return with Harlan, as Niel, Ash, Barak, and Nahum waited with him.

He'd been nervous all night, ever since she left, and he

knew it was stupid because Shadow was more than capable of looking after herself, but nevertheless, he was still worried.

"Gabe, will you relax?" Nahum said from where he sat on the sofa sipping a beer, completely at ease in a loose t-shirt and cotton trousers.

Gabe was standing at the window, looking out on the dark fields behind the house. "I'm trying, and failing."

"We know," Barak said, dryly. "Have a beer."

"I want to keep a clear head, just in case." Gabe glanced at his watch. "They should be here soon." He turned back to the room, unnerved to find his brothers reclining in their respective chairs, ignoring the TV and watching him with amusement. "What?"

"You," Ash said, smirking, "are worried about Shadow. You going to fly in and rescue her?"

"If necessary."

Niel laughed. "How very gallant of you."

"Piss off. All of you."

Barak winked. "Like the feel of her in your arms, brother? Don't think we haven't noticed how you like to take her flying."

He knew they were teasing him, but right now he wanted to punch them. "I can count on one hand the amount of times I've done that, so don't exaggerate!" They all just smiled at him with infuriatingly knowing expressions, and Gabe added, "Besides, she's our business partner. I like to keep her happy."

"Uh-huh," Nahum said. "I bet you do."

Gabe was about to offer a more scathing response when he heard the front door open, and the clatter of footsteps down the hall. He turned toward the door, relieved when Shadow walked in, closely followed by Harlan.

Shadow beamed and waved the cardboard roll. "Success,

renegades!" She glanced behind her at Harlan. "I've persuaded him to let us look at it."

Harlan nodded in greeting. "I'd say she threatened more than persuaded me."

"Yeah, she does that," Nahum answered, a smirk still on his face.

Shadow hesitated, looking around the room suspiciously. "What's with you guys? You look...weird!"

"Nothing!" Gabe said hurriedly. "Show us the bounty!"

Shadow headed to the low coffee table, and aided by Nahum, cleared the space and extracted the map. "You're going to like this, boys."

"We will?" Gabe asked. "Why?"

"It's a map that tells you where to speak to angels." Shadow smiled triumphantly as she started to unroll the document.

Gabe exchanged a troubled glance with the others. "It does *what*?"

Harlan held his hands up. "Don't get too excited! It's long been thought to be fantasy."

"Until now," Shadow pointed out. She looked at Gabe, her violet eyes mischievous. "Someone else wanted this, too. I stole it from her."

"Tell us everything," Gabe insisted.

For the next few minutes, Shadow and Harlan told them about their evening, and the Nephilim clustered around the table as Shadow secured the map. She pinned down the edges with nearby objects, revealing a large, detailed drawing of a place called Angel's Rest and the surrounding area. It was fantastical in design, filled with images of mythical beasts, winged creatures, and many symbols.

"Where's this?" Niel asked, studying it intently.

"In the Mendips, which is in the southwest of England,"

Harlan explained, making himself comfortable on the sofa and taking the beer that Gabe held out to him. "Have you heard of it?"

Nahum shook his head. "No, but that's not surprising. There are lots of places we don't know."

"Fair enough. The Mendips is a huge area, and parts of it are designated nature reserves. It's riddled with limestone caves, gorges, woods, and small villages. There has been mining there in the past. Angel's Rest," he said, nodding to it, "is a village, very picturesque, but otherwise unremarkable, other than being in a place of natural beauty. It still exists, obviously, so we can pinpoint the area where this map covers with reasonable accuracy. But none of it is in proportion." He ran his finger along a craggy line on the map. "Here, for example, is where Ebbor Gorge runs." He shrugged. "And, yes of course, the landscape has changed, but even at the time the map was made it didn't make sense."

Gabe was still standing, his back to the fire as he looked at the map. "I presume the area was explored many times over the years?"

"Absolutely, and nothing was found. The spot right here on the gorge," his finger hovered over a drawing of columns and an apex roof, "is a tiny drawing of a temple, and underneath it says *The Temple of the Seeker*—but it doesn't exist." Gabe drew closer to look, squinting at the tiny, precise lettering as Harlan continued. "Even if it did, there is some kind of path that must be followed in order to allow the seeker to speak to angels." Harlan scratched his head, looking slightly embarrassed. "Everyone thought Phineas had manufactured a hoax. And he wasn't that well-respected as a magician anyway, partly because, I think, he hadn't accrued a huge amount of money and resources, and that goes a long way in the alchemy world."

"You mean he wasn't a gentleman," Gabe said, already knowing how the world of alchemy worked.

"Exactly. And he wasn't thought to be a genuine medium, either."

Ash nodded thoughtfully. "So, the map was ignored and forgotten."

"Yes." Harlan took a sip of his beer. "But, it is beautiful, and very typical of manuscripts of the time."

Shadow had been listening quietly while she examined the map. "There are pictures of angels and fantastical creatures, and even the trees are detailed. I can't believe Henri didn't display this on the wall."

"So Shadow stole this is for JD?" Barak asked, and it was obvious his interest was already stirring.

"Yes," Harlan nodded. "Now that The Path of the Seeker has been found, the second part of the trinity, he is determined to find the temple. As I explained to Shadow, he can no longer talk to angels the way he used to—it frustrates him."

Gabe wasn't surprised. He had spent hours talking to JD on the two occasions he'd met him, and he eventually had revealed he had long since lost the ability to communicate with them. His obsession with angels, however, was baffling, and it had made Gabe rethink his own desire to try to contact his father. He was conflicted about the whole thing. But he said to Harlan, "I take it that you will be buying the document at the auction?"

"Yes—I hope. We have deep pockets for this one. But potentially, considering what happened tonight, someone else will bid strongly for it as well. On the plus side for us, The Orphic Guild is known for our work in the occult world, and it won't seem strange for us to want to buy it."

"Won't the theft of the map make your interest in the

second document suspicious?" Nahum asked, looking between Harlan and Shadow. "Henri might suspect you."

"Maybe," Harlan admitted, "but we weren't seen anywhere near Henri's house, so that's in our favour."

"You hope," Gabe said, frowning.

Harlan continued, a brief nod of the head his only concession to that concern. "When news of the auction breaks, Henri might think we're buying it to sell it on for a high price—maybe to him!" He tried to look innocent and wide-eyed. "I had *no idea* that the map was stolen!"

Ash groaned. "Oh, this is so underhanded!"

"Which is why it's so perfect," Shadow said, smiling sweetly.

"Why not approach Henri directly to buy his map?" Gabe asked.

"Because that *might* have made him suspect we have something," Harlan told him.

Gabe crouched down to examine the map, squashing between Ash and Barak. It *was* a work of art. It was drawn with incredible skill, and considering the detail of the landscape it was odd that nothing had been found, even if the distances weren't accurate. It made it seem all the more likely it was a hoax—or to be more charitable, a work of fiction and hope.

"Wow," Barak said, looking both surprised and impressed. "So, JD is really going to try to find it. What makes him think he'll be successful now?"

"Because he has you." Harlan looked at them and smiled. "It's likely this place is below ground with an as yet unfound access point. And of course we have to remember that the whole thing sent Phineas mad."

Nahum laughed. "Okay. Now it's getting interesting!"

"Hold on," Shadow said, her hand on Harlan's arm. "JD wants *our* help with all of this? You didn't say that before!"

He looked sheepish. "I wanted to secure the map first. And we need The Path of the Seeker as well, but it doesn't mean we shouldn't start work on finding the temple."

Niel looked at him, amused. "You called it The Trinity of the Seeker and mentioned a key. Aren't we missing an important part, even supposing we find the temple?"

Harlan leaned against the back of the sofa, and although he looked tired, his eyes danced with excitement. "Yes, we are. But The Path of the Seeker hasn't been seen for *hundreds* of years! To find it changes everything! The trinity has become more tangible—less like a hoax."

"*If* you can buy it," Nahum reminded him. "What if you're outbid? Does that mean we steal that, too?"

Harlan scratched his chin and smiled ruefully. "It might."

Shadow threw her head back and laughed. "I like this. It's more convoluted by the minute."

"However," Harlan added, "I'll be able to examine the document soon, before the auction. I'm hoping it will give us more clues to the key—even if I don't buy it. There'll be photos." He grimaced. "It's unfortunate, but everyone will have access to its contents. But the key has to be out there somewhere."

Gabe drained his beer. "And everyone will have access to copies of the map, surely?"

"Maybe. The current images are poor, and Henri certainly never shared any. And," Harlan laughed, "this isn't treasure we're talking about—it's a gateway to the angels. How many people are really going to be interested in that? Anyway, we have the map now, thanks to Shadow. I'll take it back to London tomorrow. Once I've shown this to JD, we can decide what's next. I'll be in touch about arranging a visit to the site." He looked suddenly uncertain. "Of course, this is presuming you're interested?"

Gabe saw the interest in everyone's eyes, and he answered cautiously. "I think we are."

"Good," Harlan said, rolling the map up. "I'll talk to him and call you tomorrow."

Gabe watched as Shadow stood to see Harlan out, and once they'd left the room, he sank into the closest chair and sighed. "That was unexpected."

Nahum had been gazing into the fire thoughtfully, but now he nodded, suddenly alert. "It was. What do you think?"

"I think it will be a dead end, but I admit I'm curious."

"And we're going to get paid," Ash pointed out, "so why not?"

Niel grunted. "Because I'm not so sure we want the angels —fallen or not—knowing we're here."

"You think that would be a bad thing?" Barak asked, eyes narrowing.

"Don't you?" he replied, ominously.

They looked up as Shadow re-entered the room, and she sat on the sofa, her eyes full of intrigue. "You all look serious!"

Gabe grimaced. "We're debating how likely this is to be true—it sounds like medieval madness."

Shadow peeled off her black leather boots and socks, and sat cross-legged, her elbows on her knees. "I agree, but it is interesting that someone else was trying to steal it. Surely that gives it some merit."

"I think," Nahum said, "that it probably gives the map more value, now that the path has been found. That's all." He cocked his head at her. "You sure you weren't spotted?"

"Very sure. But I'd love to know who the mystery woman is."

"Me too," Gabe mused. "Any whiff of the paranormal about her?"

"Not that I saw." She shrugged. "But I could be wrong."

Barak feigned choking on his beer. "You admit *what?*"

"It's rare, I know," she said, shrugging his sarcasm off. "But we're in, right?"

Gabe felt his blood already stirring with excitement. "Of course we are."

he Orphic Guild's London office was bathed in spring sunshine when Harlan arrived the next morning. He had opted to drive to the office, rather than risk the tube with his precious cargo.

As he strolled through the front door into the wide reception hall, Robert Smythe, Mason Jacobs's secretary, was coming down the stairs and he narrowed his eyes at Harlan. "There you are! We thought you'd got lost."

Harlan bit back a stinging retort and opted for sarcasm. "I have many abilities, but flying over London traffic isn't one of them. Is Mason free?"

Robert was a prissy man who thought he ruled the London branch just because he was Mason's secretary, and his tone was abrupt with pretty much everyone except for Mason. Harlan was aware that his jeans and leather jacket didn't endear him to Robert either, who was already fussing with the cuffs of his expensive shirt. "Not until eleven. He's in a meeting right now."

Harlan checked his watch. "Excellent. Time for a coffee before I see him. Book me in, will you, just so he knows to expect me." Harlan walked past him and up the stairs to his office, not waiting for a response. Robert brought out the worst in him. He shouted over the banister, "Are Aiden or Olivia here?"

Robert barely bothered to slow down, "Olivia is, Aiden will be here later."

Harlan nodded and continued to his room, noting a new stack of files on his desk, and curious, he checked their contents. All the files were prepared by the small administrative team. It was their job to keep an eye on upcoming auctions and prepare reports for the collectors. They also took phone calls from prospective clients, gathering details of each possible case for the collectors to review. They were divided equally between Olivia, Aiden, and Harlan, except if they were returning clients who were then always referred to the respective collector. Only when they had reviewed the information and sometimes discussed them together did they take them to Mason for the final call. More often than not, he approved their decisions.

The files were a mixture of the usual requests: old occult manuscripts, weapons, jewellery, and magical objects. One caught Harlan's eye. A new client had requested help finding a cursed painting. *Interesting.* He moved it to the top of the pile, and then made himself a coffee from his state of the art espresso machine. While Harlan liked to use the staffroom on the ground floor, sometimes it was easier and quicker to have his machine at hand. Once he'd downed the first cup, he made a second and carried it down the hall to Olivia's office. He knocked and opened the door, peering in cautiously. He grinned when he saw she was free. "Is this a good time to talk?"

Olivia was seated behind her desk going through her own files, and she looked up and smiled. She was a similar age to him, slim and toned, a result of regular workouts that included running, climbing, and boxing.

"You're back! Sure, come on in." Olivia's mid-length, caramel-toned hair had a soft curl to it, and she pushed it away from her face and leaned back, picking up her cup as she did so. "I see you brought your own coffee."

He looked rueful. "It's my second, and I've only just walked through the door. I've been driving for hours and needed a shot of caffeine."

"Of course. You've been in Devon. How did it go?"

"And Cornwall," he reminded her. "I picked Shadow up last night to steal the map and stayed at Alex's flat."

Olivia nodded as she recognised the names. "The witch in White Haven and our fey friend. How did it go?"

"Successfully, but it wasn't without problems. Someone else tried to steal that map, but Shadow beat her to it. I'm trying to work out who it was. Shadow described a young woman with spiky black hair. Any ideas?"

Olivia narrowed her eyes and tapped her cup with her manicured fingers. "It rings a bell. I think I saw her at an auction only a couple of weeks ago."

"An auction for what?" Harlan asked, leaning forward.

"Dark Age grave goods and stone carved idols." Olivia frowned. "I can't be sure, because they weren't sitting together, but there was something about their studied avoidance of each other that made me think she was with Nicoli."

"Damn it," Harlan said, groaning. Andreas Nicoli ran The Order of Lilith, another occult organisation that had far shadier morals than The Orphic Guild, and one of the more prominent groups they competed with. "I hoped it wouldn't be them. Any idea what they were after?" It was always an advantage to know what the opposition was up to.

"No. They brought a couple of very ordinary stone idols, with no valuable occult or paranormal connections that I could discern. However," she said, also leaning forward and putting her now empty cup to the side, "she could be working for someone entirely different, or be a private operator. If she *is* working for Andreas, it's worrying they want the map. That means they'll be bidding for The Path of the Seeker, too."

"If they don't steal it first."

Olivia's eyes widened. "You think they would?"

"I think it's a possibility," Harlan said, running his hand across his chin and realising he really should have shaved that morning. "What the hell day is it?"

Olivia laughed. "Monday. When's your auction?"

"Wednesday night. Good. That doesn't give them a lot of time."

"Which auction house?"

"Burton and Knight."

"Even better," Olivia said, looking relieved. "Nicoli wouldn't dare to piss them off."

She was right about that, Harlan mused. Burton and Knight was a small auction house specialising in the occult. No one working in the paranormal world would want to get on their bad side, or they'd find themselves banned from future auctions. It had happened once before, as far as Harlan knew, to an organisation called The House of Sigils, and they had ended up collapsing. It was a sober reminder to everyone else.

"True," he said brightly. "But I think it will get expensive."

"And if you win, we need to find somewhere very safe to store it."

"But if we lose, *we* need to steal it."

"Wow." Olivia folded her arms across her chest. "Are we that serious about this?"

"We stole the damn map, Olivia. JD wants this!"

"A map to angels?"

"Yes!" Olivia had no idea who JD really was, and it galled Harlan not to tell her. "But who else would want it so much that they'd be willing to steal for it, too?"

She fell silent for a moment. "I don't know, but Aiden will be in later. We should talk to him."

"Good suggestion. But now," he said, rising to his feet, "I need to see the boss. Catch you later."

He headed to Mason's office, and five minutes later, after Harlan had explained everything, Mason looked very annoyed. "Bloody Nicoli? JD won't like this."

Harlan decided now was the time for his request. "We need to act quickly to find the location. Gabe and Shadow are keen to help. They're just waiting for our permission."

Mason sighed thoughtfully and nodded at the map, still rolled up on his desk. "Will it really be that difficult?"

"Yes. I know you want JD to study it first, but under the circumstances, I don't think we should wait."

"All right. Send them as soon as possible."

"We'll have to book them in somewhere."

"That's fine. Liaise with them and see what they want." Harlan stood, and Mason pushed the map towards him. "Take this with you, and get admin to photocopy it—or scan it—as good a quality as possible, and send it to them. I'll phone JD." But as Harlan was heading out the door, he spoke again. "By the way, I heard from Chadwick's solicitors yesterday. He left us his house in his will."

Harlan paused at the threshold, confused. "William Chadwick left us his house? As in The Orphic Guild?" Chadwick had commissioned them to find the druid Kian's tomb, and had then been possessed by Kian's ghost, and was subsequently killed by Shadow.

Mason was leaning back in his chair, looking solemn. "Yes. It's a stipulation of his will that we leave his collections intact, and has requested that we properly curate them, but we can use the house as a base for anyone we choose. Contractors, for example, who need to stay in town for a couple of nights."

Harlan was momentarily stunned and leaned against the doorframe. "Why us? Why not any relatives?"

Mason shrugged. "I think in many ways we were his family, and I was a good friend, of course." He absently stroked the lapel of his suit jacket. "I am honoured, obviously, and also relieved, if I'm honest. All that work he put into his collection." He shook his head. "It would have been terrible to split it up. I'm going to pick the keys up and visit there later."

"Do you think anyone will contest the will?"

"No, I doubt it. He left enough money to his surviving relative—a nephew, I believe."

Harlan thought of the night that Chadwick died, and felt a wave of regret wash over him. "I'm sorry, Mason. I wish it hadn't happened, and I know Shadow does, too."

Mason brushed his concern away. "It was Kian's fault, not Shadow's." And then he bent over the papers on his desk and Harlan shut the door softly behind him.

Shadow was riding Kailen, her cherished horse, when her phone buzzed in her jacket pocket, and she halted on the rise of the hill overlooking the sea below.

The coast stretched out on either side, the cliffs high in places, and the waves crashing against their feet. She could see the occasional walker on narrow belts of beach, a few others taking the cliff path, and lots of seagulls. One wheeled on the air above her, screeching as she answered. "Hi, Harlan."

"Hey, Shadow. Good news. Mason wants you to go to

Angel's Rest as soon as possible. Any chance you can get there today?"

Shadow grinned triumphantly, as Kailen fretted beneath her. "I think so. Gabe is at Caspian's right now, but he's making arrangements to cover security." The Nephilim still worked for the shipping branch of Kernow Industries, but Gabe was planning to leave Barak in charge.

"Good. I thought I'd book you in somewhere close by. Any preferences? We're paying, obviously."

"Some place outside the town, the bigger the better, and at least three bedrooms. Niel will probably come with us."

"Okay. Leave it with me," Harlan said, already sounding distracted. "I'm going to get you a copy of the map, and I'll send it on as soon as it's done. And Shadow, be careful. There are others looking for this, and I'm not sure how ruthless they will be."

Shadow felt a thrill of excitement rush through her. She never felt more alive than when she had opponents. It made her blood sing. "That's no problem at all."

She ended the call and turned Kailen back towards home, urging him to a gallop, and dropping low against him. It was a shame she wouldn't be able to take him with her, but the others would take care of him; all of the Nephilim were excellent riders. When she arrived back home, she spent some time rubbing Kailen down before stabling him, and then she headed inside to shower. By the time she emerged, Harlan had phoned to confirm their accommodation and Gabe had arrived. She could see his SUV in the courtyard.

Shadow's hair was still wet when she walked into the kitchen where he and Niel were chatting at the kitchen table, and her skin was damp from the shower. She'd been so anxious to speak to them she'd barely dried herself. She was hot and barefoot, wearing only a sleeveless t-shirt and her slim fitting jeans. She saw Gabe try not to stare at her figure, which gave her immense satisfaction.

"Heard anything?" Niel asked.

The big, blond Nephilim was cradling a cup of coffee, and he leaned back in his seat, watching Shadow with lively blue eyes. The hair on either side of his head above his ears was shaved, and the rest of it was tied back, making him look more Viking-like than usual.

She helped herself to coffee and dropped into a chair at the end of the table. "I certainly have. Harlan has given us the go-ahead and booked us a place starting today. Are you both ready to go?"

They nodded, and Gabe said, "We've been checking the area. Angel's Rest still seems like a small village, although from what I can recall, there are a few more roads and buildings than on the old map."

"Not surprising though, is it?" Niel said. "Six hundred or so years have passed since its creation."

"Harlan is sending us a copy of the map. How long will it take to get there?" Shadow asked.

"Not long, about three hours," Gabe told her. He checked his watch. "There are a few more things I need to do, but I can be ready in an hour. Does that sound good for you two?" They both nodded, and Gabe rose to his feet. "Good. Let's take weapons, ropes, and other useful supplies. Who knows where we'll end up, or who might be there waiting."

$\mathcal{B}$y the time Gabe, Niel, and Shadow arrived at the house that Harlan had booked for them, Gabe was cranky and feeling cramped.

The traffic from Cornwall to the Mendips was heavy, and because they had set out mid-afternoon, they hit lots of commuter traffic, too. Once they'd left the M5 they followed A roads, heading east through Cheddar, and then took a minor road to the house. The Mendips was a designated Area of Outstanding National Beauty and was a popular tourist attraction, for good reason. The route wound through a beautiful landscape, and they had all been quiet as they absorbed their surroundings.

Fortunately, they were outside the holiday season, but Gabe knew the place was popular with walking groups, and potentially that would be an issue. The Mendips was also huge, but the area they were focussed on was in the south-east, near Ebbor Gorge and Wookey Hole. However, the concerns they had talked about on the journey disappeared as he stopped the car at a gated entrance situated on a leafy lane, and gazed at a large, medieval manor house built in warm mellow stone.

"Are you sure that's it?" he said over his shoulder to Shadow, who had been giving him the directions.

"Yes," she answered impatiently. "I know how GPS works."

"But that's enormous!"

Niel was in the passenger seat, and he laughed. "That's Harlan for you. I daresay he'll be staying at some point, and so will JD, and maybe even Mason. I guess they won't want to slum it!"

Gabe whistled softly. "Well, if you're sure." He put the SUV into gear, rolled through the gate, and parked on an immaculate gravel drive.

"I did tell Harlan we needed privacy," Shadow said as she exited the car. "And I think we've got that."

As Gabe shut the door, he looked around at the surrounding high wall and trees. "This place must have cost a fortune."

Niel grabbed their bags from the boot. "How do we get in?"

"There's a key safe around the side," Shadow told him, already crunching across the gravel. "I've got the code. I'll get it."

Gabe took his overnight bag from Niel and hefted a box of food into his arms, and as they walked to the entrance, he said, "This is a good choice. I like that it's so private."

Niel shrugged and grimaced. "Too many trees for my liking—people can hide there."

"But it hides us, too. The first thing I want to do is get our bearings. I want this map narrowed down as much as possible, or we could be here for weeks."

Niel laughed dryly. "More like years."

Shadow rounded the corner of the house with the keys in

her hand, and stepping past Gabe onto the double height porch, she let them in and disabled the alarm system. As Gabe followed her inside, his mouth dropped open as he gazed at the immense hall in front of him and the large staircase that swept up to the next floor. "Wow. It's really quite something!"

Shadow smirked. "Best place you've ever stayed?"

Gabe looked at her, amused, as memories of other homes flooded back from millennia ago. "I wouldn't say that. Didn't you know I was royalty in my day?"

She cocked her head as she appraised him. "Royalty? No, I did not!"

"Well, I was—for a while, at least." He walked across the hall and put his bag on the side table. "My palace was made of marble and decorated with priceless silks. I was groomed and oiled, ate only the best food, and hunted on my own lands." He enjoyed watching her surprised expression as her gaze swept from his head to his toes. He looked at Niel, who was sniggering. "And him, too. A palace in a forested land on a mountain ridge, surrounded by snow and ice."

Shadow's gaze slid to Niel, who was still laughing, his arms folded across his chest. A memory flashed into Gabe's mind of Niel wearing his bearskin cloak that he wore in the mountains above Mesopotamia. Despite his northern European appearance, he had been born in the Middle East. His fallen angel father was a white-blond warrior with ice blue eyes and wings the colour of freshly fallen snow. Gabe shook his head to clear his vision. It had been a long time since either of them had seen him.

"Well! Aren't you two full of surprises?" Shadow said, looking marginally annoyed. "I thought you were warriors and mercenaries, not pampered princesses."

Gabe continued to tease her, knowing she was trying to get him to bite. "We were that, too. There's so much more you don't know about us! But, now's not the time. Let's check this place out, find bedrooms, cook, and plan."

———

Half an hour later, after they investigated the house from top to bottom and chose bedrooms, the trio met in the conservatory at the back of the house that connected to the large, well equipped kitchen. It was full of plants, and had a central table surrounded by wicker chairs on a tiled floor. It was light and airy, and late evening sunshine slanted through the windows.

On their way to the Mendips they had stopped and printed the scanned copy of the map that Harlan had sent Shadow. It was good quality with a high resolution, and they had been able to print a large size. They had also bought a detailed map of the surrounding area, and Gabe laid out both side by side, and stood staring at them with his hands on his hips.

"Bollocks. There are differences."

Niel grunted. "Not surprising. Harlan said Hammond's map wasn't geographically correct."

"Where was he from?" Gabe asked, aware there were many more questions he should have asked Harlan and hadn't.

"Hammond? Right here in Angel's Rest," Shadow said, glancing up at him, her violet eyes bright in the fading light. She'd relaxed her glamour, allowing her Otherness to shine through, and she seemed almost ethereal, making Gabe feel like a block of stone in comparison. "But what does that matter?"

"I wondered if he'd drawn this from his vision or from memory, or both." Gabe ran his finger across The Map of the Seeker, tracing lines and hills. "The fantasy images are so detailed, but it's odd the map itself is inaccurate."

"I don't think it's odd," Shadow answered. "Maps are very hard to get right, unless you're a cartographer—vision or not!"

Gabe sighed. "I suppose. Harlan said there were other records, like his diary. They must give some background."

Niel was standing on the other side of Shadow, and he frowned. "What if it's just a product of his fervent imagination?"

Shadow shook her head. "No. Places on it actually exist. Angel's Rest, for example. That's half a mile up the road. And Deerleap Standing Stones. And Ebbor Gorge, of course—the temple is marked partway along it. Although the gorge's shape is different on Hammond's map, it's clear that it's still Ebbor Gorge." She shrugged. "I don't see what the problem is. It's in the gorge, somewhere. And Harlan has thoughtfully booked this house very close to it."

"It doesn't mean it isn't still fantasy," Gabe said. He looked out the windows towards the setting sun. "Let's eat, and then when darkness falls we can fly, Niel. We'll see better from overhead."

"And what will *I* do?" Shadow asked, looking put out.

Gabe grinned at her. "You can stay here and study the map."

She narrowed her eyes at him, and Gabe was pretty sure she'd be doing nothing of the sort, but he winked and headed to the shower, leaving Niel to cook.

When it was fully dark out, Gabe and Niel walked onto the lawn at the back of the house, unfurled their wings, and lifted easily into the night.

The moon was waning, covered occasionally by scudding clouds, and Gabe felt his spirits lift as he climbed higher, using the currents to carry him. Below were clusters of lights from the small villages, but large areas were swathed in darkness. He took a moment to orientate himself, noting Angel's Rest below, a short distance from their house that had a few lit windows visible. A little farther up the valley he could see other isolated buildings, and he smiled. This was quite some place. If nothing else, he would enjoy being here. It was important for them to know their new homeland, and he resolved they should travel more often.

For a while he drifted on the wind, enjoying the freedom that flight gave him, and the feeling of power. His strong build gave him advantages over humans, but that was nothing compared to this. His conversation with Shadow earlier had set him thinking, and all evening he'd been mulling on the past and his history, and it had made him restless. He wondered if it had affected Niel, too. Sometimes, it seemed as if the other Nephilim were more comfortable with their present circumstances than he was. But that changed too, depending on his mood. He blinked in an effort to clear his thoughts and focussed on the landscape below.

Gabe's sight had adjusted quickly to the night, and he noted the rugged cliffs, patches of woodland, and wide-open fields that unfurled below him. Dropping lower, he saw the tangled trees that filled the Ebbor Gorge, and he drifted downwards, finally landing on a rocky outcrop overlooking the valley. Within minutes, Niel had joined him.

"There are caves spread below here, did you know?" Niel asked.

Gabe nodded. "I read about them earlier. Many have been explored. There'll be nothing for us to find there, I'm sure."

"True. But potentially the temple will be hidden by some kind of magic, and could be in a cave," Niel reasoned. "It's certainly not above ground."

"Yeah, to hide it in the open would use a lot of power…

but angels are powerful!" Gabe pointed down the valley. "Wookey Hole is an attraction now, and so is Cheddar Gorge. Thousands of visitors pour through there, and the caves."

"But back when Hammond drew his map, far fewer people would have been in there—not like today."

"But it can't be in one of the main caves," Gabe said, shaking his head. "The temple is nowhere near them, according to the map. I think, wherever it is, it hasn't been found—for centuries, at least."

"But this whole area has been inhabited for millennia."

"I know. But surely a place where humans can talk to angels must be one that is hard to get to?"

Niel smiled, his teeth white in the fractured moonlight. "You mean you have to earn the right?"

"Of course. When have the fallen or the other angels ever made anything easy?" Gabe flexed his wings as he surveyed the area below him. "The fallen never made it easy for us, and we're their *children*!"

"I must admit," Niel said softly, "that I wonder if they know we're back."

Gabe turned quickly. "What do you mean?"

"They killed us, brother. Drowned us all. Do they know that a handful of us have returned?" Niel's eyes were intense, dark pools. "Here we are, thousands of years later, having made a miraculous escape from the spirit world. You would think they would have detected us somehow."

Gabe considered his words for a moment. "That's an interesting thought, but why would they? We're living quietly. Unobtrusively. You can't find what you're not looking for."

"True. But we're independent right now—and that's what I like. What if this place really exists? What if somewhere beneath our feet is a channel to the angels, and we draw unwanted attention to ourselves? We could make our new life very hard."

Gabe gazed at Niel's hard, angular face and felt the conviction of his words. "What if *they* don't exist anymore?"

Niel barked out a laugh and looked up at the stars spread above. "Oh, I think they're out there somewhere, far less involved in the human world than they used to be. And I think we're below the radar right now, as humans say. I think we should stay that way."

"You're having second thoughts? Already?"

"I'm torn, if I'm honest. I feel as if we're in a void of sorts, out of touch with our roots. But equally, I like the opportunities it affords us."

Gabe nodded, aware that he thought the same, but still…

Niel gripped Gabe's shoulder with his large hand, callused from years of fighting. "Food for thought, friend. I'll see you back at the house." And with that, Niel plunged over the cliff and then rose majestically as his wings caught the uplift, carrying him over the valley below.

Food for thought, indeed.

As soon as Shadow was alone, she strapped her knives to her thighs and ran across the lawn to the bottom of the garden.

She nimbly climbed the high stone perimeter wall and perched on the top, looking at the vista beyond. There was a copse behind the house, and then for a short distance there were open fields, and then a deeper darkness marked the edge of the tree line that ran up into Ebbor Gorge. She dropped down, threading between the trees, fresh air renewing her energy and resolve. After they had eaten, the three of them had examined the map some more, still bewildered at where to start. They would search in daylight, but

Shadow also believed that hidden things were more likely to reveal themselves at night. It was fey belief, and one she often found to be true.

She crossed the fields, and once under the trees again, was forced to slow down. There was no path here, and she edged through the thick undergrowth until she finally found a stony trail leading up a narrow gully into the gorge. At this point it was wrong to call them cliffs, but as she progressed they rose in height around her and she paused, listening to the scurry of wildlife, the hoots of owls and the *whoosh* of bats in flight. But no human noises reached her, and she pressed forward, past crevices leading into the rock, and the scrub trees clinging to the stone. It was an ancient landscape, barely scarred by humans, and the weight of many years was heavy here. There was so much still to find, she was sure. *But not tonight.* Tonight was just a chance to get a feel for the place, and smiling to herself, she pushed on.

5

*O*n Tuesday morning, Harlan found Aiden in the library of The Orphic Guild, bent over a book on a table under the window.

Weak spring light lit up his dark hair, and as he heard Harlan approach, he looked up and smiled. "Harlan! It's been a while. How are you?"

Aiden was the youngest of the three collectors based in the London office, and Harlan estimated he was in his early thirties. Like himself and Olivia, Aiden had been immersed in the paranormal world for years, and was resourceful and clever, but also more cautious. He also spent a lot of time out of the office, and his clothes reflected it. He was wearing old army fatigues today paired with heavy tramping boots, and it looked like he had barely slept.

"I'm fine, I guess, but how are you?" Harlan asked as he sat down in a chair at the table. "If I'm honest, you look like shit."

Aiden laughed, rubbing his hands through his hair. "I know I do. I arrived back later than expected. I grabbed a couple of hours sleep, and then headed in."

Since the last time Harlan had seen him, Aiden had spent weeks in Scotland tracking down treasure in a castle and had then been in York looking for clues to Viking gold.

"Did you have success in York?" Harlan asked.

Aiden held his hand out and wiggled it. "Maybe. I'm here to check a couple of documents and then I'm leaving again. I heard your druid business was tricky."

Harlan rolled his eyes. "Yeah, but we got there eventually. I take it you've heard about Chadwick's death?"

Aiden nodded. "I have, and am sorry to hear it. Our life-long obsessions don't always turn out the way we want, do they? Anyway, I hear you're on the path of angels now with a fey and seven Nephilim." He grinned. "Sounds like a fairy tale."

"Yeah, well, that remains to be seen. The fey is wayward, and the Nephilim...well, let's just say they're different! And I'm not sure what to think of angels." Harlan leaned forward, his fingers playing idly with the pages of the book in front of him. "I wanted to know if you recognised a description of someone. I discussed it with Liv yesterday. We think she's a new member of Nicoli's team."

Aiden immediately sobered. "Go on."

"Short, slim, black short, spiky hair. Liv thinks she saw her at an auction a few weeks ago."

Aiden thought for a moment. "It doesn't ring a bell, but I'll keep my ear to the ground. I think Nicoli has someone in York, too."

Harlan narrowed his eyes. "Why?"

"Let's just say that I've had a few great ideas, and yet someone is always there before me."

"Lost your touch?" Harlan teased him.

"Not yet, old man. But," Aiden looked out of the window for a moment, his gaze unfocussed, before turning back to Harlan, "I think Nicoli is increasing his operatives. There's nothing I can put my finger on, other than my recent experiences. It's just a feeling."

"You think he's trying to compete with us?"

Aiden shrugged. "Anyone! There are always clients who are willing to try anything to get what they need—and Nicoli is prepared to do that. Maybe he's decided to grow his operation."

Harlan leaned back in the leather chair, hearing it creak beneath him, and his fingers tapped the smooth, varnished wood of the armrest. "I think we're too established to suffer from it, if he is."

"I agree. But competition is bad for auctions, and could make some work more dangerous. Your current job, for example. Tell me about how you saw this mystery woman." Harlan filled him in on the details, and Aiden grunted. "Catering? If it was Nicoli, he must have used that route before if this was such short notice—or, he knew about the path going on sale before you did."

"True," Harlan said, nodding. "I hadn't considered that. You can't just stick someone in a legitimate catering team with no background." He sighed. "Thanks for complicating things, Aiden."

"My pleasure." Aiden pulled the book back to him. "I better get on. I have a train to catch at three. Good luck."

Harlan rose to his feet. "You, too."

Talking to Aiden had made Harlan restless—and worried.

The Orphic Guild had long known about Andreas Nicoli and The Order of Lilith, and they occasionally competed for occult items, especially in auctions. But this encounter was different, and if Aiden was right, it could happen more often.

Harlan returned to his office and immediately started

pacing. He shouldn't leap to conclusions—none of them should—and although he trusted Aiden's judgement, he should explore the other options. As he'd discussed with Olivia yesterday, there were several individuals and collectives that hunted for occult and magical goods, and he was pretty sure the loners wouldn't have teamed up with anyone.

He ran through the obvious single operatives, reconsidering them. There was Jackson Strange, who was strange by nature as well as name. A shaggy-haired, forty-something man who was charming, eccentric, and never to be underestimated. He would never team up with anyone, however. Dana Murphy, an Irish woman with jet-black hair and the bluest eyes, was more ruthless than she looked. She also worked alone, employed by a couple of big museums. He doubted she would team up with anyone, either.

There was someone else he was missing. Harlan paused at the window, looking over the street below, but failing to see anything. Then it came to him. *Samson Randolph. Of course.* He'd met him at a few auctions. His family was originally from Jamaica, but he was third-generation English with a First Class History degree and an endless thirst for knowledge. Harlan shook his head. *No, he wouldn't work with anyone, either.*

Harlan considered the other organisations that were active players in the field. There were The Seekers of the Lost, The Grey Order, The Order of the Chalice and Blade, and The Finders of the Forgotten. Not all of them were based in London, and a couple were family-run affairs that probably couldn't compete for The Trinity of the Seeker. There were potentially others he wasn't familiar with.

That line of thinking brought him back to Nicoli and The Order of Lilith, who would go after anything and everything —much like the guild. Nicoli's organisation had been going for about five years, and he estimated there were maybe three people he employed—depending on need. There was Andreas, of course, a thirty-something Greek man with deep pockets and questionable morals. He had no idea if his employees were full-time or contractors, but he'd seen a few at auctions, clearly stating they worked for Nicoli. There was a big guy with a long beard and red hair whose name he had never learnt. A blonde-haired woman, Gabriella Anderson, who'd bid very high one night to get an obsidian stone with magical properties. And Jensen James, a cocky boy in his twenties who Harlan refused to call a man; he was shifty, watchful, and distinctly untrustworthy.

Harlan ran his finger across his lower lip. Aiden was right. Unless this new woman worked alone, working for Nicoli was the next obvious choice. It might be sensible to find out more about her and what Nicoli was up to—and more importantly, who they were stealing the map for. But what was the best way to do that? He had no idea where Nicoli was based. Was it an office, or his own home? *Shit. Too many questions and not enough answers.* But Harlan knew that whatever was happening, they needed to get ahead of the game, and he needed information to do that. *What contacts did he have that could help?* Burton and Knight Auction House would be the most obvious place, but the auction wasn't until the next evening. He reached for his phone, intending to call Rose Donnelly, his contact there, but maybe that would be a bad idea. He didn't want to give himself away. *Damn it!*

Before he could exasperate himself with more specula-tion, his phone began to ring, and he picked it, answering impatiently. "Harlan Becket."

"Harlan. Are you all right?" The smooth tones of Mason's voice made him focus.

"Yes, sorry, Mason. Can I help?"

"I just wondered if you had an update for JD? I'm going to see him now."

"Not much at this stage, I'm afraid. Gabe and Shadow are onsite now, but I haven't heard from them. Not surprising, really. They've only just started their search." Harlan was surprised JD hadn't taken possession of the map yesterday, and he couldn't resist saying so.

"He arrived back in the country last night," Mason told him. "So he couldn't. I'm taking it to him now."

"I presume JD's place is secure."

"Very. Don't worry, Harlan. It will be safe there."

Harlan nodded absently. "That's good." He checked his watch. He could be in Angel's Rest in three hours. "I'm heading out too, Mason. I want to see the site in person, but I'll be back for the auction tomorrow. I don't think there's much I can do here before then."

"That's fine. I'll see you soon."

As soon as Mason had hung up, Harlan took a cursory glance around his office, grabbed his overnight bag that he always kept ready, and headed for the door.

Shadow stood in the cave called The Witch's Kitchen and smiled. It was lit up with ghoulish lights of green, pink, and purple, and the cool, damp air made her shiver.

They were at Wookey Hole cave complex, being tourists, and so far Shadow was enjoying herself. When the three of them had woken up that morning, they decided the best way to get a feel for the area was to see what had already been discovered. It was interesting to see how the humans had celebrated these caves, making them an experience for those who would never travel far beneath the earth's surface otherwise. And she'd found out they had actually been used for millennia. Bones had been found going back years, from when man had used caves to shelter in.

"Well, this is something, isn't it?" she said to Gabe, who was also looking around with amusement.

"I guess so."

Gabe's arms were folded across his chest, and he turned slowly as he examined the cavern. Ahead of them was a small boat on an underground stretch of water, and Shadow grimaced at the thought of the dark tunnels that hadn't been discovered yet, or were inaccessible to all but the hardy. There were caves in the Otherworld, especially in Dragon's Hollow, where they mined for precious metals, and the dragons hoarded their gold. She'd had one particularly unpleasant encounter in one of them once, years ago, with a vicious creature that almost killed her. The experience had put her off caves for a long time. While there might not be any dragons here, this was still an unnerving place to be, but at least the lights made her appreciate the unusual beauty.

"You know," Gabe continued, "this place was discovered in about the fifteenth century. I read it."

"Me, too." Shadow considered the heights of The Great Hall, one of the aptly-named caves they had already passed through, and said, "Maybe Phineas Hammond was inspired by them. They could have influenced his visions."

Gabe shook his head, half watching Niel walk around the other part of the cave. "It's too obvious, and too populated."

Shadow looked at him like he'd gone mad. "Now! But not in the fifteenth century. Now it's all lights and experience, and years and years of cave diving and exploration. They're even blasting through to a new cave," she told him, partly impressed and partly horrified at the thought of tons of stone coming down on their heads.

Gabe faced her. "I admit, The Great Hall is impressive, cathedral-like, a fitting place to talk to angels, but I expected to *feel* something, and I didn't. Nothing angelic or divine, or anything of the sort."

"You're right," she reluctantly admitted with a heavy sigh. "This temple will be something different. Come on. I'm cold. Let's get some coffee."

It was only when all three of them were sitting outside Captain Jack's, the restaurant in the Wookey Hole attractions, and Shadow was eating a large slice of cake and Niel and Gabe had burgers, that they discussed their options again.

Niel wiped ketchup from his chin and said, "It's too obvious, too big."

"And it's not where the temple's placed on the map," Gabe added. "But it could be part of the complex. Further in and further up."

Shadow swallowed a mouthful of cake. "As you know, I'm willing to try and do most things, but caving is not one of them."

Gabe pushed his sunglasses on top of his head, and his dark brown eyes looked amused. "Not one of my favourites, either. And besides, from what I can gather, we are much too big to go squeezing through some of these tiny passages that link the caves."

Niel laughed. "Phineas had a *vision*. As far as we know, he never actually came here. Maybe this temple is somewhere in the middle of hundreds of tons of rock. In that case, it can stay there, locked away for eternity. And it's probably a good thing, too."

The day was warm, and Niel had a short-sleeved t-shirt on, revealing his tattoos, and both he and Gabe drew a few curious glances. Shadow could see herself reflected in Niel's sunglasses, unable to see his blue eyes. "Why do you say that?"

"Like I said to Gabe last night, dealing with angels has a cost."

"But what about JD?"

"What about him?" Niel shrugged. "From what we found out, angels did him no favours. For all of his intelligence, which is considerable by the sound of it, he was—is—a brilliant mathematician, he was side-tracked by angels. People lost faith in him. Sounds to me like he was duped by his friend, Kelley, and he ended up losing more than he gained. If he'd never spoken to angels, his life would have been far better for it." Shadow and Gabe exchanged an uneasy glance that Niel saw. "Don't panic, I'm here to help. Just saying, is all."

Gabe's expression was unfathomable. "Niel thinks we may attract the attention of angels, which could cause us problems. And he might be right. They did kill us once."

Shadow leaned back in her chair, considering them both. "It's unlikely they'd send a major flood to kill seven of you though, right? Talk about overreacting!"

Gabe laughed, giving Niel an amused glance. "I think she has a point."

Niel grunted. "There are other ways to kill us."

"I think the angels—if you insist on calling them that—don't give a crap about anything in this reality anymore, so I wouldn't give it a second thought," Shadow told them, suddenly impatient. And then she realised that wasn't a very charitable way to talk about their fathers. She tried to modify her tone. "The important thing—*the thing we're being paid to do*—is the job. And then there's JD. I don't think it's up to us to tell him what he should or shouldn't do. What now?"

Gabe grinned. "Let's go for a drive. I passed over Cheddar Gorge last night; I'd like to see it in the day. You both up for that?"

"You don't want to visit Dinosaur Valley?" Niel asked, feigning surprise.

"Strangely, no," Gabe said, wincing as a group of moms and toddlers settled at the next table, the children already shrieking. He rose to his feet and pulled the car keys from his pocket. "Let's go."

Shadow was only too glad to follow him, and she cast one final glance at the table of small humans, wondering why anyone would want to deal with *that.*

6

*W*hen Harlan arrived at the rental house later that afternoon, he was relieved to find Gabe's SUV on the driveway, and the house looking as good as it did in the photos. He hadn't phoned to warn them he was coming, so it was only as he was close that he realised he might be waiting outside for hours.

Niel answered the door to him, saying, "Oh, it's you! We wondered who'd be calling."

He led the way down the hall, and Harlan dropped his bag at the bottom of the stairs before following him.

"How's it going?" Harlan asked him.

Niel laughed. "How isn't it going would be a better question."

Harlan tried to brush away his concerns. He'd known this wouldn't be easy. Niel led him to a modern, gleaming kitchen that already showed signs of use. A pot was simmering on the hob emitting a mouth-watering smell, and Harlan's stomach rumbled. It was something rich and garlicky. "That smells amazing. What is it?"

"Nothing flash. Spaghetti Bolognese—enough for you,

too," Niel reassured him as he headed to the fridge and grabbed some beers. "Want one?"

"Yes, please."

Harlan took the proffered beer and followed Niel to the large conservatory at the back of the house, where the doors to the terrace were open, and a cool breeze carried the promise of rain. The day had turned dark, thick clouds gathering overhead, and consequently the lamps were already on, banishing the gloom. Shadow and Gabe were sitting and talking quietly at the centre table that was covered in maps, along with dirty cups that had been pushed to the side.

They glanced up, smiling in greeting as Harlan and Niel joined them, and Harlan said, "Hey, guys. I hear there's not much progress yet."

Shadow's violet eyes already narrowing. "Did you really think there would be?"

"Calm down, tiger. No, I didn't. It's called a conversation starter."

"Tiger?" Shadow's eyes narrowed even further.

Harlan decided to tease her. "It's an animal. A big cat, known for its viciousness."

"I know what it is," she said coolly.

Gabe sniggered. "If you really want to rile her, call her a screwball."

"Don't you start," she said, flicking her bottle cap at Gabe with startling speed.

He caught it in his large hand just before it hit his face, and he grinned at Harlan. "See what I mean?"

Harlan raised his bottle in salute. "I'll remember that one. Thanks."

Shadow folded her arms and leaned back in her chair. "Have you finished your male bonding? Can we continue?"

Gabe gestured at the maps. "Please, go ahead. We're all ears."

Shadow leaned forward, casting Gabe an annoyed glance. "I believe I was suggesting that we concentrate further up the ridge." She pointed to the old map. "The spot where the temple is marked looks like it could be further into Ebbor Gorge, even though it doesn't really align with modern maps." She turned to Harlan. "While these two flew over it last night, I walked part of it. It's a bit of a scramble, and quite wild in places, but it's possible that there's something in there that has remained undiscovered for years."

"That's what's been worrying me," Harlan admitted. "It's National Trust property. Surely if there was something there, it would have been found by now."

Gabe shook his head. "The trees are thick in places, and it's very rocky. And, it could be hidden by magic."

"The angels like to challenge people," Niel said. "It's not going to reveal itself just like that."

Harlan started to grin. "Of course! Maybe we need The Path of the Seeker first? They might need to be used together!"

"So you mean us searching now is pointless?" Shadow asked, annoyed.

"No, not at all," Harlan said, trying to reassure her, and relieved to see her hands weren't going for her knives that he knew would be hidden somewhere on her body. "I might be wrong. I'm as much in the dark about this as you are."

"And what about the third part of the trinity? The key?" Gabe asked softly. "Without that, we get nowhere."

Harlan sipped his beer thoughtfully. "I know. But I'm hoping that once we find the place, it will become clear what type of key it is, because I don't think it will be what we expect. I'm hoping we'll get clues as to where to go next." Harlan looked out the window at the increasingly gloomy afternoon. "What if we look now? We might beat the rain. I really want to get a feel for this place."

Gabe drained his beer and stood up. "Have you got hiking gear?"

"In my bag."

"Let's go, then."

However, by the time they arrived back at the house two hours later, they were all wet and miserable, and Harlan felt none the wiser.

They had walked partway up the gorge when the rain started, making the rocky path treacherous in spots, but they persevered, clambering up through the narrow, rocky ravine until they came into woodlands. There they'd sheltered for a while, until it became clear the rain wasn't going anywhere. By the time they neared the entrance again, the streams that crossed the track had swollen, and they all got even wetter. Harlan felt guilt ridden and cranky. The walk was his suggestion and the others had agreed gracefully, but he realised it was a waste of time. They hadn't walked far enough, and it was a bigger area than he'd realised—which conversely gave him renewed hope, too. The temple could be there. *No. It had to be there.*

"Damn rain," Gabe grumbled as he shook water off himself like a dog in the hallway of the house. "I'm heading in the shower."

Niel kicked his boots off, going straight to the kitchen. "Food will be ready in thirty minutes, so you all better get a move on!"

Shadow ducked past Gabe and ran up the stairs, yelling, "Ladies first!"

Gabe yelled back. "Since when are you a lady?"

But she'd disappeared already, and Harlan said, "Please tell me there's more than one shower."

Gabe nodded. "Sure there are. But I warn you—she uses *a lot* of hot water. Nice place, by the way."

Harlan grabbed his bag and walked up the curving staircase next to Gabe. "Thanks. I use this company all the time. Never been here, though."

Gabe grunted as he headed through a door leading off the main corridor. "It's a good choice…defensible."

The door slammed behind him, and Harlan wandered onwards until he found an empty bedroom that overlooked the back of the house. The rain was heavy now, and everything beyond the perimeter of the garden was a misty blur. One thing was for sure—they wouldn't be doing any more exploring that night.

Gabe opened a bottle of red wine, grabbed a couple more beers, placed them and some glasses on a large tray, and carried it into a cosy dining room that led off from the kitchen.

He felt better after his shower, and the smell of Niel's cooking always cheered him up. He'd have liked to return to the conservatory, but it was deafening in there because of the heavy rain, and was now distinctly chilly.

He almost fell over his own feet when he walked in and he caught his breath, hoping that Shadow hadn't noticed as he placed the tray on the table. Her back was to him as she fed the fire that crackled in the grate, and her grace was breathtaking.

She wore loose cotton trousers and a slim-fitting t-shirt, revealing bare arms that looked silky smooth in the light. Her hair was caught up in a messy knot on her head, exposing her slender neck, and he caught a whiff of musk and rose. She finished prodding the fire and rose swiftly to her feet, turning to him with a satisfied smile.

"That's better. A room is not complete without a fire."

"Even in the summer?"

She grinned. "Even in the summer." She shrugged. "Although, I cope with candles. Fire is life."

"I know that. Beer or wine?"

"Wine, please."

He poured her a glass and passed it to her, trying to avoid touching her fingers. They looked beguilingly gentle, but they were lethal killing machines. Not that they worried him too much. He was more concerned about what the feel of her soft skin would do to his scrambled brain right now.

Gabe gestured at the rain. "You know, this will have a nightmare effect on cave systems. Water levels will rise, and some caves will be filled completely with water. What if our temple is the same?"

She took a sip of wine and wandered to the window. "Then we'll be in trouble. But water levels drop quickly—and I don't think our temple will be affected. I think it will be protected, somehow."

"By magic?" Harlan asked, and they both turned to see him walk in and head straight to the fire, warming his hands.

"I think so," Shadow said, watching him. "Or what's the point if it would be inaccessible half the time?"

"Maybe it's part of the challenge," Gabe suggested.

Niel's booming voice filled the room. "I need help with plates!" He appeared in the doorway, carrying a steaming bowl that he placed on the table. "Sit," he commanded to Gabe and Shadow, as Harlan scooted past him to help.

In a few minutes, after pasta and garlic bread had been placed next to the Bolognese sauce and they had all filled their plates, Harlan said, "This is fantastic. Thank you."

Niel smiled. "Cheers. My specialty is breakfast, but this is my other staple."

Gabe laughed. "If you're lucky, Harlan, you might get to try some of Shadow's rabbit stew. That's her specialty."

She looked affronted. "I have several, I'll have you know."

"And what's yours, Gabe?" Harlan asked.

"Barbeque and meat, Middle Eastern-style—koftas, kebabs, that sort of thing."

"Sounds great," Harlan said. "You guys have some sort of cooking roster, then?"

Gabe shrugged. "I wouldn't call it that. We're not all home at the same time. There's lot of midnight cooking, too."

Shadow rolled her eyes. "They eat like horses." She gave Gabe and Niel a sidelong glance. "I think their limbs are hollow."

"You're doing a pretty good job of putting that away," Niel pointed out.

"You're a very good cook."

Niel feigned choking. "Wow. I'm going to remember that one."

They chatted and joked over dinner, the food and alcohol loosening their tongues as they relaxed. When they'd finished eating and had stacked the dishwasher, they moved to the chairs around the fire, and Shadow prodded it back to life again. The rain was falling even harder now, and Niel put some music on, low in the background.

"So, how long are you here for, Harlan?" Gabe asked him, watching as the American stretched his feet towards the fire.

"I head back tomorrow. The auction is tomorrow night." He turned towards them, making himself more comfortable. "Mason delivered the map to JD today, so I'll be interested to see what he thinks of it."

"You think he may have some insight?" Niel asked.

"Maybe. I know Mason will ask me more tomorrow, too.

I thought coming here today would help. And I guess it has, sort of."

Niel nodded. "Ground reconnaissance is the best."

"Speaking of which—" Harlan looked at Shadow. She had curled up in the corner of the sofa, as sleek as a cat. "Do you want to come to the auction with me?"

She sat up, suddenly alert. "Why?"

"I think the woman you saw at Henri's will be there. I'm pretty sure I'll recognise her from your description, but I'd like first-hand confirmation."

Gabe felt a stir of worry in his gut. "You think she'll bid?"

Harlan nodded. "I have no doubt. If they wanted the map, they'll want the path."

"Even though we have the map?" Shadow asked, her face flush with intrigue.

"Oh, that won't put them off!"

"Who's *them*?" Gabe asked.

"I'm not one hundred percent sure, but after chatting to my colleagues, we think a man called Andreas Nicoli is behind this. His organisation is called The Order of Lilith. We cross swords occasionally."

"Lilith?" Niel asked, his eyes narrowing with suspicion and an edge entering his previously relaxed voice.

Gabe felt the worry in his gut turn into a twisted knot of panic. Lilith's name could have an unpredictable affect on Niel.

"Who's she?" Shadow asked.

"Adam's first wife, if you believe the myths," Harlan told her, giving Niel a puzzled glance. "But an unsuitable one. She wouldn't do as she was told."

"Adam—the first man?" Shadow's tone was already laced with contempt, a sign of her disbelief, Gabe knew. "I like her already."

"A demon wife, or witch, depending on what you read,"

Niel said, his face now turned towards the fire, his gaze distant. "But she was actually none of those things."

Harlan's eyes widened. "You knew her?"

Gabe watched Niel, noting his hands were clenched in his lap, his beer forgotten on the floor, and Gabe answered for them both. "Once. A long time ago. She was a strong woman who was neither demon nor monster, but who wanted to live as she chose. She was demonised for it. She died for it."

"Died for her independence?" Shadow was already bristling with anger.

Niel looked at Harlan and Shadow, seeing the confusion on their faces, and then looked at Gabe. Gabe shrugged. *This was Niel's past, not his.*

Niel sighed as he came to a decision, heavy and world-weary, and he stared into the flames again. "Lilith was my wife."

Harlan's mouth dropped open, a flood of emotions crossing his face. "Your *what*? I'm sorry I made light of it."

Niel shook his head. "Forget it. You had no idea, and it was a long time ago—even for me."

Shadow was silent, and her eyes burned. Gabe knew she'd be teeming with questions, but she swallowed them, only saying, "I had no idea you were married, Niel."

He smiled sadly. "We were all married once, Shadow. Some of us, many times."

Shadow looked at Gabe. "You were married?"

He felt odd confessing it. "Yes. Just once." Just that simple word brought his memories rushing back. He would dream of her later, he knew it. *But what did it matter that Shadow knew?* She was still staring at him. "Were you? *Are* you?" he asked her. Shadow never spoke of whom she had left behind.

"No. Marriage is not common for fey, and I was always too busy travelling for a long term relationship." Shadow glanced across at Harlan. "What about you?"

"Me?" Harlan looked incredulous. "I don't think anyone would put up with me. Not long term, anyway." He glanced at Niel, who was still staring into the fire. Harlan seemed anxious to make amends, and it was pretty clear Niel wouldn't say anything else. "Anyway, I was talking about Nicoli's order. They have lots of connections—lots of people who may want the map. They'll be there tomorrow. So will you come?" he asked, looking at Shadow again.

She nodded. "Of course." She settled back into her corner, cradling her glass of wine. "Tell us more."

For the next couple of hours, Harlan chatted about the different occult organisations he knew about and how The Orphic Guild fitted in with the rivalries and characters. It was useful knowledge and Gabe was grateful for it, but he noticed Niel remained quiet, participating with only occasional good grace, and it was clear his thoughts were elsewhere. By ten, Harlan made his excuses and went to bed. Shadow soon followed, leaving Gabe and Niel in companionable silence.

Gabe headed to the kitchen and came back with two glasses of whiskey and the bottle — just in case. He thrust a glass at Niel, and Niel took it from him, a wry smile on his lips.

"I'm fine, Gabe."

"Are you?"

"Of course. It was a long time ago, and her name was bound to come up eventually. It just wasn't how I was expecting it to." He sipped his drink and leaned back in the chair, watching the amber liquid swirl as he turned the glass. "It's odd how you think you've buried your memories, and yet they come back so swiftly, like a knife in the darkness."

Niel wasn't an emotive man. None of them were. But it didn't mean they didn't feel deeply, or love, or mourn lost relationships. It was assumed that anger and violence was their reason for being, but their lives were far more complex than that. Over the last few months they had all mourned in different ways, while simultaneously celebrating their new existence. But Niel hadn't lied earlier. Lilith had been gone for years, even before the flood.

"She was a good woman, Niel," Gabe said softly. "I miss her, too."

"Her death was unjust…unfair. It still burns."

"And it always will." Gabe sipped his drink, enjoying the warmth as it rolled across his tongue and down his throat. "It should. It's a reminder of our limitations—in case we forget."

"I can't forget. I don't want to, not really."

"Then let's drink to memories." Gabe lifted the whiskey bottle and topped their drinks up. "And share a few."

This could be a late night, but that was fine. He'd be up as late as Niel needed him to be.

7

*S*hadow and Harlan were halfway to London when Shadow couldn't contain herself any longer.

"What's the deal with Lilith?"

Harlan glanced at her, before concentrating on the road. The rain was still heavy, and the journey was slow. "That's an excellent question, and one I'm not sure I'm equipped to answer."

Shadow had taken a while to go to sleep the previous night. She'd sat up in bed, the drumming rain a backdrop to the research she'd done on her phone. While she knew that the Nephilim had led rich and full lives prior to the flood, for some reason she never considered wives to be a part of that. *Maybe because she'd never been married herself?*

She said, "I find it hard to believe she really was the first woman for one thing."

Harlan laughed. "You have a hard time believing in creation myths, full stop."

"Don't you?"

"I will admit they seem simplistic. But like most myths, they are there to frame our lives, to give meaning where there was none—especially hundreds and thousands of years ago, when life was complicated and confusing. Don't you have creation myths?"

Shadow shrugged, watching the competent way Harlan threaded through the traffic. "Not like yours. We are fey. We have existed since the dawn of time. Our magic is woven with the elements and the earth. Magic is everywhere for us. But this Lilith—she seems to have significance."

"It's odd, isn't it," Harlan mused, "which names survive time. Who sticks around, who disappears. I think she gets tied up in patriarchy and the church and the rights of women —well, for some people."

"That's what I think, too." Shadow stretched her legs out. "I read about her online last night. The stories are many and varied, too confusing."

"Well, it seems you can have a first-hand account, if you want one."

"I'm not sure Niel will want to talk about her."

"Maybe not right now, but I'm sure he will in time. He seems like a reasonable man."

Shadow nodded. "He is. They all are." She'd wait, and when the time was right, she'd talk to him—and Gabe. They were partners and friends, and she wanted to know more about them. She thought back to her research the night before. "For all that I read, though, I still couldn't get a picture of her."

"For a historical perspective, I think you'd have to talk to theology scholars for that—or a man of God. But only your guys can give you the real deal. Certainly not me." Harlan grinned at her. "Is this the way all of our car journeys are going to go from now on?"

Shadow laughed. "Maybe. I have lots of questions about lots of things." She liked Harlan. He was easy company. And intriguing. Their conversation the previous night had been instructive, and she realised now more than ever that Harlan was deeply embedded in the arcane and magical world, and she appreciated that. "How did you get involved in all this?"

"By 'all this,' do you mean the occult?" he asked.

"Yes."

"Well, that's quite the story, but in a nutshell, I watched too many adventure films and read too many books about the occult, myths, and magic. I fancied myself as a bit of a rogue trader, and ended up making a few finds and some dodgy deals with some very *interesting* characters. This was in the U.S., of course."

"Which bit?"

"West coast, mainly, but I travelled around. And then I met Olivia, who already worked for The Orphic Guild, while we were both searching for an Incan statue, and I ended up getting a job with them—based in San Francisco, at the time."

"And when did you come to London?" Shadow asked, wondering exactly how dodgy Harlan's past had been.

"Almost ten years ago, when Mason offered me a chance to move here." He flashed a smile at her. "I miss California weather. And what about your past?"

"Ooh." She grimaced. She should have been expecting that. "It was eventful."

He laughed loudly. "I bet. Come on, Shadow, you gotta share something!"

Shadow mentally filtered through her varied jobs, wincing at the memories of some. "I've been a mercenary on occasion—for kings who waged war for land or castles. I've hunted dragon gold, chased and killed murderous creatures, stolen a few things, and searched for a lot of lost treasure." She shrugged. "That type of thing."

"And left family and friends behind?" he asked.

"Yes." She fell silent, thinking of the band of fey that had become her family; the ones she worked with. "I miss them."

"I bet. But you have the Nephilim. That's lucky, right?"

She nodded. "Very." She decided it was time to change the subject, and realising she had no idea what would happen after the auction that evening, she asked, "You asked me to bring my bag. Are we staying in London tonight?"

Harlan nodded. "Yeah, probably best. These things can go on for a few hours, and sometimes there are after-auction drinks. They're good for networking."

"Where will I sleep?"

"If we need to, I'll check you into a hotel, but I think I have a better solution. Remember William Chadwick?"

Shadow squirmed. "The man I killed? Of course." She still felt guilty about that, even though it was her life or his.

"He's left us his house. The Orphic Guild, that is." He grimaced. "Mind you, we only got the keys a few days ago, so it might need airing out."

"You're going to let people stay there?" Shadow remembered the strange Victorian Gothic building with its extensive occult collection and rich decorating. That would be a *very* interesting place to stay.

"A chosen few. I'm sure you'd make the cut." He cast a sidelong glance at her. "As long as you don't steal anything."

"I can promise that—for you."

"So grateful!"

"S'okay."

"I tell you what. Let's head to the office and see who's around. I have some prep work to do before the auction, and I think you should meet Olivia."

Shadow was about to answer when Harlan's phone rang, and he answered it, the Bluetooth in the car kicking in so that Shadow could hear, too. She recognised Mason's voice.

"Harlan, where are you?"

"On the way back to London now, with Shadow." He

glanced across at her. "We're in the car, so she can hear you, too."

"Good. Don't go to the office. Come to JD's estate. I'll send you the address. Any idea when you'll be here?"

"How's one o'clock sound?" Harlan asked after a quick glance at the time. "We should eat some lunch first."

"Don't bother. You can eat here," he said, and then hung up abruptly.

Shadow felt a stir of excitement. "We're going to JD's place? Have you been there before?"

Harlan grinned. "Nope. A first for both of us."

———

"This home is well off the beaten path," Shadow observed, after it seemed as if they had been driving through the countryside for ages.

"You know," Harlan said, as he negotiated the quiet lanes of Surrey, "JD used to live right by the river in Mortlake, in London. But when he was officially declared dead, it became something else. A Tapestry Works. I imagine that would have been annoying. He had an observatory, I think."

"Not much you can do when you're dead, though," Shadow pointed out as she looked around at the green fields and narrow lanes. "Is that why his house is called Mortlake and he has the same last name?"

"I guess so," Harlan replied, keeping an eye out for the number of the house. "He must have been very fond of the area."

"Seems obsessive," Shadow said, thinking that dwelling on the past was never a good thing. "This place looks expensive."

"Parts of Surrey can be."

They had just driven through a small village, and the

houses were becoming sparse as they drove further out. Harlan slowed and he eventually turned onto a drive, finding their way blocked by a large gate and an intercom. He reached out of his window and pressed the button. Shadow saw a camera blink to life, and without needing to speak, the gate swung open and Harlan pulled in.

A house in warm, mellow timbers was at the end of a brick-lined drive, a large garage off to the left. The gardens were a mixture of lawns and borders, and another car was already on the drive.

"That will be Mason," Harlan said, pulling to a halt. "The house is Elizabethan. Not surprising."

"You guys like your big houses," Shadow observed, as she exited the car. It had stopped raining, but heavy clouds were still gathered overhead, looking as if there might be more rain due soon. She stretched as she stood, easing her cramped muscles, and rolled her shoulders before walking to Harlan's side.

"JD certainly does! You know," he said, lowering his voice, "he used to have a lot of money troubles. I guess that with longevity comes wealth—if you invest properly. And there's lots of money in the occult business."

Shadow was taking in the extensive gardens bordered by trees, and the home so isolated from its surroundings. "I guess he likes privacy, too. I wonder how he manages immortality. He must have people he trusts."

"Well, Mason knew, and you're right, there must be others."

"Didn't you say there are other Orphic Guild offices? Maybe they know, too?"

"Excellent point, Shadow." He cocked his head at her, a speculative look in his eyes. "You're not just a pretty face."

She smiled. "But it is disarming, yes?"

"Very." He led the way to the front door, but it was

already opening, and an older woman with grey hair cut into a blunt bob stood on the other side, giving them sweeping glances. "Harlan and Shadow, I presume?"

"At your service," Harlan said, extending his hand, and Shadow did the same, surprised by the strength of the woman's grip.

"I'm Anna, JD's assistant. Come in. They're in the map room."

As they stepped inside, Shadow admired the gleaming hall that had a tiled floor and doors leading off on either side. The walls were decorated with a mixture of wooden panelling and wallpaper, and a broad staircase swept grandly to the upper levels. But what was more interesting were the strange sigils, runes, and alchemical shapes carved into the woodwork and the plaster of the ceiling, and she wondered if they protected the house in some way. Oil paintings of figures in old-fashioned clothing, dark and moody, lined the walls, and although Shadow would have liked to examine them closer, Anna was already heading down the hall, and she hurried to follow her. Partway down Anna led them up a small, winding staircase, finally emerging into an attic space, where Shadow looked around, shocked.

The entire back of the roof and walls of the attic had been replaced with glass, and a deck ran out from it onto a flat section of the roof. But the most surprising thing was the large telescope in the middle of the room, pointing skyward.

The remaining walls were covered in maps of the world, old and modern, as well as maps of the night sky, with sections of the universe enlarged and places of significance marked. Hundreds of pictures of planets, moons, and stars jostled for position, and a desk at the far end was surrounded by stacks of paperwork, covering a large area of the floor. On it was a single map, and Shadow could guess which one it was.

Shadow was aware her mouth was hanging open, but she couldn't stop staring, and she noticed that Harlan wasn't doing much better. A cough disturbed her, and she swung around to see JD smiling. "Do you like my map room?"

Shadow laughed. "Sorry. I was being rude. Yes, I do. It's not what I was expecting." She swept her arms wide. "None of this is. You have an observatory!"

"It's very impressive," Harlan added.

JD beamed with pleasure, his chest swelling slightly. He looked the same as the last time she had seen him, but a little less groomed. His white beard and thick head of white hair looked a little more unkempt but he still exuded elegance, intelligence, style, and wit. He wasn't wearing a smart shirt and suit, but was instead in a cotton shirt, full at the sleeves and covered in ink, the cuffs rolled back, and he wore old corduroys and braces. It suited him.

Mason leaned against the edge of the desk, watching with an amused expression. "I'm glad to see I'm not the only one to find this room fascinating," he told them. "Good to see you again, Shadow."

"You too, Mason." Shadow was glad to see Mason hadn't changed. He was as immaculate as when she'd last met him.

"Anna, will you bring coffee and lunch, please?" JD asked.

Anna was waiting at the threshold, and nodded before she left, shutting the door behind her.

"I'm glad you could make it," JD said, heading to the desk. "Mason tells me you've been to the site." He stood over the map, his eyes burning with curiosity, his mouth in a firm line. "I've been aware of this map for some time. I even owned it, at one point."

"You did?" Harlan asked, surprised. "What happened?"

"It was stolen while I was abroad, along with other books I had collected for years." He shot a glance at Shadow. "Some of them I want you to help me recover." He sighed and looked back at the map. "I didn't pursue this because I hunted for the temple at the time, and found nothing. I had presumed that it was a work of fancy."

"But now that The Path of the Seeker is up for auction, that all changes," Harlan said softly.

"It certainly does." JD pulled on soft, white cotton gloves and then ran his finger across the map, finally stopping on the site of the temple. "Back then, Wookey Hole, the village, didn't really exist. There was only a smattering of houses. Wells, the town, was there, of course. There were no roads through the area like there are now. Cheddar Gorge was spectacular, but difficult to get to." He shook his head. "It was hard going, and I toiled for months. Of course I found caves, but nothing that could be a temple. The path could change everything." He looked at Harlan. "You have to get it."

"I plan to," Harlan said decisively. "Shadow is coming, too. It's clear someone else is interested in this. Mason told you about what happened?"

JD nodded. "I don't care what it costs, just buy it."

"It could get very expensive."

JD shrugged. "It doesn't matter. Bring it here as soon as you have it." He gestured to the map again. "Have you found anything yet?"

"No," Shadow said, "but of course we've only just started looking. The map is inaccurate, obviously fantastical, but we'll find it." She sounded sure of herself, but she wasn't. It seemed improbable, but failure wasn't an option.

"Bidding tonight will make us a target," Mason said. "You could be vulnerable to attack by whoever's working against us."

"I think we're equal to it, aren't we, Shadow?" Harlan asked her.

"Of course."

69

"Have you had an advance look at it yet?" Mason asked Harlan.

"Not yet. Burton and Knight are being cagey and leaving it quite late."

"Is that unusual?" Shadow asked, not entirely sure how auctions worked.

"In order to generate interest in a lot, it's normally well-advertised." Harlan scratched his head, perplexed. "So, yes, this is unusual, and worrying."

The door opened behind them and Anna came in carrying a large tray stacked with food, which she put down on a low table on the other side of the room. "I'll be back with more," she called over her shoulder.

JD peeled his gloves off elegantly. "Excellent. Let's eat."

8

*B*urton and Knight Auction House was situated in an unassuming building in Chelsea. Unlike many other auction houses, it didn't have a large sign over the entrance advertising what it was; instead, there was a small brass plaque next to a door painted shiny black with a medusa's head brass knocker on it.

Its familiarity soothed Harlan as he stepped inside the entrance hall, Shadow next to him. He spent a lot of time there, and he knew many of the staff well. Burton and Knight specialised in the occult and arcane, and it was rare he went elsewhere. Tonight they were in one of the smaller rooms, and Harlan led the way down the corridor, grimacing as he arrived on the threshold. Even though he had purposely arrived early, it was already half full.

They sat at the end of a row at the back of the room as he said, "This will be harder than I originally thought. No sign of the woman yet."

It was more of a statement than a question, but Shadow shook her head. "No."

A couple of people nodded their way, and he nodded

back. *This didn't bode well.* There were many objects for sale that night, so with luck, the other bidders would be more interested in those items. After talking with JD and Mason earlier, they'd decided he should bid on a few other objects in an effort to mask their real objective. Some of the lots were an obscure collection from the home of a private collector of medieval objects, and they would fit in with the kind of thing The Orphic Guild would obtain.

Harlan fidgeted in his seat, running his fingers under his collar and adjusting his jacket. He'd dressed in a suit, and the place was overly warm, making him sweat. It didn't help he'd just had a good workout at the guild's gym, followed by a hot shower. Shadow had decided to spend her time strolling the streets of Eaton Place. He was relieved he hadn't needed to entertain her, and she sat next to him now, composed and alert.

He opened the leaflet on his lap, reading through the descriptions of the lots for sale, and pulling his pen from his pocket, he marked a few that he should examine when allowed.

Shadow had been flicking through her own copy with interest, and she now lowered her voice and brought her lips close to his ear. "Are we actually going to be able to look at the path before the bidding opens?"

He nodded and checked his watch. "Any minute now, I hope."

They waited impatiently for a while longer, and then Rose Donnelly, his contact, appeared at the entrance to the adjoining room and addressed the attendees. "The lots are now open for inspection."

Rose Donnelly was a short, plump woman with a porcelain complexion and red hair, and she acknowledged Harlan as she saw him across the room, and then immediately headed through the door.

Harlan left his jacket on the chair, and followed by Shadow, trailed after the growing crowd. Immediately beyond the door was a series of tables, well lit by spotlights, but he ignored them for now, heading to Rose's side.

Her face creased into a frown as he reached her. "Sorry, Harlan. I know you wanted to see this earlier, but it hasn't been possible."

"Why the hell not?" he asked, trying not to lose his cool.

"Things are a little odd right now," she said, lowering her voice. "Who's your friend?"

"Shadow, she's a new contractor," he said, quickly making the introduction. "What do you mean by 'odd?'"

"It seems there are a couple of interested parties, and they're trying to make life awkward." She glanced around as they talked, smiling and nodding at other bidders. "Look, I can't talk, but I suggest you keep on your toes tonight. I think there's more to The Path of the Seeker than originally thought."

"Is it genuine?" he asked quickly, before she walked away.

"Absolutely. We've had it dated and compared it to records of The Map of the Seeker. They are of the same date and hand. Unfortunately," she paused and looked at Harlan suspiciously, "the actual Map of the Seeker has been stolen. We approached Henri Durand for it on Monday. There was quite an uproar, as I'm sure you understand."

Harlan tried to look as shocked as possible, and he felt Shadow still next to him. "Stolen? How?"

"Henri has no idea, but he's quite upset."

"I'm sure he is," Harlan said, smoothing his hand down his tie, and nodding in concern. "Pass on my regards if you see him again."

Rose nodded before walking away, and Harlan started to inspect the lots, examining each one carefully, and making notes in his sales pamphlet. "Keep your eyes peeled, Shadow," he said softly as they progressed.

"I don't need to," she replied. "She's here."

Harlan resisted the urge to jerk his head up and stare. "Where?"

"Where do you think? By the document."

Harlan casually lifted his head and scanned the room, immediately seeing the woman Shadow had described. She was shorter than he had pictured, but her black, spiky hair was immediately recognisable. And it looked as if she was with Jensen James, the cocky young associate of Andreas Nicoli.

Shit.

Trying not to appear rushed, he eventually arrived at The Path of the Seeker, and nodding politely at Jensen he leaned forward to inspect the document, wishing Jensen would piss off. He was aware of their eyes on him as he noted it was a long, one-page manuscript, the paper thick and slightly yellow, but otherwise in remarkably good condition. The title at the top read, *The Second Part of the Trinity of the Seeker. For those who would dare to seek the knowledge of the angels.*

Harlan frowned. This wasn't what he was expecting at all. The document was filled with strange drawings and symbols, very alchemical in nature. Some were laid out in a grid, as well as what appeared to be verse written in Latin. However, the paper matched the map, to the naked eye at least, and Rose said it was genuine. He hoped JD could make more sense of it.

Rather than leave him in peace, Jensen spoke up. "Something you're interested in, Harlan?"

His cocky cockney tone grated on his nerves. "Perhaps." He looked at Jensen coolly. "Are you, Jensen? You look like you're guarding it."

Jensen smirked. "No, mate, just looking, like you." He nodded at Shadow. "You brought a friend?"

Shadow smiled disarmingly, simultaneously releasing a wash of glamour. "I'm Shadow."

Jensen's eyes widened with surprise and he blushed to his roots. "A pleasure."

Suppressing a smile, Harlan nodded at the would-be thief next to him. "Have you brought a friend, too?"

Jensen tore his gaze from Shadow. "This is Mia."

Mia was staring at them both with a suspicious look on her face, but she nodded, remaining mute.

"Well, we must get on," Harlan said, turning his back and returning to their seats in the increasingly crowded room.

"The manuscript wasn't what I was expecting at all," Shadow said, looking worried.

"Me neither. I couldn't make heads or tails of it. I found the words, 'For those who would dare', quite ominous." Harlan scratched his neck. "I have a bad feeling about this. Where's Mia?"

"I can't see her, but Jensen is over there, near the front."

The energy in the room had risen as everyone settled in to bid, and Harlan felt the prickle of nerves and excitement that he always had at the start of an auction, but the feelings generally disappeared when the bidding began.

Another familiar face appeared across the room, and he raised a hand. Olivia headed swiftly to his side, and as she sat down, her silk dress fell in waves around her calves. "Evening, Harlan. Mason suggested I join you tonight." She smiled impishly. "Perhaps he doesn't trust you."

"Funny. Are you my support crew?"

She laughed. "I'm here to keep tabs on the room while you bid."

"That's a good idea." He noticed her eyes slide to Shadow. "Sorry, you two haven't met."

He introduced them, and they greeted one another warmly, and not without a fair degree of curiosity. He realised with a sinking feeling that they were, for all of their physical differences, horribly alike, and were going to get on far too well—probably to his detriment.

Shadow's eyes slid across Olivia's dress, watching as she crossed her legs to show a tanned calf, her Louboutin shoes on full display, the red sole unmistakable.

"I like your shoes," Shadow told her, looking envious. "I normally wear boots, but those are *different*!"

"Thank you. A treat to myself, after finally getting a *very* nice commission." She leaned across Harlan to get closer to Shadow, and lowered her voice. "They're my third pair."

"I bet you don't wear them in the field," Harlan said, already feeling out gunned.

"Of course not!" She grinned at him. "I'll stick to my steel toecaps for that. So, tell me, where are we at?"

"We have a feeling things aren't going to be that straightforward," he told her.

Shadow lowered her voice. "I still can't see Mia. Does this place have a back door?"

"Two," Olivia answered. "A regular entrance for the staff, and a warehouse door for delivery vans further along, both at the back of the building."

A speculative look crossed Shadow's face and Harlan said, "What are you thinking?"

"I need to be outside."

"You suspect trouble?"

"Don't you? I think I should position myself for an alternative solution."

Olivia grinned. "Oh, I like you. Harlan?"

Harlan inwardly groaned, but knew it was a good idea. "All right. Be careful—and discreet!"

Shadow smiled as she edged past both of them, her eyes as mean as a snake. "Always."

Olivia watched her leave. "She's the fey, right?"

"Right."

"She doesn't look it."

"That's her glamour. It's very effective. When she drops it, it's actually quite unnerving. It's her stealth, however, that's even more unbelievable. She has this knack for disappearing."

Olivia frowned and then smiled. "Really? How very useful."

"Oh yes. And deadly. I suggest we never cross her."

The bang of the gavel interrupted them, and they both turned to the front of the room.

———

Shadow made her way quickly down the main street, looking for the road that would take her to the back of the building.

After a couple of false starts, she found the one she needed and increased her pace, knowing the auction would be starting imminently. From what Harlan had said, The Path of the Seeker would be auctioned towards the end, so she could have a while to wait, but it would give her a chance to position herself.

The lane was quiet, which wasn't surprising. It was evening, and she imagined most deliveries would take place during normal working hours. Buildings crowded around her on both sides, and overflowing bins and boxes were piled outside most rear entrances. She wrinkled her nose as the smell of rotten food reached her. Some buildings backed directly onto the street, while others had what looked to be rear courtyards. A few vans were parked, pulled in close to walls. There was some activity outside a couple of buildings, and she could hear chatting and music. The kitchens would be here, for the restaurants that lined the street.

It didn't take long for Shadow to find the rear of Burton and Knight. She spotted the warehouse door straight away. It was a large roller door, padlocked to the ground, with a camera and alarm system in place. The normal door to the rear entrance was a short distance away. It was already gloomy in the alley, the light fading rapidly, and she watched and waited across the street, sheltering in the recess of a wall.

Shadow was sure that Mia was up to something. If she wasn't in the auction room, she suspected that she would be finding a way to take the document in case Jensen failed. *Or maybe she was just going to steal it, anyway.* Harlan had told her that thefts were rare from here, but she had a feeling that they were willing to risk the consequences for this. Shadow wondered if Mia would exit this way, or if it would be more likely that she might steal it and stroll out the front door? As far as she could tell, Mia wasn't supernatural, so evading the auction staff would be tricky. *Surely she couldn't hope to steal it from under their noses?*

Shadow ran her finger over her bottom lip, pondering the possibilities, and her gaze drifted up to the windows above. From what Harlan had said, Burton and Knight owned the whole building. A drainpipe ran close to a couple of windows, and if she needed to, she might be able to get in that way. *But no, waiting was the key.* So, she shuffled into a more comfortable position and watched.

It was dark when her phone vibrated in her pocket, and she read a message from Harlan saying that Mia was still nowhere in sight and the auction for the path was about to begin. She put her phone away, and within minutes a loud and persistent alarm rang out, shattering the silence. It was coming from the auction house.

A diversion—it had to be.

Within minutes, the back door burst open and a dozen people exited, pacing and chattering excitedly. In the confusion, a small, petite figure separated herself from the others, and walked quickly down the alley. *Mia.* Shadow followed, hugging the wall as she kept her in sight. Mia was walking briskly, but not fast enough to be suspicious. She could see her short, spiky hair as she passed beneath a light, and Shadow allowed her to reach the far end of the alley, well away from the auction house and the gathering crowd, before she caught up.

Mia was angling to the left, no doubt to head down the network of small lanes. Shadow waited until she was close to the wall and then ran up behind her, throwing her arm around her neck and dragging her to the side. Mia immediately reacted, kicking back as she tried to shake off Shadow, but she threw her against the wall, Mia's face slamming into the brick, and pinned her in place, wondering how best to search her. Mia grunted and her elbow jammed back, catching Shadow in the stomach, and she almost lost her grip. But she was taller and stronger, and although Mia squirmed, she couldn't get free.

Although Shadow wanted to question her, she knew her voice could give her away, and so far Mia hadn't got a good look at her. Besides, she was using her fey magic, which would make her hard to see. Mia took advantage of Shadow's hesitancy and this time she kicked out, catching Shadow in the calf, and Shadow lost patience. She punched Mia, hard, and the woman went limp. Shadow lowered her to the ground, pulled her behind a large skip, and started to rifle through her coat. But there was nothing within it. Frustrated, she patted her down and then rolled her over, wondering if she'd secured the document to her back. But again, nothing. *Herne's bloody horns.* Mia was groaning, her eyelids flickering, and Shadow debated interrogating her, but it was pointless. She'd either hidden the manuscript, or passed it on. *Jensen. Where was he?*

Leaving Mia, Shadow watched the growing number of people clustered around the back of Burton and Knight. She returned to them, again keeping close to the wall, but there was no sign of Jensen, Olivia, or Harlan. She came to a quick decision and doubled back on herself, running down the alley. Mia had already gone, but Shadow turned left, just as Mia had intended to. She couldn't have gone far.

Shadow reached the end of another narrow road and paused on the corner, spotting Mia's limping figure hurrying down the street on the right as fast as her gait allowed, looking over her shoulder nervously. Shadow pursued her, hoping she would lead her to Jensen. But Mia paused on the corner, beneath a streetlight, and within moments a car pulled up to the kerb, picked her up, and drove away.

9

*H*arlan and Olivia had just sat in Harlan's car when Shadow opened the back door and slid inside.

Harlan turned to look at her, but he could already tell by the set of her shoulders and her bleak stare that things hadn't gone according to plan. "I take it you haven't got it."

"No." Her lips were set in a hard line.

It was an hour after the fire alarm had gone off and Harlan and Olivia had evacuated Burton and Knight. They'd hung around on the pavement waiting for the fire brigade to declare the place safe, hoping that all of Harlan's suspicions were wrong, but within minutes of them getting back inside the building, the staff confirmed that The Path of the Seeker had been stolen. Jensen and Mia were nowhere in sight. The staff were furious, and also profoundly apologetic, but Harlan was still annoyed. His only hope had been Shadow.

"Shit," he said forcefully.

"It was stolen, then?" she asked.

"Of course. That damn alarm was a diversion. What happened?"

"I caught up with Mia, but she didn't have it. She must have passed it to Jensen, or someone else. Or she never had it in the first place, and she was a false trail to start with."

"Damn it!" Harlan smacked the wheel with a clenched fist. "I knew I should have followed that weasel, Jensen, instead!"

Shadow leaned forward, her head between Harlan and Olivia. "She got into a car on the corner of one of the back streets, but I wouldn't recognise it."

"Did she see you?"

Shadow looked at him scornfully. "Of course not. I attacked her from behind, and I didn't say a word."

That was something at least, Harlan reflected.

"It doesn't matter," Olivia said, looking far calmer than Harlan, which infuriated him even further. "We know they're working together, and although we didn't see it get stolen by either of them, we know it has to be them. Let's face it, Jensen disappeared after the fire alarm sounded, and that's highly suspicious. But this means Nicoli is behind it all." She looked beyond them both to the pub on the corner. "May I suggest a drink? It's not exactly like we need to flee the scene of the crime."

"Great idea," Harlan said, already exiting the car, and within minutes they had bought drinks and found a spot in the cosy pub.

Harlan's fingers drummed on the table with nervous energy. He scanned the room, and satisfied no one was close enough to hear them, especially over the hum of conversation, said, "We need to plan our next move."

"Have you told JD yet?" Shadow asked.

"Of course not. I've barely had a chance to think."

"No need for snarkiness," she told him.

He sighed and rubbed his face, feeling stubble beneath his fingers. "Sorry. I'm frustrated. I really thought we'd gotten the drop on them."

"Me, too." Shadow smiled ruefully. "But, I must say, I'm impressed. When did Jensen disappear?"

"Not until the alarm went," Olivia said. She looked composed and thoughtful, with not a hair out of place. Neither had Shadow, Harlan observed, feeling more unkempt by the second. "I was keeping an eye on him. The bidding for the path had just started, and there were at least another two interested parties."

"Did you recognise them?" Shadow asked.

"I did. One of them was a man who I've seen a couple of times but don't really know. He brought a few items, and I think he was bidding hopefully rather than energetically. He seemed to drop out quickly, but the other man," she raised an eyebrow as she watched Harlan, gauging his reaction, "was Jackson Strange. He arrived late. Did you see him?"

Harlan blinked, and felt even more annoyed. He'd arrived at the auction feeling in control, but now everything had changed. "No. He was bidding on the path, too?"

Olivia nodded. "He arrived just as the auction started and lurked at the back of the room. You were too focussed to see him." She smiled. "But that's why I was there. He put in a couple of bids, and had every intention of keeping going by the look of it, until, of course the alarm went off."

Harlan thought back to the scrambled events when the alarm sounded and they had all hurriedly left the room. "But I didn't see him afterwards, either."

"No." Olivia sipped her gin and tonic thoughtfully. "He obviously didn't hang around—and that might mean something, or it might not!"

Shadow leaned forward, her eyes bright. "Who is Jackson Strange?"

Olivia smiled again. "He's quite the lone wolf, Shadow. Charming, with a dangerous undercurrent of sexiness. He's a hunter of occult objects like the rest of us, but has no known associates."

"Could he be behind the theft?"

Harlan shook his head. "I doubt it. I'm not saying he's not capable of theft, I just don't think he's behind this one."

"Unless they're working together," Shadow suggested.

Harlan looked at Olivia, but she shook her head too, obviously agreeing with him. "It's unlikely," he said to Shadow. "That's why we call him a lone wolf. I've never known him to work with any other hunter."

"So, he either wants it for himself or a private client," Shadow speculated. "And that's means there are three of us after it, but only one of us with the map."

A horrible thought occurred to Harlan, and he mused on it for moment before voicing his concern. "There's a third part to this—the key. I wonder if one of them already has it."

"I must admit, it had crossed my mind," Olivia said. "You should call JD sooner rather than later. What if someone knows he has the map and tries to steal it—tonight!"

"There's no way anyone can know he has it," Harlan reasoned.

"Except for the fact that you were bidding on the path tonight," Shadow told him.

"But that just means we want it, or someone we work for has it, or we have it locked in our offices. There's no reason to think JD has it."

Shadow nodded, seemingly satisfied, and leaned back again, sipping her drink. "So, what now?"

"Well, I have to phone JD, and I'm not looking forward to that."

She waved her hand as if swatting a fly. "But we have to find it and steal it back, right?"

Harlan watched her over the top of his pint, aware that Olivia was smirking. "I suppose that's one possibility."

She snorted. "That's *the only* possibility. We have the map, we need the second part. And frankly, if we find who has the key—*if* someone has the key—we need to steal that, too."

Olivia laughed. "I knew I liked you! But first things first. Path first, then we'll focus on the key."

"We need both," Shadow persisted. "But, let's start with weasel-face and Mia. Where are Nicoli's offices—The Order of Lilith, is that right?"

"Right. I think it's somewhere in Camden," Olivia said thoughtfully, "but I'm not sure exactly where."

"If you find it, I'll watch it. And then I'll break in."

Harlan laughed, despite his reservations. "You make it sound so easy."

"I'm sure it won't be, but that's part of the fun isn't it?" Shadow finished her drink and wiggled the glass. "Time for another?"

"My round," Harlan said, rising to his feet. "Then we'd better decide where you're going to sleep tonight. And you should call Gabe and let him know what's happening."

Gabe topped his glass of whiskey up and stared at Hammond's map on the table. "What are we missing?"

"An accurate map." Niel's arms were folded across his chest. "You'd think after five hundred or so years, something would have revealed itself."

"Not if it's been hidden well by angels," Gabe reminded him. "They always liked their tricks and fancies."

They were both sitting around the table in the small dining room, the fire blazing and the whiskey bottle in handy reach. It was late now, closing in on midnight, and they had spent the day exploring the area, trying to orientate themselves to the map and work out what some of the more obscure illustrations meant. They had also hiked through Ebbor Gorge again. Fortunately the day had been dry, but the ground was muddy, and the streams were full. After that they had revisited Cheddar Gorge, but after some debate, discounted it.

Niel pulled a bowl of crisps towards him and took a handful. "Maybe this is a good thing," he said softly.

Gabe looked up at him and frowned. "Why?"

"Because I don't think any good can come of it."

"Not even for us?"

Niel swallowed a few crisps, and in the silence of the room, Gabe heard their distinctive *crunch*. "There were a host of angels, Gabe. Thousands of them. Some minor, many not, but all with a power we can barely conceive of. And some of them fathered us. We know that humanity was seen as something lowly and insignificant by most of them. Beyond their care. Humanity was something that *we* were made to control —to keep them in their place. The angels were far too embroiled with divinity. You know this, but I need to remind you because I'm wondering *why this temple even exists*." He tapped the map. "Because for it to exist, it means an angel willed it so. Carved it out of rock and earth. But why? Just because some faithful human could ask him questions? Can you see any of them wanting that?"

Gabe stared at Niel, an uncomfortable prickle of worry crawling beneath his skin. He was absolutely right, but Gabe had been so caught up in wanting to find it, he hadn't really questioned why it should exist. He took another fiery slug of whiskey, enjoying the heat as it coursed down his throat. "It is a good question."

"I know."

"We keep talking about *angels*, but maybe it was the design of one angel, rather than many. Maybe he was curious about humans?"

"I don't buy it," Niel said belligerently. "Say it does exist, out there in the rock somewhere. Why put it *there*? This place, as far as I can gather, has no significance historically."

"Apart from the fact that thousands of people have sheltered within the caves here for millennia. That might be significant."

Niel shrugged. "So, people have sheltered in caves all over the world."

"It *is* called Angel's Rest," Gabe pointed out. "That must mean something."

"And there's a village called Wookey Hole! I don't think there's a bunch of Wookiees down there!" Niel huffed. "And why give the vision to Phineas Hammond, of all people?"

Gabe shook his head, feeling weary. "Niel, I have no idea. Some people *do* talk to spirits and demons on other planes. I have no idea why some have the gift and others don't!"

"But no angels existed where we were in the spirit world," Niel said forcefully. "Not one! And we were there a *long* time."

Gabe remembered the swirling chaos of the other dimension with revulsion. "But angels communicate slightly differently. You know that."

Niel nodded, his gaze vague, before becoming argumentative again. "True. But based on our past experience of them, this temple sounds … suspicious."

"And we also can't forget that JD spoke to angels. They shared reams of information with him."

"But we haven't seen any evidence of that—or rather, you haven't. In the hours you spent with JD, he showed you nothing! And this Enochian language sounds highly suspicious."

He was right, Gabe reflected. *JD was greedy for knowledge, but shared little.* "Despite that," he conceded, "we still have a job to do. And in the event we cannot find the temple after searching as long as is reasonably possible, only then can we stop."

Niel fell silent. Gabe knew what Niel was like when he had something fixed in his mind, and this was well and truly stuck. He'd had misgivings since the start.

Finally, Niel spoke. "All right. But if we find out something more sinister, then we need to really consider whether to continue. Especially once we have The Path of the Seeker. That will hopefully reveal something more useful."

"And the key," Gabe muttered. "Don't forget that." His phone rang, and he saw it was Shadow. He answered, relieved. He hadn't heard from her all day, and he was getting worried. "Hey, Shadow. Success?"

"No," she answered abruptly, before launching into an explanation of what had happened at the auction. He leant back in his chair, rubbing his eyes, and for a moment he thought as Niel did. *Maybe this was a good thing? Maybe this was fate?* Then she told him she'd be staying in London for another day or so, and he asked, "Where are you staying?"

"With Olivia tonight, Harlan's associate. I'm not sure about tomorrow yet."

"Okay. Don't do anything rash."

He heard the smile in her voice. "When do I ever?"

She hung up, and Gabe pocketed his phone and picked up his whiskey, quickly summarising the conversation for Niel.

Niel groaned. "So now there may be two different parties, as well as us, looking for this?"

"Yep."

"We're missing something."

"Maybe."

Niel pulled the map closer to him, frowning at the page. "These images don't make sense now, but they must mean something. Maybe they signify clues in the landscape?"

"Perhaps. Some look alchemical to me." Gabe pointed.

"That signifies water, that fire. But," he added, growing sick of debate, "that's JD's specialty, so hopefully he will decipher it."

"True." Niel pushed the map away, suddenly impatient. "Want to fly again? Have another search?"

"Despite your misgivings?"

"If there is something dodgy about all this, I'd rather we find it than anyone else. We're equipped to deal with it."

Gabe laughed. "Are we? That's good to know."

Niel drained his glass and stood up. "Of course we are. Or more than most. Which is why I'm still in the game."

10

_____

*S*hadow watched Olivia as she prepared coffee and breakfast on Thursday morning in her modern kitchen, and felt suddenly homesick.

She'd slept well, but Shadow missed the chaos of the farmhouse and the banter of the Nephilim. She shook her head, annoyed with herself. It was something she needed to get used to. She could be travelling a lot with this job, and that was a good thing.

Olivia was fun and easy company, and she'd offered Shadow a bed the previous night without hesitating. Shadow had accepted because it was getting late to book into a hotel, and she realised she didn't want the anonymity of a hotel room. Olivia lived in Chelsea, not far from Burton and Knight and the pub where they had drinks and food. Harlan had looked relieved too, and once he'd dropped them off, he promised to be in touch the next morning. And it was a good decision. Olivia's flat was warm and comfortable, decorated with all sorts of interesting objects that Olivia told her she'd bought in many different countries. Photographs of exotic places covered the walls, and Shadow hoped she'd be as well-travelled in this world as she had been in her own.

Olivia placed a cup of coffee in front of her and said, "You look thoughtful. Everything okay?"

"Fine," she answered, picking up the cup and cradling it. "Just contemplating the strange turns my life has taken recently."

Olivia had returned to the counter to collect cereal and toast, and she placed them in the middle of the table, before picking up her own coffee and taking a seat. "I gather you've been here for about six months, is that right?" She gestured to the food in front of them. "Help yourself."

"Thanks, Olivia." Shadow started to butter her toast as she answered. "Yes. I arrived at Samhain. Since then, it's been a bit of a rollercoaster."

"And you live with Gabe?"

"And six others." Shadow frowned. "I presume Harlan or Mason has told you who they are?"

Olivia took a bite of her toast, liberally spread with jam, and nodded. "Nephilim. They sound fascinating."

Shadow laughed. "They are, and they're not. They're like any other men—well, sort of, they're huge — until you remember their past."

"Which makes them useful for this job in particular, I guess."

"Yes," Shadow nodded, as she buttered another piece of toast.

Olivia smiled. "I must admit, I'm quite looking forward to meeting them."

"Well, you seem to be more and more involved in this job, so I'm sure you will." She took a bite of toast and asked, "How did you come to work for The Orphic Guild?"

"Crikey," Olivia said, raising her eyebrows. "It was sort of convoluted. I studied Art History at university, and my passion was the Renaissance. I got a job with a museum as a researcher, and ended up being involved with a very curious collection of objects. It sent me down a rabbit hole of the occult, and I ended up meeting Mason. One thing led to another, and I decided The Orphic Guild had interesting prospects." She grinned. "And I have a passion for adventure. And money."

"Harlan said you worked in San Francisco for a while."

"Yeah, that's where I met him. He was quite the rogue." She winked. "In the nicest of ways!"

"And still is, I think," Shadow said conspiratorially. "So, what's the plan today?"

"I've got a couple of calls to make," Olivia said, topping up her coffee, "and I know Harlan has, too. We both have contacts who may know where Nicoli is based."

"Good. As I said last night, if we find it, I'm happy to watch it all day, if necessary."

"Nicoli is a tricky customer," Olivia warned her. "You've probably gathered that already."

"That's okay, so am I."

It turned out that Nicoli's office was in an old warehouse in Camden. Shadow and Harlan sat in Harlan's car, which he'd parked far down the street, and they hunched in their seats, watching it.

Shadow frowned. "He's obviously not going for the upper class look that The Orphic Guild is."

"I guess not. The Order of Lilith has more threatening overtones though, don't you think?"

She laughed. "I guess so. And therefore, he's looking for a different type of client."

"Oh, I don't know," he said, shrugging. "The occult

attracts a certain type of client, whether they are rich or poor, morally upright or not. In the end, depending on how much someone wants something, many are always willing to do something underhanded—including us, as you so rightly pointed out the other night." He turned to look at Shadow with a sly grin.

"It's an interesting line of work," she agreed, remembering the many scrapes she'd got into in the Otherworld. "It seems it doesn't matter what world you live in when it comes to this business." She checked the time on her phone, feeling impatient. "We've been here for over an hour, and no one has gone in or out. Are you sure we shouldn't just march up to the door and rattle our swords?"

Harlan looked at her, clearly intrigued. "What do you mean?"

"Well, rather than subterfuge, we could just accuse him and see what he says."

"Won't that tip our hand?"

"It has already been tipped, surely. You gave that document a very thorough inspection yesterday, and Jensen watched you like a hawk. And then, of course, you started bidding."

Harlan shook his head. "Too soon. It may be that confrontation or negotiation will be needed before this is over, but not just yet."

Shadow's phone buzzed, and she read a text from Gabe asking if she was busy. She called him back immediately. "I'm with Harlan, watching Nicoli's building. How are things there?"

"I'm bored and frustrated," Gabe answered, his voice low and oddly soothing.

She smiled. "Me, too. What do you suggest?"

"We want more details on how Phineas received his vision."

She groaned. "More research? That's not what I had in mind, Gabe."

"Niel has made some very good points, and I want more background. I'm sure Harlan can provide it."

"Hold on." She turned to Harlan. "Gabe wants more info on Phineas's vision. Have you got some?"

"I think so. Well, JD does." Harlan looked puzzled. "Why?"

"Captain Fantastic here has concerns."

"I like that name," Gabe crooned in her ear. "You can call me that more often."

"It was supposed to annoy you," she shot back.

"That's okay, screwball. You can't be right all the time."

Shadow bit back a response, instead turning to Harlan. "Can we get this info to Gabe? It might actually keep him quiet."

"I miss you too, sugar buns," he said, teasing her.

Harlan sniggered. "Did he just call you *sugar buns?*"

Shadow ignored him. "Gabe, I swear I will have my revenge if you don't shut up, right now."

"Send me the info, then?"

"As soon as I'm not stuck in a car watching The Order of bloody Lilith!" She cut him off and glared at the warehouse.

Harlan suppressed a smirk. "I'll call Mason and get him on that—" And then he stopped and stared, shrinking down in his chair even further. "Shadow, get your head down."

She scooted down, glamouring herself and extending it to Harlan, blurring both of their features. "What?"

"There's a man approaching the warehouse. I know him."

Shadow stared, trying to decide which of the people wandering down the pavement it could be. And then she saw a small, round man head to the entrance of the warehouse. "The little fat man?"

"The very same."

"Who is he?"

"Erskine Hardcastle, necromancer and demon conjuror extraordinaire."

"What? Are you kidding?"

"No." Harlan hadn't taken his eyes off him, and he kept watching until Erskine entered the building. "Well, this changes everything."

Shadow twisted to look at Harlan, still low in her seat. "Why? He's a buyer, like anyone else. Who cares who he is?"

Her glamour still blanketed both of them, and Harlan twisted to look at her, too. "What have you done? I feel weird."

"It's my glamour. I'm going to keep it on us for now. Answer the question."

"He's a well-known user of black magic. He supposedly has a demon at his beck and call, and we refuse to do business with him."

Harlan's normally blasé demeanour had changed dramatically, and for the first time, Shadow saw real concern on his face.

"But you just said that many occult collectors resort to all sorts of things to get what they want. Why refuse him?"

"He's bad news. Rumours of unexplained deaths and mysterious disappearances have dogged his past. He has few friends, and fewer enemies. Most people steer clear of him, and he likes it that way. Fear and intimidation are his friends." Harlan glanced at the road again, and certain that Erskine had gone inside, he straightened up and started the engine. "Time to go."

"But The Path of the Seeker is in there!"

"And that's exactly where it can stay for now. I'm serious, Shadow. We need to find out more before we proceed. I think Gabe's concerns could be legitimate."

Harlan was rattled. *Erskine Hardcastle.* He'd met him a few times, and each encounter had given him the serious creeps. And now, sitting at Mason's desk in his office at The Orphic Guild with Shadow next to him, Harlan knew that Mason was rattled, too.

There was something about Erskine's intense manner and pale, grey eyes that spoke of dark secrets, and power swirled around him. Harlan could never work out if it was actually magic, or just the sheer force of his personality. He had to admit that Erskine had been nothing but polite when he'd met him, usually at the auction rooms and once at a private dinner, but he still didn't like him.

The feeling had been compounded when he tried to manipulate the guild to do business with him, but Mason had smoothly declined citing several good reasons, and they had all breathed a sigh of relief when he exited the building that day. Erskine had never approached them again.

"Damn it," Mason said, immediately standing and pacing around the room. "That is the last name I wanted to hear."

"I can assure you, he was the last person I wanted to see."

"We don't know for sure though, do we, that he went there for The Path of the Seeker?"

"No," Harlan admitted. "He could be there for any other purpose. But it is suspicious timing." He felt compelled to add, "I presume Olivia told you about Jackson?"

"Yes. Something else to worry about." That morning, Mason had been clipped with Harlan, annoyed about the loss of The Path of the Seeker. But now, that annoyance had been pushed well into the background. "What does a demon conjuror want with angels?"

Shadow had been silently watching their exchange as she leaned back in her chair, twirling her dagger and balancing it on the point of her finger. Harlan had tried not be distracted by her dexterity. Still turning it idly between her fingers, she said, "I guess this is why Niel has more questions. He hasn't got a very high opinion of angels. None of them do. They question why such a place would exist."

Mason paused by the window, his eyes also falling to the knife. "They suspect a darker motive?"

"Yes. Have you got what Gabe asked for?"

Mason walked back to the desk, bent down, and opened the bottom drawer, extracting a bundle of papers. "Here are the copies of Hammond's dairies and notes pertaining to the period. The copies are good, the originals not so much. They are not easy reading. I read them a while ago, but not recently—and certainly not today." He handed them to Shadow. "I hope they tell you something of use."

Shadow placed them in the messenger bag on the floor next to her, while Harlan said, "I want to speak to Rose again, from Burton and Knight. She couldn't talk last night, but I'm hoping to get information today. I'm also hoping to get a copy of the path."

Mason frowned. "I thought you said they hadn't released any photos."

"They didn't. But that doesn't mean they haven't got any," he told him. "Of course they'd take pictures."

"I guess the involvement of Erskine would explain the pressure Rose was referring to," Shadow pointed out.

Harlan stood up abruptly, aware that their only option could be taken away at any moment if they didn't get to the auction house quick enough. After all, if Nicoli was willing to steal the path, he'd want to get rid of photos of it. too. "Come on, Shadow. We need to speak to Rose, now." He looked at Mason. "Warn JD. We'll send copies when we get them and then head back to Gabe. And maybe, Shadow, Gabe should call for backup."

11

*G*abe and Niel sat outside The Witch's Cauldron pub in the centre of Angel's Rest, bathed in bright sunshine.

They had a second pint in front of them, and the remnants of lunch were pushed to the side of the table, but despite that, Gabe felt on edge. He'd just ended the call from Shadow about the necromancer, and he'd updated Niel.

"Gabe, will you relax?" Niel said. "So, there's a necromancer. We've faced worse."

"I can't. We are now involved in some mad race for something that has existed for six hundred years, and all of a sudden, it's hot property! And some of my worry is your fault."

Niel laughed, and its boom disturbed the couple at the next table. He looked at their shocked faces and immediately lowered his voice. "My fault?"

"Yes you, voicing your worries about Hammond's map and vision and the whole Trinity of the Seeker."

"Better to be forewarned than forearmed."

Gabe just groaned. "Oh, shut up."

"Come on, you knew this wouldn't be an easy job. There's no such thing."

"I don't mind hard. What I dislike are the layers of subterfuge."

"You used to thrive on it."

"I was younger then."

Niel fell silent, and Gabe enjoyed the moment's peace as he debated their next steps. They were leaning back in their chairs, the wall of the pub behind them so they had a good view of the street, and both wore sunglasses.

Then Niel spoke softly. "Don't make any sudden movements, but I see a young woman with short, spiky black hair strolling down the high street."

"Are you thinking it could be our thief?"

"Yes. She's small and petite, just like Shadow describes her, and even from here I can see the bruise on her cheek." He gave a short laugh. "Shadow doesn't hold back, does she?"

"Okay. You've convinced me. Whereabouts?"

"She just exited the church."

"The church?" Gabe couldn't keep the disbelief from his voice. "What would she be doing in one of those?"

"Well, maybe she's a believer, Gabe? That happens. There are quite a lot of them. In fact, strictly speaking, we are, too."

"Not in the worshipping sense, we're not," Gabe answered, turning casually to talk to Niel, and looking down the street as he did so. "I see her. Looks like she's got a slight limp, too."

"Has to be her, right?"

"I guess so. I doubt she's here alone. Maybe that skinny Jensen kid Shadow mentioned is here, too."

"Should we follow her?"

"This place is quiet, and we stick out. We'd never pull it off."

"How dare you!" Niel said, looking at Gabe, affronted. "I can be discreet."

"You're the size of a mountain."

Niel shrugged, and the muscles across his shoulder flexed impressively. "It's a gift. Especially to the ladies."

"Don't even suggest attempting to speak to her," Gabe said, trying not to laugh. "I wonder where she's staying. There are lots of holiday cottages here, so I doubt it's far."

"Unless they've got somewhere just outside the town, like us."

"I tell you what," Gabe said, watching discretely as she passed them, heading to the far end of the high street where the antique shop was. "Why don't we visit the church? I want to know what she was looking at."

"Fair enough," Niel said, draining his pint. "Let's hope we don't burst into flames as we walk through the door."

St Thomas Church in Angel's Rest was a solid old building, built of pale grey stone with a tiled roof, surrounded by well-kept lawns and a hedge. It exuded peace, and Gabe couldn't help but feel he was intruding when he stepped inside the stone porch and pushed the heavy door open.

It was small but immaculate, and smelt of furniture polish. It had an arched ceiling, stained glass windows at the far end, narrow windows on either side, lines of wooden pews, a spectacularly ornate pulpit, and an altar. Fortunately, they were alone.

Gabe strolled down the nave, feeling confused. "This is old," he observed. "I wonder if it was here when Hammond was alive."

"It's possible. It's distinctly medieval in design. Maybe it has a connection we haven't figured out yet."

Gabe noted the wooden floor and smooth, plastered walls painted white. Nothing looked mysterious or as if something could be hidden, like in some churches; he thought particularly of the Church of All Souls in White Haven with the sealed chamber below it. "We need to check the date it was built."

Niel was standing by the altar, looking at the stained glass windows behind it. "But nothing appears disturbed in here. Maybe she was in here for personal reasons."

"Come on," Gabe said, "let's check the grounds."

Gabe led the way back outside, and for a few minutes they strolled across the grass and around the small cemetery behind it. He pointed at the tombstones. "Look at those dates —all from the 1430s and onwards. That's Phineas's time."

"So it *was* here when he was alive! I wonder if he's buried here."

Niel set off across the cemetery with purpose and Gabe searched with him, Niel's shout eventually calling him to his side. In front of him was an old gravestone, covered in lichen, the engraved name faded over time. "There. *Phineas Hammond. Died 1432.*" He stared at Gabe. "That's the year he completed the trinity."

"Interesting," Gabe said, feeling that this was another layer of weirdness. "Let's hope Shadow has got his diary."

———

Gabe watched Shadow place the bundle of papers and images on the table next to the map, and heard the frustration in Harlan's voice as he said, "They're here already?"

"'Fraid so," Gabe told him, turning to see Harlan's face wrinkle with annoyance. They were in the conservatory again, enjoying the warmth of the afternoon sun. Gabe picked up a page from the stack, glancing at lines of scribbled text. "Well, Mia is. We didn't spot anyone else, but I doubt she's alone. You made good time."

Gabe hadn't expected to see Shadow and Harlan until the

evening, so he was surprised when he heard the growl of Harlan's car on the drive later that afternoon.

Harlan thrust his hands in his pockets. "We left as soon as we saw Rose at Burton and Knight. There didn't seem any point in hanging around."

"You got copies of the document?"

"They gave me *one* copy, but it's a high resolution photo and we made more - some close ups too." He jerked his head to the table. "They're in that pile. We were right about Jensen. He did try to pressure Burton and Knight. He didn't even want them to display the path, but they basically told him to get lost, and conceded only the photos. I'm surprised they even did that. It's an ominous sign."

"Especially after what you told me," Shadow said. She'd finished emptying her messenger bag, and she stared at Harlan accusingly.

"What do you mean?" Gabe asked, looking confusedly between them both.

"Just that Harlan assured me Burton and Knight would never be intimidated, and yet..."

Harlan grimaced. "I feel Erskine's oily touch on this."

Niel had already pulled a chair up to the table to look at the new paperwork, but he said, "Tell us about him."

"I know very little, really. He's in his late thirties, short, round, and has these horrible, pale eyes that seem to look right through you. He appeared in London a few years ago and immediately started bidding on anything relating to demonology."

"Is that a common subject?" Gabe asked, leaning against the table's edge.

"For study? Reasonably so. The medieval period was obsessed with it, the church in particular. That's the type of material that Erskine typically goes for."

"So the fact that he seems to be interested in a document

about angels is curious," Gabe noted. He watched Niel shuffle through the new pages, pulling out a couple that caught his eye.

"Very," Harlan agreed. "But the timeframe is right—medieval period, I mean." He started pacing. "I just need to do something to try and get a breakthrough! I feel we're getting nowhere."

"It will come," Gabe told him. "We've only been on this for a few days. I'll grab us a few beers and we'll start searching through the new material. Have you sent JD what you have on the path?"

"Sure. With luck, he'll make more sense of the text than I do."

"Is it that bad?"

Niel interrupted. "See for yourself." He'd extracted the file with the images of The Path of the Seeker and placed it on the table. "I was expecting to see instructions, but there are more diagrams in here than writing!"

"Alchemical symbols," Harlan explained as he pointed some out to Gabe. "It doesn't matter how many times I look at these, they never seem to stick in my brain."

"I can understand why," Gabe said. "But this is where JD excels, right?"

"Correct. He's been immersed in this for centuries."

"I guess we should familiarise ourselves with them anyway," Gabe said. "Although, I doubt they'll make much sense. It's less about identifying the symbols than interpreting them, and that requires a whole other level of understanding." He sighed, feeling like this was getting more complicated by the second. "Do we all want beer?" Everyone nodded, and he left Harlan and Niel talking while Shadow followed him into the kitchen. "How was London?" he asked her.

"Frustrating." She leaned down to a cupboard to grab

some snacks, and he couldn't help but take in her curves. He looked away, feeling guilty, and stuck his head in the fridge to cool his thoughts, as she added, "But I met Olivia."

He grabbed four bottles of beer, shut the door, and turned back to her. "What's she like?"

"Cool. I think she'll end up joining us on this. Harlan says she's useful in a fight, and I think we'll have one. There's definitely more to this than we first thought."

Gabe opened a couple of bottles and handed her one, and after he'd sipped his own, he asked, "What did you make of the demon conjuror?"

She leaned against the counter. "He was a long way down the street, so too far away for me to get a feel for him. But Harlan doesn't strike me as a man who scares easily, so there must be substance to his concerns. The church thing sounds odd, too."

"With Mia? Yes, it is."

"Have you called for backup, yet?"

"A couple of hours ago. Nahum is arriving tomorrow, and Ash is on standby."

She sat on the countertop, took another sip of beer, and looked at him speculatively. "What's your demon fighting like?"

Gabe laughed. "That's a good question, and I can honestly say I'm not sure. What's yours like?"

She'd relaxed her glamour again, and her violet eyes glowed with mischief. "I'm not sure, either. They don't exist in my world, and I have yet to come across one here. Didn't you meet one on the other plane?"

It was a place he didn't like to think of, and it felt nightmarish now, like some drug-addled dream of fire, darkness, and chaos. "I did on occasions, but it was different there. They were shapeless, ever-changing things—well, some of them. Others had more substance. But we didn't engage them. They did their thing, and we did ours."

"Which was?" She leaned her elbows on her knees and watched him.

"Well, we didn't go fishing, or to the gym."

She rolled her eyes. "I'm serious. What was it like?"

"I can't describe it, not really." He considered the words he could use, and none of them seemed adequate. "We existed. It was both endless and seemed to last for mere seconds. Like time had no meaning. But I was aware of my brothers—sort of." He shrugged. "It certainly wasn't heavenly, but neither was it like the depictions of hell I have read, either. I was simply nothing."

Shadow teased him. "I'm sure you could never be *nothing*, Gabe."

He became acutely aware of her physicality, and for a second they just stared at each other, until Niel's shout broke the moment. "Where's my bloody beer?"

Gabe smiled ruefully and pushed away from the counter, grabbing the other two beers as he did so. "You're suggesting we develop a battle plan, then?"

"I'm presuming that a demon conjuror will use his tools to get what he wants. I've got the Empusa's sword, so I'm hoping that has demon-fighting properties, and of course I have my dragonium sword. That metal has many useful qualities, too. Whatever happens will prove interesting."

"Maybe we should have brought a witch with us."

"They're only a phone call away."

Gabe's thoughts immediately flew to Alex. He was the best at this sort of magic, and he'd always offered help where needed. Potentially, if nothing else, he could put up some protection for the house. "Good point. Let's see how the next couple of days go."

---

12

*T*he sound of the Bee Gees echoed through the ground floor of the house and into the conservatory, and every now and again Harlan heard Shadow singing. Harlan couldn't help but laugh. "Shadow never ceases to surprise me."

Gabe grinned at him. "I know! Who would have thought that she'd be a disco fan?" He shook his head in disbelief. "This is Zee's fault."

"Zee is a fan?" Harlan thought he must be hearing things.

Niel snorted. "No! Zee is responsible for our musical knowledge—well, he, Ash, and Barak—and this particular period was Zee's."

"Does she have the dance moves, too?" Harlan asked, unbidden images filling his mind of Shadow dancing.

Niel and Gabe laughed, and Gabe said, "Oh, yes. Wait until you hear Chaka Khan. Then the dancing really starts!"

"Barak dances with her!" Niel reminded Gabe. "That man has moves!"

"What an interesting household you have," Harlan said,

comparing their farmhouse to his own quiet flat and suddenly wishing it was filled with a bit more life.

Niel rolled his eyes. "Never a dull moment." He looked around as Shadow came into the room with more beer. "Having fun in there?"

Shadow smiled broadly. She was barefoot and wearing a t-shirt and skinny jeans, and she danced rather than walked over to them. "Of course! I'm cooking to music. What could be better?"

Niel took a bottle from her outstretched hands. "Thanks for relieving me of that burden."

"My pleasure." She handed the rest of the drinks out and frowned at the paperwork on the table. They had split the work between them; Gabe was studying the map again, and Niel had opted to read through the copies of Hammond's dairies. "Better than doing *that*. Have you found anything interesting?"

Harlan looked at the images of The Path of the Seeker. "No, actually. It makes less sense now than it did earlier." He could feel a headache beginning and wasn't sure if beer would help, but then again, it was probably just what he needed. "I don't even know why I'm trying. I'm not an alchemist."

Shadow slid into the seat next to him, squinting at it as if it would bite. "Heard from JD?"

"No. But I didn't expect to yet. He'll have his entire library to use for reference. It makes sense that he'd stay at home, rather than come here."

"I've found a few interesting things," Niel said as he leaned back in his chair. "It seems Hammond's vision was spread over weeks. That's not surprising, really. The trinity is so detailed, it couldn't possibly have been given to him in a few hours."

"I doubt it can be interpreted in a few hours, either," Gabe said.

"Maybe not," Harlan admitted. "But the pressure's on now that a few others are involved." He looked at Niel. "Any mention in there of who gave him the vision?"

"Not specifically. Just frequent mentions of the angel who visited his dreams."

A thought suddenly struck Harlan. "Is this difficult for you two? I mean, angels were your fathers!"

Gabe shook his head, but his dark eyes assumed a faraway look. "No. It's intriguing, more than anything. I still have a hard time believing that they—or even just one of them—are giving instructions to humans."

"I'm the first to admit my Bible history is poor, but didn't they used to appear with reasonable frequency in those stories?" Harlan asked.

"I'm not a Bible scholar, either," Gabe said. "I know it exists, and Ash has read bits of it, but it was written well after our time. And the New Testament? Well, that happened a long while after we were killed by the flood."

Niel laughed. "Yeah, we are *old* testament! But, in real life," he sobered quickly, "the angels appeared to a certain chosen few only—and I mean *a few*. Aside from the fallen and their willingness to mate with human women. But they didn't hang around playing happy families."

Harlan rubbed his face, perplexed. "Now my brain really hurts." He stood and walked to the doors to the terrace, needing a break from complicated symbols and the confusion of the past. "It's clouding up again out there. I think we'll get more rain later."

"I hadn't planned on exploring outside tonight, anyway," Gabe said. He stood too, stretching his arms above his head. "We need more direction first. Otherwise, we're just stumbling about blind." He turned to Niel and Shadow. "I can see us returning home for a while until JD can decipher the path."

Harlan nodded. "I guess that makes sense. We can't stay here for weeks doing nothing."

His phone started to ring and he pulled it from his pocket, noting it was an unknown number. "Harlan here."

"Excellent," a cockney voice crowed in his ear. "I've been trying to get you all day."

Immediately, adrenalin flooded Harlan. "How did you get this number, Jensen?"

"That doesn't matter." Harlan was aware that the room had gone silent as the others listened. "What matters is that we need to chat about The Map of the Seeker."

"I don't know what you're talking about."

Jensen laughed. "Bullshit, mate. Why else would you be looking at The Path of the Seeker?"

"It's my job, idiot."

"Let's cut the crap and talk deals. You have the map, we have the path. I'm not sure how you pulled off that particular heist from under our nose, but I'll admit I'm impressed. Why don't we work together?"

"Because you're a sneaky little shit, that's why," Harlan answered, abandoning all pretence. They may as well draw the battle lines now. "And you're working with Erskine Hardcastle."

Jensen fell silent for a second, and Harlan knew he'd surprised him. *Good.*

When he eventually answered, Jensen's voice was threatening. "Then you know that Erskine always gets what he wants, and you'd do well not to cross him."

"You're not the only one with powerful clients."

"But we have deep pockets, Harlan."

"Your money doesn't interest me," Harlan told him. "Go

away, and try to be a good boy." He hung up and turned to find the others staring at him.

"Does he know that we're here?" Gabe asked. "In this house?"

"No idea," Harlan admitted. "And I'm not sure how he got my number, either. But from this moment on, consider us under attack. Jensen pretty much threatened me with Erskine's power."

"In that case, we take it in turns to be on watch tonight," Gabe said, "and we bring all the weapons in from the car."

Shadow volunteered to take the second watch, and by 2:00am she was wide-awake and standing in the darkness of the living room next to Gabe, looking onto the shadowed drive.

It was raining again, and its steady drumming broke the silence of the night.

"I take it nothing has happened?" she asked Gabe.

His arms were folded across his chest and he shook his head. "Nothing at all. I've been around the perimeter, but it's as quiet as the grave out there. However, that was an hour ago. Let's have another look together before I go to bed. We'll start at the back."

He led the way through the house and into the conservatory, moving quietly despite his size, and had his hand on the door to the garden when Shadow saw movement beneath the trees. She placed her hand on his arm, his muscles like steel beneath her fingers, his skin warm.

"Wait. There, beneath the trees. Something moved."

Gabe paused, drawing them both back from the window and into the deeper darkness of the room. "Are you sure it's not the rain?"

Shadow didn't answer for a moment. She had sharp eyesight, and was pretty sure she hadn't imagined it. And then she saw it again. "To the right, beneath the oak. The shadows look all wrong." Something was creeping along the border, keeping to the shrubs.

"I see it," Gabe said softly, his voice barely audible. "Just one person, I think."

"Mia, perhaps."

"Unless it's an animal. Probably too big."

"I can leave from the front door and make my way around," Shadow whispered, eager to act. "I could get close enough behind to grab whoever it is."

He was unmoving for a moment, and then he looked down at her, uncertain. "You're stealthy, but not as strong as me."

"My blade is my strength." She glared at him, challenging his decision.

"We'd be better off waiting. Cover the window and doors, and then strike when they enter."

"That's passive."

She sensed rather than saw him smile. "Slow down, tiger. It's wet out there. It's harder to fight when you're slipping in mud."

"Spoilsport," she protested, adrenalin already surging through her.

"And besides," he added, "if I wanted to be passive, I'd just turn the lights on and scare them away. But they'd come back another night. I prefer to fight now."

She had palmed her dagger in anticipation, and was watching the garden again, spotting the creeping figure a little closer to the house. "Good. I want to see the fear in their eyes."

"You're scary, you know that?"

She shrugged. "When I need to be."

"Go wake Niel and Harlan. I'll wait here."

She seethed. "An order?"

"A request, you awkward madam!"

He refused to look at her, watching his quarry like a hawk, and although Shadow hated to go, she had to admit his size made him harder to get past.

She turned and ran, but before she'd even reached the bottom of the stairs, she froze. A black silhouette was at the front door, visible through the glass—the distinctive shape of someone tall and skinny. *Jensen?* She waited, and the figure moved to the right towards the windows in the sitting room where they had been only minutes before. Silently, she crept forward, all thought of waking Niel and Harlan forgotten. *How long had she got? And were there more than two of them?*

She followed the direction of the intruder, spotting the quick dart of the silhouette towards the side window, and she made a snap decision. *If there were more, they needed everyone awake.*

She raced up the stairs, barrelling into Niel's room, and he sat up abruptly. She hissed, "Niel! Get up, now!" Within seconds he was on his feet, already in jeans, but his chest was bare. "There are at least two intruders, one front, one back. Get Harlan. I'll be in the front room. And be *quiet!*"

Shadow didn't wait for a response, instead running back downstairs and approaching the sitting room with stealth and draped in glamour. But those minutes had cost her. The sound of rain was louder in here, and she saw that a side window was open bare inches. She sensed magic. *Was this intruder a witch?*

She dropped to a crouch, hoping the intruder was still in here and that Gabe wasn't being attacked already. But there was no sound from further in the house, and she had surely been too quick for them to get very far. She waited, confident she had melted into the darkness, and within seconds was rewarded when a figure emerged from the dark bulk of the curtains.

It edged across the room, pace quickening as he or she grew bolder, and Shadow saw the distinctive weasel face of Jensen, and the glint of hard steel in his palm. She waited until he passed her and paused in the hall at the bottom of the stairs, and then finally stepped behind him and kicked the small of his back. He crashed forward and landed with a thump on the floor, but in seconds had rolled to his feet, blade flashing. He lunged at her, but Shadow sidestepped and dropped, sweeping her leg out and bringing him to the ground again.

Out of the corner of her eye, she saw another figure emerge from the darkness of the other room across the hall. It wasn't Gabe or Harlan. Deciding to immobilise Jensen first, she smacked his arm on the hall floor and his knife skittered away. But he was wiry, and already trying to get to his feet. She punched him, and he groaned, barely moving. She was already crouching, knife out, but just as she was about to tackle the third intruder, Harlan appeared halfway down the stairs and leapt on the unknown assailant.

And then she heard a scream from the back of the house —a very *female* scream—and realised Gabe was fighting in the conservatory.

The sound galvanised the other two intruders into action.

For the next few minutes there were roars, groans, punches, sickening thuds, and the sound of breaking furniture all around. Shadow pulled her sword out of its scabbard, and with her pulse pounding in her ears and the rush of battle racing through her veins she took on Jensen, as all pretence at silence disappeared. Harlan was holding his own, trading punches, too.

"What the fuck!" Jensen shouted as Shadow's sword missed his throat by inches—deliberately. As much as she wanted to kill him, she reminded herself that the rules were different in this world.

"If you want the map, you weasly-faced little shit," she yelled, "you'll have to do better than this!"

She kept a close eye on his hands, watching for any spark of magic, but there was nothing, other than some fumbling in his pockets, and then trying to grab his knife off the floor.

And then an inhuman growl reached her ears from somewhere in the centre of the house and Jensen froze, his eyes darting nervously, and Shadow froze too, sword outstretched. Harlan and the other figure had also rolled to a stop, and after another unearthly howl, Jensen turned and ran for the open window, the second figure following, and Harlan and Shadow let them go.

"What the hell is that?" Harlan asked, breathless. He wiped the back of his hand across his lips, smearing blood.

"Sounds like a demon to me," Shadow said, quickly unsheathing the Empusa's sword so she was carrying both. She twirled them in her hands, eager to put them to use and not hold back. "Make sure the window is secure, and I suggest you stay here and guard the front entrance. And yell loudly if you need help—although, I think I might be busy."

Shadow sprinted down the hall and through the kitchen, finally sliding to a halt on the threshold of the conservatory. Gabe and Niel were circling a thrashing creature, all fire and smoke with eyes like live coals.

Flames were whipping across the room. Niel stood at the far side, restraining a wriggling and distraught Mia, as Gabe fought the demon. *Was he actually trying to catch it?* No matter. She ran in, feeling the hot lash of flame whip around her leg—and then something else. The dry, rattling creep of a withered hand on impossibly long arms.

She whirled, slicing and cutting at the strange grabbing

fingers of the demon, pleased to hear its hiss of pain as her blade found flesh.

But Gabe had grabbed one of the thrashing fire whips, and was hauling the demon closer and closer as he wrapped the whip around his right hand. Her breath caught. His hand must be burning, but he didn't stop, and the creature roared, so loudly that Shadow thought her ears might bleed. Gabe didn't let go, pulling it ever closer, a look of fierce determination on his face as his muscles strained with the effort.

And then Gabe spoke in a language that set her nerves alight. Guttural, gut-wrenching noises that turned her stomach and made her shudder in revulsion.

Everything suddenly stopped.

Mia had fainted, and was hanging limply in Niel's arms. The flames that licked across the demon disappeared, and with another guttural noise that threatened to bring Shadow's dinner back, it seemed to answer Gabe.

Gabe responded, his face wild with fury, as the almost impossible language crawled from his tongue. He released his hold on the creature, and within a second it had vanished, leaving them all in shocked silence.

13

*G*abe's right hand and forearm burned with an almost unbearable pain, and he looked down to find that his skin was smoking.

Shadow was at his side in seconds, dragging him through to the kitchen and thrusting his wound under the running cold tap. She yelled, "Harlan, turn the lights on!"

They were still in near total darkness in the kitchen, and aware of noise behind him, he twisted to see Niel carrying Mia's unconscious body into the room and place her gently on the kitchen table. Niel caught his eyes. "I'll secure the building."

Niel turned the lights on as he left, and Gabe blinked at the sudden brightness. His arm still hurt like hell, the searing pain feeling like the burn was smouldering through to the bone, but Shadow's hands were cool and comforting, even more than the icy water that splashed over his skin, and she whispered something soothing, words that felt like a balm to his senses. She seemed like a dream to him.

He watched her as if from a distance, almost like his soul had retreated far away from his body, noting her soft creamy skin, the curve of her neck, and strong yet slim arms and hands, and he suddenly wanted to feel those arms wrapped around him. He swallowed, banishing the thought. *She wouldn't appreciate it.* But then she looked up at him, her captivating eyes full of concern, her lips parted, and he wondered if he was wrong.

For a second she just studied him, and then said softly, "What were you thinking? You could have died!"

He smiled, ridiculously pleased that she was concerned. "I'm still here, though."

"But look at your arm! You might have lost it! I know you're Nephilim, but can you grow limbs back?"

He still hadn't looked away. He couldn't. Her eyes were far prettier than his smoking skin. "I doubt it, but I took a chance. And besides, I heal quickly."

"That was a *demon*! It's no ordinary fire!"

"But I'm no ordinary man."

It was a challenge now. *Who would look away first?* He didn't want to. He wanted to stand here for hours, her cool skin on his, her soft voice a caress.

And then Mia groaned behind them, and reluctantly, they both turned.

Mia blinked and fluttered her lashes, and her head lifted as she looked around. And then alarm flooded through her and she leapt off the table, almost stumbling.

Shadow left his side in an instant. "Not so fast, Mia. We have some questions for you."

She looked wild-eyed at Shadow and whirled around, looking for a way out. But Harlan was already standing in the doorway, his arms across his chest, his face grim. Mia backed away towards the wall, trying to put as much distance between her and them as possible. Gabe, aware his arm was still smoking, stayed put, his arm remaining beneath the running water.

"We won't hurt you," Shadow said. She walked to the table and sat down, gesturing to the chair across from her. "If you answer our questions."

Mia shook her head. "No. I can't."

Her voice was soft, brittle, and Gabe thought she was younger than she looked. And beyond her defiance, she looked terrified. He wondered how much she remembered of the demon.

"They're simple ones," Shadow told her. "Who was the third person who attacked us tonight?"

Mia shook her head. "I don't know who you're talking about."

Shadow shook her head and started to twirl her dagger between her fingers. "Liar. Who was it? We know about you and Jensen, and we know you work for Nicoli and Erskine Hardcastle. Who was the other person?"

She looked nervously between them all, but still didn't speak.

Instead, Harlan did. "It was a man, I know that much." He shrugged when she remained silent. "No matter. I'll find out." He moved into the room, and Mia looked as if she wanted to melt into the wall. "What I *really* want to know is, did you steal The Path of the Seeker?"

"No," she said defiantly.

Harlan grinned. "Lying again? Come on. You have to answer something if you want us to let you go!"

She glared at him, some of her resilience returning. "Yes. Right from under your nose!"

"That's better. How far have you got with finding the place?"

"We haven't got the map. You have it!"

"But you'll have a copy. How far?"

Mia shook her head. "I don't know. I'm not privy to their schemes. I'm just the thief."

Gabe believed her. He wouldn't tell her too much if she worked for him.

Harlan nodded, probably coming to the same conclusion. He watched Shadow's whirling blade, then took another step towards Mia. "Where are you staying?"

"I can't say."

"*Where?*" His voice hardened.

She hesitated, and then said, "19 Barton Lane."

"With Erskine?"

She nodded.

"And Nicoli?"

"He arrives tomorrow."

"And the key? Do you have it?"

She hesitated again, and Shadow released the blade and it embedded in the wall next to Mia's head.

Mia flinched, her lips pressed close together and her eyes darting between all three of them. "I have no idea. I am just the thief."

Harlan glanced at Shadow and then Gabe, and Gabe knew she'd tell them nothing else. "You can go," he said to Mia. "Don't let me see you here again."

Her eyes widened and she trembled, but nodded silently.

Harlan stepped back, gesturing to the doorway. "I'll let you out of the front door."

Gabe watched as she hurried on shaking legs, but she paused in the doorway, turning to face him. "He has more than one demon."

Gabe nodded. "I know. It told me. I said that if it was sent here again, I would kill it. I trust it's delivering the message to his master right now." He lifted his arm from the water and showed her his smoking flesh. "I'm more than a match for it."

Ten minutes later, Gabe was sitting at the kitchen table, and Shadow, Niel, and Harlan were sitting with him.

Harlan had seen Mia safely off the property, and then helped Niel finish searching the house. Satisfied that they were secure and the paperwork was still safe in its hiding place, Niel brought the first aid kit in from the SUV, and its contents were now spread before them.

"Good. We have burn gel," Niel said, plucking the packet off the table and opening it.

Gabe's flesh had finally stopped smoking, and the burning pain had dulled, but he could still feel it. He looked at his skin dispassionately. A weal of red, burnt, and peeling skin spiralled around his forearm, and his hand had blackened flesh on it, particularly in a strip on his palm and across the back, where he had gripped the coiled flaming whip and pulled the demon towards him.

Shadow took the gel from Niel. "Let me. Unwrap a dressing."

"Yes, ma'am," Niel muttered, and Gabe suppressed a grin, grateful that he would feel Shadow's cool fingers again.

Harlan was leaning back in the chair, his arms crossed and expression bleak. Day-old stubble covered his chin, and dark circles were visible beneath his eyes. The kettle boiled, and he stirred. "What's that for?"

"Just put it in a jug and then in the fridge," Niel told him. "We need it to clean the wound when we redress it tomorrow."

Harlan nodded and stood. "Sure. And then I need a drink. A proper drink. Who wants one?"

"I wouldn't say no to whiskey," Gabe said, wincing as Shadow gently inspected his wounds.

"Bring the bottle in," Niel suggested.

"Gin for me," Shadow added. "It's in the fridge."

Gabe watched Shadow spread the gel over his skin and immediately felt relief. "That stuff is good."

"Not as good as Briar's balms would be," she said. "I think I'll ask her for a kit for us."

"That's a good idea," Niel agreed. "We should write a list. I'm sure Eli could make a lot of it. He is an apothecary, after all."

Gabe grunted. "I wasn't really anticipating that we'd need field dressings."

"I didn't think you'd try to wrestle a demon," Niel shot back.

Shadow was wrapping a non-stick dressing around his wound. "I didn't think you'd actually let it live!"

Harlan re-entered the kitchen with the whiskey, and he caught the end of the conversation as he placed it on the table. "Yeah. Why was that?"

"I thought that sending it back with a message might be more impressive than killing it," Gabe explained.

In seconds Harlan returned with glasses and Shadow's gin, and he sat down, pouring everyone a hefty measure. "You were showing off?"

Gabe laughed dryly. "Not exactly. It was a warning to Erskine. I thought it might make him back off."

"It's always good to confound your enemy," Niel added. "They won't know what to make of that."

"Maybe," Harlan said, before downing his first shot in one gulp. He slammed the glass down on the table and topped it up straight away. "Damn. That was good. Although, I'm more of a Kentucky Bourbon man."

"Did *you* see the demon?" Gabe asked Harlan. In all the confusion, he didn't remember spotting Harlan in the conservatory.

"I was making sure our two intruders had gone, but I arrived at the door in time to see you 'talk' to it." He shuddered. "I don't know what I expected a demon to look like, but I am not ashamed to admit that it was pretty terrifying. Want to explain how you can speak demon?"

"I think you know we're adept at languages. Demon language is just another one," Gabe said, watching Shadow finish wrapping the gauze bandage around his arm and securing it. "Admittedly, it's archaic, a language birthed from the Earth itself. Much like the language of the angels."

Shadow picked her gin up. "That was the ugliest language I've ever heard. I thought I was going to throw up."

"Me, too," Harlan agreed. "It's like my whole body rebelled against it."

Gabe nodded. His flesh recoiled from it, too. He'd felt it in the pit of his stomach. "It is not meant for human ears. And I'm not sure you'd even survive hearing the true voice of an angel."

"Why?" Shadow asked. Her hands were cupped around her glass, but she wasn't relaxed. She was poised for action, and her swords were propped on an empty chair within easy reach.

Gabe's injured arm rested lightly on the table, but the fingers of his left hand rubbed the fine grain of the wood as he remembered the last time he had heard an angel speak. It was millennia ago. He looked up to find Niel staring into his whiskey, also lost in his thoughts. He sighed. "They speak the language of fire. It is both exquisitely beautiful and horribly painful."

"Fire!" she said, surprised.

"It is not of this world."

"You told Mia the demon spoke to you. Is that true?" Harlan asked.

"Yes. I really did tell it that I would erase it from existence if I saw it again. And then it couldn't resist boasting that the next time, he would return with more and they would be too powerful to overcome. I told him they would fail, and to tell Erskine that I doubted he would be so brave without his demon servants." He shrugged. "It went."

Shadow frowned. "He really controls them? When they appear? What they do?"

"Yes, through ritual magic."

"Although," Niel added, "it is a fine line that a conjuror walks. If they push too far, or take too few precautions, a demon will strike back. They do not like to be manipulated."

"So, in theory," Harlan said, thoughtfully, "Erskine will be sitting in a room, the demon contained in a circle of protection in front of him. He can summon it and then send it to do his bidding, right?"

Gabe nodded. "I believe so. Or, the conjuror himself is in the circle, protected from the demon that prowls without. Even in our time such men existed."

Harlan rested his elbows on the table, and leaned his chin into his left hand. "So, what does a demon conjuror want with The Trinity of the Seeker? Angels are not demons."

Niel grunted. "That's debatable."

Gabe shook his head, puzzled. "I don't know. But Niel is right. I have read some people's interpretations of angels, and many are wrong. While some angels undoubtedly protected humans, others despised them for being less than them. They were also insanely jealous of their free will. Angels had none. They were there to do the will of their God."

"Which is why some had fallen," Niel added. "Then they were independent. Free to do as they chose. And they created us."

"To control humans," Harlan said. "But if they had fallen, why not influence humanity directly? Why mate with women?"

"Angels do not belong in this world," Niel patiently explained. "They were never made for this existence. The fell to Earth, but were never a part of it. To assume human form and mate with women was difficult, and in the long term they couldn't sustain it. But they still resented humanity's free will. Their mission was control, and we were created to do that."

Gabe's old grievances started to stir in his gut, and he felt his anger rising. "And not all fell by choice. Some were sent to fight the ones who willingly fell, and some of those created us, too. Either way, we were slaves to their will. Until we rebelled."

"Wow." Harlan stared vacantly at the table for a moment as he absorbed the information. "This is too weird. So there was division among the angels."

"Huge division. There were factions, battles, insurrections. Betrayal."

Niel reached for the whiskey bottle and topped his glass up, his face grim. "And that's why I doubt that this temple, or whatever it is, can be good. Fate is stacked against that likelihood. Did you know that after Hammond completed the trinity, he died?"

"Did he?" Shadow asked. "How?"

"I don't know the details, yet," Niel told her. "We found his grave earlier, in the cemetery behind St Thomas's Church in Angel's Rest."

She stared at them all. "That's ominous."

"Yes, it is," Niel agreed. "I'll keep reading tomorrow. I haven't finished his diary yet."

Gabe nodded, rubbing his chin with his good hand. He still hadn't touched his drink, mainly because he thought he needed a clear head, although he was also sure the demon wouldn't return that night. "I'll call Alex tomorrow, see if he can put some protection on the house...something to deter demons. It worries me that Erskine can send them inside the building."

"You also need better weapons," Shadow told them. "The ones you have are not magical. El could strengthen them with properties that do more damage against anything supernatural. My dragonium sword was pretty effective, as good as the Empusa's, and that's because it was forged by fey. Magic is bound into the metal."

"It's a good point," Niel said. "A spell to enhance my axe would be very welcome. And it would be good to have a sword again—a good one."

Shadow leaned forward, animated. "Her friend Dante could make you all swords, or whatever you need, but in the meantime, El can improve what we have." She paused for a moment. "You know, I thought Jensen had used magic to get through the window, but he's not a witch. I'm wondering if he was given a spell to use…something a witch made for him. El told me they'd done something similar for the three ghost hunters."

"Like a one-off spell?" Niel asked, confused.

"I think so."

Gabe sighed. "Great! Magic for hire. That's all we need. All right. I'll ask Alex if El can come with him, to juice up what we have here."

Harlan sighed and stretched. "That sounds good. And now I'm going to bed, because I have a feeling that tomorrow will be another big day."

"You should all go," Niel said, staring at Gabe in particular. "You're injured and need to rest. I'll watch for the rest of the night."

Gabe flexed his arm. "It's feeling better already. I'm hoping it will have healed a lot in twenty-four hours."

"Maybe. But go to bed anyway." Niel grinned. "And I'll reward our success tonight with a big breakfast tomorrow."

---

14

*H*arlan stretched in the large, comfortable bed and realised he could smell bacon.

Such an ordinary, heart-warming smell, he thought as he blinked the sleep away. Despite the disturbed night, he'd managed to sleep well, finally. But as the events came back to him, he couldn't help but wonder what JD had got them into.

Of all the strange things he'd experienced in his life so far, a Nephilim battling a demon in a conservatory was one of the oddest. And seeing Shadow wielding her sword in the hall was pretty cool, too. He laughed as he recalled Jensen's horrified face, and then sobered quickly. He may be an obnoxious pain in the ass, but even he'd been scared when he heard the demon.

Harlan tried to recall what the other attacker had looked like. It was a man, he was sure of that. Average height and build, reasonably strong, and dark hair—although, in the darkness of the hall, it was hard to tell. He had a good punch, he knew that much. Harlan's ribs and jaw ached from the blows the man had landed. No doubt he was one of Nicoli's team members he hadn't met before. He should have asked

Mia what his name was last night, but to be honest, he was more worried about Erskine. With luck, Gabe's message would have either scared him or infuriated him, or both, and that was fine with him.

The scent of bacon soon became stronger, and remembering the Nephilims' huge appetite, he decided he'd better get out of bed before it was all eaten.

Harlan shouldn't have worried. By the time he arrived in the kitchen, showered and shaved, he found Niel setting out a mountain of fresh, crusty bread in the middle of the table, and saw more food on the stove.

"That's a sight for sore eyes," Harlan said as he headed to the counter to make coffee. "Am I the only one up?"

Niel greeted him warmly. "Morning, Harlan! Nope, Shadow is already outside, trying to see where Mia came over the wall. For a little thing, she's pretty resilient."

"You're talking about Mia, right? I wouldn't call Shadow a 'little thing!'"

Niel's laugh filled the kitchen. "Hell, no. She'd have my balls for earrings!"

"Ouch," Harlan said, wincing. "And where's Gabe?"

"Helping." He looked at Harlan and gave a knowing wink.

Harlan almost spilled his coffee in shock. *Really? Are they—"* His question hung in the air. *Why was he so surprised?* They had chemistry. That was obvious. Maybe he was disappointed. He'd half wondered if he might stand a chance with Shadow himself.

Niel shook his head, a wry smile on his face, as he put bread in the toaster. "No, they are not. *Yet.* And it's not worth my life to ask."

"Fair enough," Harlan said as he processed the information. Before he could ask anything else, he heard a knock at the front door, and he immediately grabbed a knife from the counter.

"I'm hoping that's Nahum," Niel said, striding across the room and picking his axe up as he headed into the hall. "Stay here and watch the sausages!"

Within moments he heard voices, and then Nahum followed Niel into the kitchen.

Nahum was uncannily like Gabe, even in his mannerisms, and he nodded at Harlan as he picked up a slice of fresh bread and took a bite, mumbling a greeting. "Sorry," he said, once he'd swallowed. "I started early and didn't really eat before I left."

"You heard about the demon?" Harlan asked him.

"Yeah. Courtesy of my brother, at four in the morning."

Niel shrugged. "Gabe's orders."

"It's fine. Where is he?"

"Just coming now," Niel said, pointing out the window.

When Gabe and Shadow entered the room, they were in the middle of an argument, and Shadow was fuming. "Why not? They'd never see me. I can hide better than you, you big-winged idiot."

"Because I say so. What are you going to do if you get spotted and Erskine sends a demon?"

"*In the middle of the street?* Besides, he won't see me! I'm too good." She sounded incredulous, and then she saw Nahum. "Hey, Nahum. Your brother is an idiot."

Nahum just grinned. "I know. But adorable too, right?"

"Since when?" she scoffed, marching to the counter and picking up a slice of crispy bacon.

Niel slapped her hand. "Sit! Or you'll get nothing!"

Harlan saw her hand slide to her knife as she glared at him, and then clearly thought better of it. She stalked to the table and sat down with a *thump*.

Niel turned to Harlan and whispered, "Sexual tension."

Harlan tried not to laugh and failed, and was rewarded with twin glares from Gabe and Shadow.

"All of you, sit now!" Niel instructed. "Harlan, take the plate of sausages and bacon."

The breakfast was a chaotic, noisy affair, as they caught Nahum up on the events of the night and their progress, or lack of, so far.

"How's your burn?" Harlan asked Gabe.

"It doesn't feel too bad, but I guess we'll see when we change the bandage."

"It can wait 'til later," Shadow told him, gesturing with her fork. "Burn dressings should stay on as long as it's not leaking."

"Ugh," Nahum said, wrinkling his nose. "Leaky wounds. Nice conversation over breakfast."

"Like you have a weak stomach," she shot back.

"By the way," Gabe said, "I phoned Alex once I got up. He'll be here in a few hours, with El."

"And bringing some balms from Briar?" Harlan asked.

"I mentioned it, so hopefully."

Harlan nodded. "It's handy that you have witch friends. There are a couple we use in London on occasion, but I don't know them that well."

"I take it you have resources all over the city?" Nahum asked.

"And beyond."

"Good to know," Nahum said thoughtfully. He turned to Gabe. "So, now I'm here, what do you want me to do?"

"Look at the documents," he answered, "and see if we've missed something, because so far I feel we're wading through treacle."

"And I'll phone JD," Harlan said, pushing his empty plate away and standing up. "He might have news."

Harlan's conversation with JD didn't inspire him. In fact, it downright worried him.

He walked into the conservatory to update the others, relieved to see that the room looked better than it had done a few hours earlier.

The demon, and the fight in the hall, had caused damage to furniture and decorative objects that Harlan knew The Orphic Guild would have to pay the bill for, but at least there had been no windows broken. The three Nephilim and Shadow were once again sitting around the table, the paperwork shared between them, and Nahum and Gabe were conferring quietly together.

Harlan joined them at the table. "JD is struggling with the translation, too."

"Why?" Gabe asked, his dark eyes troubled. Harlan noticed he still moved his injured arm gingerly, and that was another worry he added to his list.

"Well, it seems that alchemy hasn't been the top of JD's list for many years now. He's been focussed on astronomy and math—his first love. So, although he has an entire library of alchemical documents, he hasn't really studied them for years." He looked at everyone's shocked faces, and tried to play down their concerns. "I know. To be fair, it sounded like he hadn't slept for days. He's working very hard to decipher the path. Apparently, having the original document is better—something about magic in the paper itself." He shrugged. "Anyway, the upshot is, I have no bad news to share, but JD promises to update us as soon as he can."

"Bollocks," Gabe exclaimed, annoyed. "Let's hope that Erskine is having as many problems."

"I've found something," Niel said, looking up with a frown. "From what I can gather from Hammond's diary—and it's tricky, because his writing is confusing and the account rambling in places—it seems that once he'd finished the trinity, he decided it had to be split up."

"What? Why?" Nahum asked.

Niel barked out a laugh. "He doesn't say! He just rambles about being duped and that the trinity is too dangerous for mortal eyes." He referred to the papers in front of him. "He says, 'My end is nigh, but I will do what I can in the short time I have. I cannot destroy them, he has seen to that, but I will hide them. I am more devious than he thinks.'" He looked up. "He never discloses who *he* is, or why he knows his *end is nigh*!"

"Oh, great," Gabe said, sarcastically. "He develops a conscience, but won't tell anyone anything!"

"Better than not having one at all," Shadow pointed out. "And he successfully split these documents up for years. I wonder why he couldn't destroy them?"

They all eyed the map warily, and Niel said, "This could explain why it looks so well preserved."

Without warning, Gabe snatched the map off the table and tried to rip it in half, and Harlan couldn't help but shout, "No! What are you doing?" And then his mouth dropped open as Gabe failed to tear it.

Gabe looked amused. "Well. This is something!"

Harlan's heart was still thumping. "Holy hell, Gabe. That was risky."

Nahum grinned. "Let's try something else." He pulled a lighter from his pocket and held a flame to the corner of the map. Nothing happened.

"Oh, shit. It's not even smoking!" Harlan said. He reached out his hand, and Gabe passed him the map. He ran his fingers over it. *It felt like paper, and it looked like paper...* "What could do this?"

Shadow shrugged. "Magic. Let me try my swords." She walked over to the side of the room where she'd left them, and brought them back to the table. She held the dragonium sword up first. "Spread it on the table again, Harlan."

He eyed her suspiciously, and then reluctantly laid it flat for her. "Just try a corner!"

She nodded, and then chopped the sword down quickly. Sparks flew from where the blade made contact with the paper, and Shadow's arm jerked back in shock. "Ow! I felt that! So, the finest fey metal doesn't work, either!"

By now, all of them had drawn forward and were staring at the map, and Gabe said, "And the Empusa's?"

Shadow tried that too, and the same thing happened.

Gabe leaned back in his chair and ran his hands through his hair, looking frustrated. "Shit. Where the hell does this lead to?" He looked at Niel. "Anything else in that diary?"

He grimaced. "He rambles, and with every entry he sounds more deluded. He mutters about knowledge and the fall of man, and then it gets to the point where I can't decipher his scribbles anymore. And then they end." He squinted at the page, and then referred to another document. "According to this account, which is written by a contemporary, he died only hours after his last entry, and that was only days after he finished the Trinity—The Key of the Seeker, actually."

"The final missing part," Gabe said softly.

"What did he die of?" Nahum asked.

"He died suddenly in his sleep. Heart attack? Aneurism? A curse?" He shrugged. "We'll never know."

Harlan looked at the map in front of him as if magic would ooze out of it and infect the rest of them. "So, whoever caused this to be made, must have killed him."

"It might not have been deliberate," Nahum suggested. "It could have been the accumulation of the pressure of making the trinity. From what Niel is saying, it affected him badly."

"All very mysterious!" Shadow said, smiling impishly.

"I don't know why you're looking so pleased," Gabe said, suddenly annoyed. "This is frustrating!"

She rolled her eyes and tutted. "All good mysteries are! It's a challenge, and I like challenges."

"*You're* a challenge," he muttered. "Living with some screwball fey. I'm going to age before I should."

She snorted. "Drama queen."

Gabe studiously ignored her, instead turning to Niel. "Good work. Keep searching. Hopefully you'll uncover more useful stuff. See if there's something in the earlier entries that indicates how this all started."

Niel nodded. "Sure thing."

Nahum stood up and walked to the wall of windows that looked onto the back garden. "It's stopped raining again. I'm going to head out and walk the site. I'd like to get a feel for it, in case inspiration strikes."

"I'll come too," Shadow said, rising to her feet. "Now we know that The Order of Lilith is here, we should expect to see them everywhere, and they'll be searching, too."

"Is there anything you want me to do?" Harlan asked, feeling useless.

"Yeah, actually," Gabe said thoughtfully. "I want to know about that church in Angel's Rest—St Thomas's. Mia was in it, therefore it must have significance."

"Sounds good," Harlan agreed. He was happy to do anything that kept him busy and stopped him worrying about fiery demons.

15

Shadow stood on a crag looking over the narrow gorge, hands on hips, and frowned at the landscape around her. Somewhere beneath her feet was The Temple of the Trinity.

Nahum stood next to her. "I can see why you've been having trouble. It all sort of looks the same."

"I know. Rocks, grass, crags and crevices, and the real possibility that I may break my neck." She turned to look at him, and found that he was grinning. "What?"

"You're as nimble as a goat. It would take more than this to break your neck."

She smiled, secretly pleased. "Well, true. But I'd still rather not have to scramble up and down this slippery ravine."

He nodded to the east. "So that way is the entrance to the large series of caves under here?"

"Yes. It's a tourist attraction. Hundreds of people everywhere, and the caves have been explored for years." She shrugged, perplexed. "I don't understand why anyone would want to wriggle through tiny rock holes just to find caves for pleasure."

"I would imagine that not many people would want to engage in the hunt for dangerous occult items."

"I suppose you're right," she admitted. "To each their own."

He pulled his phone out of his pocket and opened the series of photos he'd taken of the map. "Let's see if we can make any progress." He pointed. "This line here suggests this long ravine to me. Yes, it's out of proportion, but it must be it."

She peered over his arm. "I agree. The stream runs through it, too. I know that sign—it's the elemental sign of water." She indicated the upside down triangle drawn on the map. "There are a few of those. I suspect they're small streams, or a spring, maybe."

Nahum looked at her. "Well, aren't you full of surprises?"

"I read stuff!"

"Well, those signs," he said, enlarging the picture to show her, "are runes. Hammond really did use all sorts of symbols on this. This one means power."

"You're right. He doesn't use one system at all."

"That's interesting, isn't it? Maybe it's significant," Nahum reasoned.

Shadow looked at the view, but her mind was elsewhere. "Angels speak many tongues, is that right?"

"Right, although their own language is that of fire."

She nodded. "Gabe said as much. And you speak many languages too, right?"

"Yes, although signs and symbols are harder for us. They are a type of language, but they have many interpretations." He shrugged. "Like words, I guess!"

"Are there any symbols on there that only you would know?"

Nahum didn't speak for a moment. "It's hard to say. I'm not sure. Not that I've seen so far."

"But you said the map was complex. Those strange, fantastical faces and creatures have shapes within them." An idea was forming, and she didn't like it. Not one bit.

"Yes. We've found runes in faces, alchemical symbols, and elemental signs. The runes certainly indicate strength, power, and wealth, but they don't mark one particular place. Unless that's hidden in more layers of symbols."

"Perhaps the reason this map has so many different symbols is because it was meant for someone who was good at many languages. Like Nephilim."

Nahum's deep blue eyes narrowed with suspicion. "You're suggesting this was made for *us*?"

"Perhaps. Or it was intended for those who are as clever as you, because they need to have a broad range of knowledge to decipher it—polymaths, magicians, scholars... Whatever is hidden must have great value and is deserving of only the worthy. I think we've said that before. Who is more worthy than the Nephilim? The sons of angels."

"We weren't considered that worthy at the time—well, later we weren't. We were venerated as kings for a while, until the tide turned against us. Literally!"

Shadow knew she was on to something, she could just feel it. "But *some* thought you worthy! And maybe still did many years after you'd gone." She started pacing. "Maybe an angel thought you might be back and wanted to leave you a gift. Or maybe some of you survived after all, and it was left for *them*?"

"No!" Nahum said suddenly. "Stop. This is too much!"

"Why? Because of what it implies? The temple exists somewhere beneath us. This is called Angel's Rest! Where did the name come from, Nahum? I talk to Dan a lot! Place names mean something. They retain meaning for years, and although the names modernise over time, they carry a kernel of truth in them. *Angel's Rest*! I know we've joked about this name, but it must mean something! And you know what else?"

Nahum groaned. "No, and I don't know if I want to."

"Of course you do. After our last encounter with tombs I talked to Dan about them."

"Dan from Happenstance Books?"

"Yes. Tombs were constructed for millennia. As we know, people were buried in them. Some were made to align to the sun at various parts of the day or year." She spread her hands wide. "This could be, too! Or it's specific to you!"

Nahum's tanned olive skin turned paler and his muscular shoulders rose and fell with an enormous sigh. "But we, *the Nephilim*, don't understand it. We have no idea where to look."

"The wealth sign. Where is it?"

He gave her another long, weary look and then scrolled the photos again, pulling one up and enlarging it. "This place here has wealth and power signs, a rune of victory, and," he paused, "kinship I think."

"Kinship? Where is that particular cluster?"

He looked around, finally pointing across the narrow ravine. "I estimate...there."

"Come on, then."

Half an hour later, after much scrabbling and swearing, Shadow emerged onto a narrow platform of rock, and Nahum scrambled up next to her.

"This would be so much easier with wings," he grumbled.

She smiled at him triumphantly. "Another reason why this is meant for you!"

They were on a narrow lip of stone, surrounded by tumbles of rock, bushes, and stunted trees. Nearby was a fast-flowing stream that was more of a waterfall because of the incline of the hill. The ground fell away beneath their feet, and they were both breathless.

Shadow rested her hand on the stone, warm from the midday sun that peeked through the clouds. She cast aside her glamour, allowing her fully fey self to feel the beat of the earth beneath her skin, and she closed her eyes, breathing deeply. She smiled. Despite the fact that magic was not so obvious in this world, it was still here. And there was something else.

She opened her eyes and found Nahum watching her. "What have you found?"

"You have a distinct signature. You smell different than humans, and your energy is different. It's not obvious, but I can tell because I spend a lot of time with you, and I'm fey."

Nahum rolled his eyes. "Tell me something I don't know."

"Piss off. You need to say something in your language."

"My language?"

"Yes. You must have one. Your original language, not ones you've learnt. Like mine." She greeted him in fey, enjoying the feel of it as it rolled off her tongue.

He smiled. "Give me a few more lines, like tell me what we've been doing this morning!"

"Why?"

"Just do it."

Wondering why, she spoke again, this time for much longer, and when she'd finished, he laughed and answered her, and for a moment she thought she might cry. "You speak fey!"

"All languages, Shadow. But reading or hearing a good sample first helps." He smiled gently, his whole face lighting up. "If you want, we can speak it more often."

Shadow couldn't stop herself, and she burst into tears. Her hands flew to her mouth, and then her eyes. "Sorry. This is stupid of me. It's so nice to hear my own language again. I never thought to ask."

He pulled her close and hugged her, crushing her against his chest. "Sister, just ask, any time."

"Thank you," she mumbled, and then stepped back as he released her. "Now, your turn. Although, obviously, I can't answer."

"Why not? You speak English," he asked genuinely confused.

"The Otherworld was at one point closely aligned with this one, and humans and fey crossed regularly. Human languages have been absorbed into our own."

Nahum nodded, looked around, and then uttered a string of something unintelligible, but that sounded so musical she felt it deep within her. But before she could comment, the ground rumbled beneath her feet and she almost fell off the ledge. Nahum's hand shot out to grab her, and for a moment they both staggered and then fell to their knees.

"What did I do?" Nahum asked, looking around wildly.

Shadow turned around, still on her knees, wriggled to the edge of the stone shelf, and peered over the side into the dense shrubs beneath. There in the shadows, where the sun hadn't yet penetrated, she saw a deeper blackness. "Nahum, down there! Can you see it? It looks like a narrow opening!"

Lying flat on his stomach next to her, he stared into the undergrowth. "Are you sure that wasn't already there?"

"No," she admitted. "But that looks like a fresh fall of stone, and some shrubs have been ripped from the earth."

He grinned at her. "Have we actually found the entrance?"

"I think we have!" she answered, triumphantly. "What did you say?"

"I said, 'I am here to claim The Trinity of the Seeker. Show me the path, for I am worthy.'"

"Wow. Very dramatic," she said with a smirk.

"I thought the moment called for it." He looked down at the dark entrance. "Should we? It will be a scramble to reach it."

She was already rising to her feet, anxious to explore. "Of course."

Within minutes, after a hair-raising descent that was more of a slide than anything controlled, they both halted in front of a narrow break in the rock, utter blackness beyond it.

"That's going to be a squeeze," Nahum noted, "but I'm not turning back now. Are you sure you want to after all your caving talk earlier?"

"Of course!" she said impatiently. "After you. You opened it, you should have the honours!"

Nahum gingerly stepped inside the narrow cleft, and Shadow followed. Beyond was a passage, the rock pressing closely on either side. They both stood for a moment, letting their eyes adjust to the darkness, and then Nahum continued, sometimes turning sideways to squeeze through the gap. After a few minutes the passageway opened up into a square space, and Shadow stopped, shocked.

This was no rough cave; it was elegantly carved from the rock. The walls were smooth, almost polished, and the ceiling overhead was domed, but more surprising was the doorway etched into the rock in front of them. A series of flowing shapes were carved into the surface, precise and beautiful.

"Can you read that?" Shadow asked.

Nahum was standing in front of the doorway, his hands running over the surface and the edges, and he looked bewildered.

"Nahum, are you all right?"

He glanced at her, never taking his hand from the stone. "It's the language of fire!"

"Angel language! What does it say?"

"'Welcome, Seeker. Say the words and the worthy will enter. Be sure of your intent, for all knowledge lies here. Life lies here. Death lies here. The path to glory awaits.'"

"*All* knowledge?" she asked, a thrill of excitement and trepidation running through her. "Wow. What does 'say the words' mean?"

He shrugged, finally stepping back from the doorway. "I don't know—maybe the inscription? Maybe it's something from the path? I'm not risking saying anything right now though. We need to come back with the others."

When Shadow and Nahum arrived back and told the others what they had found, Gabe looked at them incredulously. "You found it and left it unguarded?"

They were in the conservatory again, and he glared at Shadow and Nahum, his arms folded across his chest. "What if The Order of Lilith is already there?"

"It's okay, Gabe," Nahum said, trying to reassure him. "We checked that place from various angles, and it's really hard to see."

Shadow's hands were on her hips, and she glared back at him. "We're not idiots! We debated whether I should stay, and I could have. No one would have seen me! But what would be the point? It's well off the track, and there are lots of trees and bushes around it. And besides, it goes nowhere at the moment."

"Yeah," Nahum agreed. "The doorway to whatever lies beyond is sealed shut!"

"But," Gabe said fuming, "The Order of Lilith has the path! They might have deciphered it!"

"We have it, too," Harlan pointed out. "Admittedly in photographic form, and we haven't figured it out."

Gabe took a deep breath and Shadow could see he was trying to calm down, but he still looked at them suspiciously, a myriad of emotions flashing across his face that Shadow couldn't understand. "You're both filthy, too!"

"Herne's horns! Scrambling up and down muddy paths and almost falling off a narrow rocky shelf will do that to you," Shadow shot back. "The whole ravine shook when it opened, and I admit, if not for Nahum's quick reflexes, I'd have fallen to the bottom of it." She patted Nahum's arm. "Your brother's big muscles saved the day."

If anything Gabe looked even crosser, but Nahum and Niel just looked amused.

Gabe narrowed his eyes at Nahum's expression, and ground out, "Sorry. And well done for finding it!"

Niel asked Nahum, "You spoke the old language?"

Nahum nodded. "It was Shadow's idea." Nahum strode over to the table and cleared the other papers off the map. "Shadow pointed out that the symbols are varied—runes of various types, alchemical symbols, elemental symbols, some Greek, some Latin, old English... There is no common language here! But what is common is the fact that *we* speak many languages—and yes I know, signs and symbols are different. But alchemists, magicians, and many others who are interested in the occult have similar skills to us."

Shadow butted in. "This is a map for the worthy—people who can prove their knowledge!"

"To be worthy of greater knowledge," Niel said, nodding.

"I suggested that maybe this map was potentially made for you," Shadow said, almost tentatively.

"For us?" Gabe questioned, his dark brown eyes boring

into hers.

"Maybe. Speaking your language uncovered it." She shrugged. "Potentially another language may have worked, too—or whatever ritual is in The Path of the Seeker."

Harlan nodded, excited. "Multiple entryways, depending on whoever gets there first. But whoever that is has to have the right knowledge and skills! That sounds plausible!"

"And you say it's the language of fire written on the door?" Niel asked.

"Yes," Nahum answered. "Do we want to go back? Now? We deliberately didn't try to trigger anything."

Gabe looked at everyone's expectant faces, and it was clear he was wrestling with what to do, but Harlan spoke first.

"We need to inform JD before we do anything! We are here for him, after all. And, although we might be able to open the door, what if there are more doorways, more tests? We need the path deciphered before we proceed."

"I still want to see it, though," Gabe told them. "Maybe tonight. I presume you can find it in the dark?"

Nahum and Shadow just looked at him, both incredulous, and Shadow bit back a sarcastic comment. "Of course."

"Did you see any sign of Mia or Jensen or anyone?"

"No," Shadow assured him. "A few casual walkers, but no one we recognised. And as we said, the opening is well off the path."

He sighed. "All right. Tonight, then."

A knock at the front door interrupted their conversation, and Niel said, "That must be Alex. I'll go."

Within minutes, El and Alex followed him into the conservatory, carrying a pack each and holdalls. Shadow grinned, heading to El and hugging her. "Sister. It's good to see you! It's been too long."

El was a tall blonde, statuesque and willowy, and Shadow

considered her a good friend. There was something about her that resonated with Shadow. Part of it was that her height and build reminded her so much of the fey, but mainly it was El's lack of regard for convention that struck a chord. With her bold makeup and piercings, Shadow admired her free spirit.

"The last time I saw you," Shadow said, "you were dancing around the Beltane fire on the beach!"

El laughed. "I certainly was. All that Beltane magic got under my skin! You were dancing, too!"

"True," Shadow admitted. "That was a good night! It reminded me a little of the Otherworld."

"Where's my hug?" Alex asked, jokingly put out. Alex was tall, with shoulder-length brown hair and permanent stubble on his chin, and was charmingly flirtatious. He now lived with Avery, another witch in White Haven.

"Sorry." She grinned, hugging him, too. "It's good you could both come and help. Being invaded by three intruders and a demon last night was fun, but annoying."

Gabe grunted and shook Alex's hand. "'Fun' is one word for it, I guess. But thank you. I know you must be busy."

Alex shrugged. "I am, but fortunately Zee could cover me. I think he'd rather be here, though."

"By the time we're through with this, we might need him," Gabe admitted.

Alex spun on his heels, looking around. "This is quite some place."

"That's my fault," Harlan said. "JD likes good accommodation."

"Well, there's good, and there's *good*!" El said, clearly impressed. "This is a big place to protect, but I'm sure we can pull it off!"

"Thank you!" Gabe said, looking relieved.

She nodded at her bag. "We've come prepared. But Alex is

your man for demon protection."

Harlan asked, "Are you staying tonight? There's room if you need to."

"No," Alex answered, shaking his head. "We'll leave once it's done—unless you really need us?"

"Hopefully we'll be okay," Nahum told him. "Besides, this thing could go on for weeks. As long as the house is protected, we'll at least be sleeping soundly."

"Mind me asking what you're looking for?" Alex asked, a wry smile on his face. "A bit of background might be helpful."

Niel offered them chairs. "Our manners are shocking! Sit down, guys, and I'll fetch beers and some snacks while everyone explains. You can do your thing later."

While they settled into seats, Shadow asked El, "Did you bring some of Briar's balm?"

"Of course," El said, immediately rummaging in her pack. She produced a glass pot and unscrewed the top, releasing the scent of herbs into the air. "This is a thick cream you need only apply sparingly. She says it's good for all sorts of cuts, but will be really great for your burn, Gabe." She looked at him, concerned. "I can't believe you wrestled a demon!"

Gabe looked sheepish. "I think my adrenalin got the better of me." He glanced at his dressing, which now looked spotted and blood-stained. "I almost bit off more than I could chew. It still hurts a little, if I'm honest."

"I'd offer a healing spell," El said, "but I'm not as skilled as Briar."

He shook his head. "It's okay, I have strong natural healing. I'm sure the cream will be enough."

"Let's do it now," Shadow said decisively, anxious to avoid another long discussion on the trinity. "The others can explain what's going on."

He looked at her, surprised. "I suppose we could. Are you sure?"

"Of course. We'll be done by the time they've finished. I'll get the sterile water and dressings, and meet you in the main bathroom."

Without waiting for an answer, she headed into the kitchen, finding Niel preparing cheese and crackers. "We're going to the bathroom to change Gabe's dressing," she told him, grabbing the water from the fridge while also grabbing a slice of cheese.

"Be gentle with him," Niel said, grinning.

"Aren't I always?"

Gabe was unwinding his dirty bandage by the time Shadow arrived with the water and first aid pack. She wrinkled her nose as the smell of burnt flesh reached her. "Put your old dressing in here," she said holding out a paper bag.

As Gabe held his arm over the long counter next to the sink, Shadow inspected the wound and frowned. "It's healed a bit, Gabe, but it still looks bad!" The burn was still bright red, and blisters had appeared in places. But his hand was worse than his arm, and she lifted it gently, turning it over. The blackened skin had gone, revealing that the burn had bit deep into his skin. "Anyone else would have lost their hand," she told him, looking up to find him watching her. "You're very lucky."

"You don't have to do this. I can manage."

"No, you can't. Not one-handed, and the others are busy. Hold your arm over the sink." She pulled some gauze from the pack and gently cleaned around the wound, flinching as Gabe winced. "Sorry. I'm being as gentle as I can."

"I know." His deep voice was like honey. Seductive. Dangerous.

She tried to focus on the wound and not his closeness. His heat. His corded muscles that felt like steel beneath her fingers. She could hear his breath coming quicker and didn't dare look up. She took her time, making sure his wound was as clean as it could be, and then patted it dry. Only then did she stop and look around to see where Briar's balm was. It was on the other side of the sink, and before she could reach for it, Gabe leaned behind her, his broad chest pressing against her back as he reached for it with his left hand. But he didn't back away. He wrapped his left arm around her, holding the pot in front of her.

"Here you go." His breath was warm so close to her ear, and for a moment, Shadow felt giddy with his nearness.

They were in front of the mirror, and she could see his face in the reflection. As their eyes met, he smiled, slowly, sensuously, still pressed close behind her.

"Thank you." She plucked it from his fingers, trying to ignore the tingle across her own fingers as they touched his briefly.

Trying not to become flustered, because she was pretty sure he was doing this to deliberately provoke her, she took the top off the pot and started to apply the cream. "Hold your hand out."

"I like you being bossy."

She looked into the mirror and saw him smirking. "For someone who likes it, you certainly complain about it a lot!"

"I like a woman who knows what she wants, too."

"Good." She glared at him, trying to suppress her amusement. Frankly, he was looking so pleased with himself, it was ridiculous. "Because this woman needs you to back up—*if* you want your arm dressed properly without me being squashed like a fly." He shifted back a few inches, and Shadow looked down, forcing herself to concentrate on finishing the dressing, which was doubly difficult with him so close. He felt far too good. *But*, she reminded herself, *he was her partner, and he needed to stay that way.* "You know, I could probably do this quicker if you just stepped back a bit more."

He didn't budge. "I'm in no rush. Tell me what you thought about the temple's entrance."

"It was freakishly precise," she said, continuing to dress his wound. "The walls and roof were smooth as silk, polished, almost sterile. It gave me the creeps, actually, rather than any sense of wonder or awe."

"That's what worries me. JD seems to think this will be wondrous and beautiful, but I think it's more likely to kill us."

Shadow finished wrapping the bandage and secured it, and then turned with difficulty, finding her hips against the counter and Gabe's broad chest in front of her. She ignored his predatory smile and instead said, "Well, maybe you should tell him. He'll listen to you!"

"Maybe, but part of me foolishly wants to see where this leads."

"Because of the link to angels?"

Gabe nodded. "It's tangible—their handiwork is all over it. Inhuman, beautiful, awe-inspiring, but also obscure, confusing, and exasperating. And we haven't even entered the temple yet! I can't walk away now, and despite Niel's concerns, I know he can't, either."

"It seems to me that Nahum is invested, too. And if I'm honest, so am I. And of course so is Harlan." Gabe was silent, thoughtful, but his gaze was distant, and she wondered where his thoughts had fled to. "I've finished your dressing, if you hadn't noticed."

"I noticed. Do you want to go?"

"Don't you?"

"Not particularly. For some strange and inexplicable reason, I'm enjoying myself."

"Oh." Her mouth was dry, and she found it hard to concentrate.

"You didn't answer the question."

"What question?"

He was grinning now, his eyes running across her face and down to her lips. "Do you want me to let you go?"

"Oh. That one." Damn his muscles and smile, and damn her body's reaction to him.

He smiled again, seductively, and the sun glinted in low, capturing them both in golden light. He was like no other man she'd met, and she had the feeling that if she fell for Gabe, she might never recover.

"Yes," she answered, "you probably should."

"Probably? That doesn't sound convincing."

She scowled at him. "Yes. You *absolutely* should let me go."

"I'm not sure you really mean that." His head lowered, as did his voice, and Shadow inhaled his musky, peppery scent. "Give me one good reason why."

She looked around, pretending confusion. "We seem to be in the bathroom, and we can't stay in here forever."

"That's not a good reason."

Shadow smiled seductively, lifting her face so they were inches apart. *You like teasing, Gabe Malouf? I can tease as well.* "It's the best you're going to get."

For a moment Gabe didn't move, and his lips were so close to hers, she could almost taste him. And then he backed away, still grinning. "All right. Have it your way."

"I will, thank you," she said archly, her heart still pounding, as she passed through the door he held open for her, acutely aware that he watched her like a hawk.

He called after her, amusement filling his voice. "Shall I get the first aid pack?"

She turned and smiled, overly sweet. "That's a good idea. See you downstairs." And yes, she might have exaggerated the sway of her hips as she turned her back on him and continued down the hall.

16

Gabe spent five minutes pacing his bedroom after Shadow had sashayed down the hall, half regretting his actions, and half wishing he'd just kissed her.

He chided himself. Partners. They were partners.

By the time he arrived at the bottom of the stairs, someone was knocking on the front door. He dropped the first aid pack behind the door, just in case he needed both hands free, and opened it to find an attractive woman in her thirties on the other side, her wavy chestnut hair loose across her shoulders. She wore jeans and boots, a t-shirt, and a worn leather jacket.

She looked up at him and smiled, holding her hand out to shake his. "I'm Olivia James. I work with Harlan. I'm a collector with The Orphic Guild."

He smiled, shook her hand, and welcomed her inside. "Gabe Malouf, at your pleasure. It seems our party is growing in size."

She grinned. "It's not every day you find a missing part of The Trinity of the Seeker."

"I guess not." He glanced down at her overnight bag. "Looks like you're staying for a few days."

She shrugged. "Maybe, maybe not, but I came prepared, just in case."

He gestured to the bottom of the stairs. "You can leave your bag there for now, if that's okay."

"Sure," she nodded, but kept her handbag over her shoulder as she walked with Gabe down the hall.

"Did Harlan ask you to come?" Gabe asked, wondering what Olivia could offer the investigation.

"Not exactly. Mason wanted me here." She winked. "Safety in numbers."

"Well, we're sure getting that!"

Gabe heard the excited chatter of voices before they'd even entered the conservatory, and found the entire group in animated conversation, broken up in twos and threes as they pored over the documents.

"Hey, guys!" he shouted. "We have another visitor. Olivia James, Harlan's colleague, is here."

After a flurry of introductions, and Harlan's pleased but puzzled greeting, Olivia settled in, and Gabe sat next to Alex. Alex was the witch he knew best and had met first. He'd connected with him psychically when the Nephilim were still spirits, and Gabe had been impressed at the strength of his will and power. "What do you think?" he asked quietly so as not to disturb the others.

"Of the trinity, or the protection you want?"

"Both, I guess."

Alex glanced at the papers spread across the table. "Honestly, this temple looks like trouble, and you need to be careful. The whole thing reeks of traps and deception. But, you can look after yourself, I know that." He shrugged, his eyes wary. "However, I'm not sure we can add anything to your understanding of the map or the path. I recognise some runes and elemental signs, but nothing you guys don't already know. Alchemical symbols aren't our thing. But, I always find it's less about translating the meaning of the symbols, and more about interpreting their meaning."

Gabe nodded. "Yeah, you're right. But there are a lot of layers there."

Alex looked genuinely frustrated. "Sorry. But I can certainly protect the house. I'd like to start now."

"Sure," Gabe nodded, already moving his chair back. "Where do you need to go?"

"I'll head outside first. I can ward the building and the garden, and then add protection spells to the ground floor windows and doors."

"Will it keep out demons?"

"I'm doing a general protection spell," Alex explained. "There are obviously a lot of people coming in and out of here. The wards will keep out anything with evil or malicious intent." He frowned. "This Erskine guy worries me. If he decides to throw something really big at you, it may get through without us here to back the spells up, but from what Harlan says, he's a conjuror, not a witch, so that means his powers are limited. They should hold."

Gabe released a big breath, not realising how worried he'd been. "That's great, thanks."

"Any time," Alex said, smiling. "You've helped us out enough. El's brought a couple of blades with her, too."

"Has she? I didn't expect anything so quickly."

"She always has stuff at hand." He looked down the table to where El was chatting to Nahum and Niel. "Hey El, do you want to show the weapons you brought?"

El's eyes widened with surprise. "Of course. I was caught up with the map." She rummaged in the bag at her feet and then pulled out one short sword and one dagger, and laid them on the table. "I had these already," she explained as the table fell quiet to listen. "One of the reasons we're a bit late is because I wanted to add some spells to them before we left—something I needed my forge for."

Nahum picked the dagger up, turning it over in his hands. "Interesting symbols along the blade."

"The symbols and the metal are enhanced with magic. The symbols imbue the dagger with strength and promise an ever-sharp blade. It can never be broken. Whoever wields it will have added agility and speed, and the wisdom to make the right move." She nodded at the sword that Niel was examining. "That has similar spells, but with added dexterity and clarity of thought, and will pierce most armour." She grinned. "Qualities I thought would be useful in a fight."

Niel stood up and carried the sword across the room so that he had plenty of space around him, and started to practice moves. "It's very well-balanced, and surprisingly light."

He looked good, Gabe noted. But then again, Niel had always been graceful in battle, and deadly.

"You could get away with a longer blade," Shadow said thoughtfully. "Your height gives you that advantage."

"True," El agreed. "But try it out. If that's the type of magical weapon you're after, I can make you one more suited to your build. All of you," she added, looking at Nahum and Gabe. "At a good price, too."

"Can you make throwing knives?" Nahum asked, running his finger along the edge of the dagger's blade.

"I can make anything you want. But it will take time, so don't expect them overnight."

Nahum smiled. "I'll keep this for now, if that's okay. I like it. Niel is right. This is well-balanced, too. I can feel the magic running through it."

"Dante, my weapons-maker friend, is very good. I enhance them with magic as we work together. We can make you scabbards for them, too."

"He knows you're a witch?" Harlan asked, surprised.

"He does, but probably not the extent of my power," El explained, looking slightly sheepish. "I like Dante. He's a good friend. The last thing I want to do is freak him out. Although," she laughed, "that would be hard, I think."

Shadow laughed, too. "Having met him, I agree."

"When did you meet him?" Gabe asked, genuinely curious.

Shadow had barely looked at Gabe since he came in, but she met his gaze now. "He helped appraise the Empusa's sword."

Alex stood up, his chair scraping across the floor. "This conversation isn't getting the house protected. You ready, El?"

"Sure. Where to first?"

"Outside," he said, grabbing his bag and steering her towards the doors to the garden. "Before it rains." He looked back over his shoulder, a wry smile on his face. "And we could be some time, so just ignore us, and anything odd you may see us do."

"Interesting," Olivia said after they'd shut the door behind them. "Are those the witches from White Haven, Harlan?"

He nodded. "Two of them." He leaned forward, arms on the table. "You say JD sent you?"

"Mason, really. I'm free this weekend, so he thought you might need backup."

Nahum raised an eyebrow. "Aren't we enough?"

She held her hands up, surrendering. "I'm sure you are. But you're not Orphic Guild employees, and Mason is paranoid."

"Fair enough."

"So, how can I help?" She gestured at the papers. "It looks like you have three things going on here. The map, the path, and the background stuff on Hammond. Is there anything I can focus on?"

"Four things!" Harlan said. "I'm looking into the church in Angel's Rest."

"Well, Olivia," Niel said, placing the sword safely out of the way before walking back to the table. "Nahum and Shadow have found the temple—or the entrance, at least. I'm all over the diaries, so our pressing need right now is The Path of the Seeker. Or, scouting out the house where The Order of Lilith have holed up."

Her eyes widened with surprise. "Whoa! Back up. You've found the temple? How?"

"A little bit of luck and inspiration from *moi!*" Shadow said, looking pleased with herself.

"And my language abilities!" Nahum reminded her slyly.

"Yeah, and that."

"We're going back tonight," Harlan told her. "I'm presuming you want to come?"

"Of course I do!"

"Just be aware," Gabe warned her, "that we're not planning to go any further. We need to understand what The Path of the Seeker means before we do, or we could be walking into a trap!"

"Sure," she nodded. "But we still have no key, right?"

"Right."

Olivia looked at Harlan. "I've been thinking on why Jackson was at the auction. He can only be interested in the trinity if he has part of it, surely. Or else, why bother?"

"The path on its own is worth getting, Olivia," Harlan reminded her.

"I'm not convinced. Maybe we should call him, see what he knows."

Gabe could feel things slipping away from him. There were already too many people involved, as far as he was concerned. "No. It's too risky, and will give him too much information. I can do without any other threats to make life more complicated."

"But what if he could help?" Olivia said, looking at him belligerently. "We're in a race here. And Nicoli is not to be underestimated. If Jackson has the key, we should try to make a deal."

He laughed. "A deal for what? We don't even know what we're really looking for! And how do you make a deal when JD wants everything?" He looked at Harlan, appealing for support, and felt relieved when he nodded.

"He's right. We need to find the key, because there's every chance Jackson hasn't got it."

Niel laughed. "Guess what, Olivia? Add a fifth line of enquiry. You've just volunteered to help me with the diaries, and figure out where Hammond hid the key."

"In that case, I'm heading out," Gabe said. "I want to stretch my legs and scope out that house, just to see how many are on Nicoli's team." He looked at Nahum and Shadow. "And seeing as you two had so much success earlier, I'll leave you to investigate the path."

Gabe was glad to be out of the house. He'd been looking at paperwork all day and he felt gritty-eyed. Now he needed to do something, anything.

He also needed space from Shadow. Perhaps distance would bring him to his senses. He was flirting with her like some giddy teenager. Pushing those thoughts to the back of his mind, he set the GPS and followed the directions until he arrived on Barton Lane in the outskirts of Angel's Rest.

The lane curved through a shallow valley, and the further it was from the village, the more spaced out the cottages and houses were. He eventually found the right one, a large stone dwelling behind a hedge. Gabe didn't linger, and he didn't want to park too close, either. There was every likelihood someone would be watching out for them, because he was pretty sure Mia would have confessed to telling them their address. He wondered if she was okay, and hoped she hadn't been punished for being caught.

The valley rose on either side, wooded in places, and he might be able to find a spot to watch up there. He checked the map and decided to turn around and head back to the village, taking another road that wound around the back of the hills. He pulled into a lay-by and hiked up the rise, finally emerging on the top of the ridge in a copse of trees over-looking Barton Lane below.

It took him a few moments to orientate himself, and then he set off, keeping out of sight, until he finally spotted the right house. The ground was damp beneath the trees, but he didn't care. He lay down on his stomach, shuffling forward until he had a good view, pulled out his binoculars, and settled in to watch.

Two hours later, he'd watched Mia and Jensen arrive, dressed in hiking gear, and another man who he didn't recognise, but who Gabe thought could be Harlan's attacker —the mystery third intruder. He was of average height with a muscular build, and had short sandy brown hair; he had returned with bags of what looked like food. Harlan had described Erskine Hardcastle and there was no sign of him, but that didn't mean he wasn't there. Gabe didn't know much about demon conjuring, but from what Alex had told him, the closer you were to where you wanted to send your demon, the better. *Pet demon.* Gabe rolled his eyes.

Just as Gabe was about to leave, he spotted someone else exiting the house—someone that he hadn't seen before. This man was tall, with a slim and wiry build, deeply tanned skin, and brown hair. He looked like he was from somewhere in the Mediterranean, and Gabe presumed he must be Andreas Nicoli, the head of The Order of Lilith. He paused on the threshold, and Gabe saw a very round man step into the doorway. They exchanged a few words, and then Nicoli turned his back and walked down the drive to his car, a black Mercedes, the other man still talking to him. *That* was Erskine Hardcastle.

Gabe studied them both, watching the way they interacted, and thought he detected tension. Nicoli appeared brusque, and after a short exchange, he got in his car and left, and Erskine watched him go, a calculating expression on his face. *Interesting.* Erskine finally shut the front door, and Gabe watched the house for another ten minutes, but when there was no more sign of movement, he decided to leave.

Gabe had just got back inside his SUV when his phone rang. "Hey, Harlan. How's it going?"

"I think I've found something interesting about the church. Niel and Nahum think it's bad news."

Gabe froze, his injured hand on the wheel. "Why?"

"I've been reading about the stained glass windows and the images they depict. They're all original, restored over the years, and apparently the angel in the central panel is holding a book."

Gabe tried to remember the images he'd seen when he was there with Niel. He honestly hadn't studied them closely. "I have a vague recollection of an angel, but there are always angels in stained glass windows."

"This one is the Angel Raziel. He is holding his Book of Knowledge."

Gabe slumped back in his seat, no longer seeing the lane in front of him. "Raziel? Are you sure?"

"That's what it says on this website I've found."

"And he's holding a book?"

"I believe it's actually called *The Book of Raziel the Angel.*"

"*Sefer Raziel HaMalakh,*" Gabe said softly, his mind whirring with possibilities. "The book he gave to Adam."

Harlan fell silent, and Gabe knew he had a million questions he wanted to ask, but to his credit, all Harlan said was, "Nahum said it is the book that leads to Eden."

Gabe closed his eyes, and the heat and dust of an afternoon millennia earlier flooded back to him. He had been tasked to find that book, and had searched for decades, before he finally admitted defeat. *But now...*

"I'm going to the church," he said, abruptly ending the call.

Clouds were once again thick overhead when Gabe drove down Angel's Rest's main street. He found a parking spot a short distance from St Thomas's Church, and he was so distracted by Harlan's news he almost didn't notice the Mercedes parked a few cars down from him. *Nicoli.*

He paused, his mouth dry, not from the prospect of seeing Nicoli who may also be in the church, but of the images the stained glass might contain. He looked at the church sitting quietly, encompassed by smooth green grass, the tiny graveyard behind it, and the enormous yew tree by the lichgate, and wondered why he had thought the church so peaceful. Now he found it ominous.

He crossed the lane quickly and walked up the path before his courage failed him, but when he pushed open the heavy door, he found himself alone. The church was dim, the stained glass windows at the far end the one patch of colour, but even they were dull because of the impending rain. But in the centre panel, the Angel Raziel seemed to emit his own light. *Or was that his paranoia?*

Gabe looked around the nave carefully before he advanced, ensuring he really was alone, and then walked up the centre aisle, his footsteps loud in the hushed place. He paused in front of the altar, studying the angel. The design was large, his face serene, his wings partially folded behind him. *The wings were always so small*, Gabe thought, *too small*. An attempt to humanise, make them appear kindly, protective, approachable, while the reality was all too different. Raziel was holding a large, open book, yellow splinters of glass radiating from its open pages, and he stared into the church, his eyes on the pews; Gabe felt pinned beneath his gaze. Raziel held the book out as if offering it to him. *A temptation.*

Gabe sat on the front pew, his face impassive, but his mind was anything but. It churned with memories, stories, possibilities, and the growing certainty that the temple was something to flee. Raziel had the old God's ear. He was privy to every secret, every plan, every order. He heard everything, and recorded everything, and his book was considered a book of magic—straight from the old God's mouth. And he had given it to Adam and Eve to find their way back to Eden, or so Christian history said.

Such childish stories, Gabe thought. *Such simplifications.* Adam was not the first man, and Eve was not created from his rib. The old God had not made him from clay, or placed him in a heavenly garden that they were expelled from because Eve had been swayed by the angel Lucifer. *Utter drivel.* Adam was a man like any other, but blessed with intelligence, drive, and the need to succeed, and so was his wife. But the Gods disliked intelligence when it led them away from worship and towards independence. The Book of Knowledge, as it was so simplistically called, was the gift of life itself. Gabe looked up at the three stained glass panes again. The panel to the left of Raziel was of the traditional image of Adam and Eve, naked except for fig leaves, walking in the Garden of Eden. Lush leaves and flowers filled the image so that the figures were barely visible. The panel on the right was made of glass in varying shades of blue depicting huge waves, and lost within them was a boat. *Noah's Ark and the flood.* Within the waves were floundering figures—animals, men, women.

His blood thundered in his ears so loudly he didn't hear the door open behind him.

Only when footsteps echoed around the church did he turn. The man he presumed to be Andreas Nicoli walked halfway down the aisle and stopped, staring at Gabe. He looked from him to the stained glass and said, "They are quite something, aren't they?"

Nicoli's voice was authoritative, but he spoke quietly, calmly, and Gabe heard the Greek accent through the faultless English.

Gabe turned to face him fully. "They are."

Nicoli scanned the panels before finally appraising Gabe. He stared at his bandaged hand. "You must be the man who questioned Mia."

"And you're the man who sent her, and the other two intruders. And let's not forget the demon. Andreas Nicoli, I believe."

Nicoli smiled, tilting his head as he shrugged. "I am, but I did not send the demon."

"I know. It was sent by Erskine Hardcastle. Don't send them again, or they won't walk out of there. Demon included."

"Mia told me of your fight." He narrowed his eyes, and Gabe knew he was trying to work out who he was. *What* he was. "Not many men could do that."

Gabe smiled. "I'm gifted."

Nicoli folded his arms and leaned his hip against the edge

of the pew next to him. "You have my name. I know you work with Harlan Beckett and The Orphic Guild. What is yours?"

"Gabe Malouf."

"Well, Gabe Malouf, you have something we want. I am willing to pay for it. Anything. Our pockets are deep."

"What would that be?" Gabe asked, playing dumb.

"Time is too short for games. You have The Map of the Seeker. I don't know quite how you pulled it off, but you stole it from us."

"I don't think so. It was owned by Henri Durand."

Nicoli laughed. "You're splitting hairs. Mia had it. You stole it. Somehow. There's a woman on your team." He tapped his nose. "My instincts suggest it's her."

"Talking of stealing," Gabe said, ignoring his probe. "You stole The Path of the Seeker, in the middle of the auction. Not convinced your pockets were deep enough?"

He didn't answer, instead saying, "Let's deal. I'll make you an offer; take the map off your hands."

"I'm in no position to make deals. It isn't mine. Besides, why do you need it? You must have photos."

"We want the original."

"What do you think the trinity leads to?" Gabe asked, watching Nicoli closely.

"The same thing that you do." Nicoli glanced up to the image behind Gabe. "This place is called Angel's Rest for a reason. Raziel's book lies in that temple, and it contains the knowledge of a God. It's not a path for the unworthy."

"What makes you think I'm unworthy? If anyone is unworthy, it is your demon conjuror. They aren't popular with angels."

Nicoli laughed, a broad grin spreading across his face before he sobered quickly. "Take my offer to Harlan. I'll give you twenty-four hours."

"Or what?"

"We come and get it."

Gabe walked up to Andreas, so he was inches away, and he looked down at him, pleased that the man had to lift his head to meet his eyes. "Or perhaps we'll steal yours."

And then he walked away, feeling Nicoli's eyes on his back until the door slammed shut behind him.

17

*H*arlan needed fresh air. The conservatory felt small, hemmed in, and too full of people after the conversation he'd just had.

He walked outside to the paved patio area overlooking the garden and sat in a wooden chair, sheltered beneath the overhanging eaves. The late afternoon had turned still. The wind had dropped, and thick clouds pressed on the land, muting all sound. Rain was due, lots of it. And maybe thunder. Alex and El were walking slowly around the perimeter of the garden, one on either side, and he watched them slowly arrive at the rear boundary together. They joined hands, and although Harlan couldn't hear them, it looked as if they were saying something—a spell, no doubt. He wasn't sure quite what happened next, but he felt a ripple of power flow around him, something comforting, like he was being wrapped in a soft, warm blanket. He smiled. *The protection spell.* Then they turned and headed back to the house.

Harlan looked across at the conservatory, an impressive structure of high-arched windows and brick, glowing with yellow lamplight. Shadow, Nahum, Niel, and Olivia were still in there, and he watched them talking animatedly, still clustered around the table. Harlan took a deep breath and ran his hands through his hair, trying to sort through his jumbled thoughts and emotions, but in the end he kept circling back to Raziel, the Keeper of Secrets, who disobeyed his God to share forbidden knowledge.

As soon as he'd read about that, he knew it was what The Trinity of the Seeker led to, and the others agreed. He laughed to himself, feeling half deranged. When he'd taken on this hunt for angels, he hadn't really understood the potential implications. It seemed distant, vague, and unlikely to produce much. Now it felt very real, but at the same time, just as unlikely. He'd been unnerved by Nahum and Niel's response, plus Gabe's curtness on the phone, and he suspected there was more to learn. But for now, he needed to call JD.

He picked up within moments, sounding distracted, and Harlan decided to cut to the point. "Hey JD, it's Harlan, I have news. Lots of news, actually."

"Ah, Harlan! Have you? So have I! You first."

"We've found the entrance to the temple, but the way onward is sealed."

"You have? That's excellent! How?" JD's was suddenly focussed.

"Hold on, we have other news. We think we know what the trinity leads to—what the temple houses—and it's not just the opportunity to communicate with an angel. It's something different. We think it is storing the angel Raziel's Book of Knowledge."

There was silence, and Harlan thought the line had gone dead. "JD?"

"I'm here. What makes you think that?"

Harlan sighed and relayed what he'd read about the church. "It seems a logical assumption to make."

"Yes, yes it does," JD said hesitantly, as if he still had some doubts. "Actually, that makes my interpretation of the path a little easier."

"Why? What's your news?"

"The path is what we thought—a passage to the inner temple, with instructions and tests. I think I have deciphered some, but others still tease me, and the ultimate test is unclear. But actually, knowing that this could lead to Raziel's book..." He went silent again, and Harlan could hear him shuffling papers. When he finally spoke, his voice was filled with steely determination. "This is the pinnacle of all prizes. We have to get in there."

"When do you think you can come down, JD?"

"Not yet. I'm not ready. Is there any news of the key?"

"No."

"Are you guarding the entrance?" JD asked.

"It's well hidden. But we have competitors. Nicoli is here. I don't think they are any further ahead of us, though."

"I cannot work any quicker!"

"I know," Harlan said, trying to sound calm. "But if we don't have the key—whatever the hell that is—then it's all pointless, anyway. And I'm not sure Nicoli has it, either. Although, he might." Harlan's head hurt. "Maybe he's had it all along." *But where did that leave Jackson Strange?*

"Focus on the key," JD instructed, "and before you go, tell me about the entrance to the temple."

By the time Harlan ended the call, his head felt like a vice, but before he could move indoors, his phone rang; it was an unknown number. He answered cautiously, but he knew the voice on the other end. It was Jackson Strange.

"Hi, Harlan. I have a proposal. Can I come and see you? It's important."

He sighed and made the arrangements, and when he re-entered the conservatory a few minutes later, Shadow and

Niel had disappeared, and he could smell food cooking and hear music coming from the kitchen. Nahum and Olivia were talking quietly, leaning close. Harlan groaned inwardly. He recognised that look on Olivia's face. She was flirting, and it looked like Nahum was enjoying it.

"Hi, guys," he said as he entered. "We have a new proposition to consider. Jackson Strange will be here this evening to offer a partnership."

Olivia's eyebrows shot up, and she leaned back in her chair. "Really? He's got the key, hasn't he?"

"He didn't say as much, but I think he does."

She grinned. "I feel smug. I knew it!"

Nahum frowned. "Do you trust him?"

"More than I trust Nicoli," Harlan said as he sat at the table with them.

"Any idea who Jackson's working for?" Olivia asked.

"No. He said very little, other than that he wanted to meet us. So, I gave him the address and he'll be here in a few hours."

"He's still in London?"

"I don't know! Maybe. He could be in Wales, for all I know." He rubbed his face. "I need a beer, and more than anything, I need to clear my head." He looked up again, abruptly. "And JD is close to working out the path. Sorry, I should have mentioned that first."

"Wow," Olivia said, wide-eyed. "We might actually do this!"

Nahum stood, rolling his shoulders with the athletic grace that all the Nephilim had. "Yeah, we might, and I'm not sure what I think about that. But, I need a shower. I'm still covered in dirt from earlier. And I think I need to clear my head, too. See you later."

When they were alone, Olivia looked at Harlan slyly. "I like these guys!"

"You're so predictable."

"Piss off. They're big and handsome, and I'm single. I can look!"

"Don't think I didn't notice that flirting."

She fluttered her lashes. "I'm playing nice with our new colleagues." Her fingers drummed on the table, and she leaned forward, suddenly serious. "This thing is feeling very real, and if I'm honest, a bit intimidating."

"Intimidating? That's one word for it. As far as occult and magical objects go, this has to be one of the biggest finds!"

"In *Christian* history. Although, maybe the Ark of the Covenant would be bigger."

"Funny."

"Why funny?" Olivia shrugged. "If this book is real, and the temple, then anything is on the table. And besides, we've found some pretty incredible things over the years."

Harlan shook his head. "Not like this." He lowered his voice. "I'm not sure of the wisdom of this, and I was hoping JD might get cold feet."

"Why would he? Imagine what we could sell it for!"

"JD doesn't want to sell it. He wants to own it."

"Really?" Olivia asked, puzzled. "Finding and selling it would make us one of the biggest occult finders on the planet!"

Harlan knew he needed to tread carefully. Olivia had no idea who JD really was. "What do you know about JD?"

"That he owns this business and is interested in the occult, just like us. I met him once, years ago. Interesting man. Very dapper. He must be well into his eighties now."

And then some. "Yeah, I met him a few weeks ago, and once since. He's old, but looks fit. And he's determined. This kind of thing is very much his personal obsession. You know how some of these people get."

"Sure. They're why we make a lot of money."

"Well, trust me, once he gets this, it will *never* see the market."

"Does he have a vault to keep this book in?" Olivia looked incredulous. "Because if this gets out, everyone will want it, and it will be all over the news. JD will have a big, fat target on his head. We might actually break the Internet. Religious enthusiasts will be coming out of the woodwork. And museums! They'll demand this should be on public display!"

"They can demand all they want. If it ain't for sale, it ain't for sale," Harlan drawled. "And besides, we're good at keeping things quiet—so are Nicoli and Strange. It's what we *do*, Olivia! Discretion is our first, middle, and last name."

She took a sharp intake of breath. "Oh, my God. I know who will want it!"

He wondered if Olivia had been drinking, because she looked decidedly excitable. *Maybe she was drunk on Nahum? She looked like she'd been inhaling him earlier...* "Who?"

"The Catholic Church! The Vatican! They'll think it belongs to them, anyway! They'll want to squirrel it away in their massive library, and it will never see the light of day again."

Harlan blinked as Olivia's words sank in. "Oh, shit. I never even thought of them."

"Who else knows about this?"

He shrugged. "Lots of people have known about the trinity for years. The site has been searched for before, when The Map of the Seeker first surfaced in the fifteenth century, and then again during the nineteenth century when this kind of thing became very popular again. Then interest waned, as it does, and it disappeared into obscurity. Hammond was dismissed as a crackpot."

"No, not the site as the place to talk to angels," she said impatiently, "but Raziel's book. This is brand new, right?"

"I guess so. But, the stained glass image in the church is

Raziel. You'd have thought someone would have connected that information to the trinity before now."

"Not necessarily. If you're looking in the wrong direction, things don't always align." Olivia started to gather all the papers together, dropping them into ordered piles. "Nahum is right. We all need a breather from this. I'm going to find myself a bedroom, grab a beer, and have a shower, too."

"So you're staying, then?" Harlan asked.

"Of course I bloody am."

Harlan glanced at the tense faces in the conservatory and checked his watch again. *Where was Jackson?*

Gabe was outside sparring with Nahum and Shadow, and the clash of swords was quite unnerving. And mesmerising. It was a good distraction, while the rest of them tried to read and relax. It still hadn't rained, and the air was getting stickier, as if a storm was imminent.

Gabe had almost growled at Harlan when he told him that Strange was visiting. "You invited *someone else?*"

"If we want to complete the trinity, we need the key," Harlan had told him, squaring up to Gabe, while at the same time trying to be reasonable.

Gabe glared at him, but Harlan refused to back down. This was his gig, and JD was his employer. Gabe didn't have a choice, despite his obvious wish to be in charge and everyone else's natural deference to him. *Tough luck.* Eventually Gabe just nodded, grabbed the sword, and headed outside to work off his anger issues. Alex and El had stayed long enough to have a meal with them and complete their spells, but then they'd left, though Harlan could feel their magic still. He'd thought Gabe was being overprotective earlier, but now he was glad for it.

"He'll calm down," Niel said, and Harlan looked around, surprised. Niel was reclining on a daybed in the corner of the conservatory, a book open on his stomach. "Gabe, I mean. He has a complicated history with the book."

"So you said earlier. Is he going to share it?"

"He will when he's ready."

Olivia looked up from her phone where she'd been scrolling for the last half an hour. "Did you know Raziel?"

"I knew of him. He had a reputation, even amongst the fallen."

Olivia twisted in her chair to look at him. "Why?"

"He was one of the most powerful angels. Enigmatic, secretive. Everything you'd expect from the one who had the old God's ear. And to give the book that contained the mightiest of secrets away to Adam…well, let's just say that his betrayal sent ripples through all worlds."

"To Adam?" Olivia cocked an eyebrow and looked at Harlan. "I can't even believe I'm having this discussion."

Niel smiled, and propped himself up so he could talk with more comfort. "He wasn't what you think. He actually wasn't the first man to be created. But he was the first man to question his existence and the word of the old God. His wife, too. Raziel decided he should have full knowledge, not bits and pieces. The other angels were horrified, and took the book back. They threw it into the ocean. The old one retrieved it, and then it was stolen again." Niel closed his eyes briefly. "It caused a fight. But that is Gabe's story to tell."

A loud knock at the front door made Harlan jump, interrupting their conversation. "It's Jackson. Get the others in, Olivia."

18

———————————

*S*hadow lounged in a chair in the corner of the conservatory, idly playing with her dagger as she watched Jackson Strange enter the room.

He was about the same height as Harlan, and looked slightly unkempt with his shaggy mane of hair streaked with grey. He seemed to lope in rather than walk, his gait fluid and easy. He wore a long, loose black coat over faded jeans and a t-shirt, and scuffed trainers; he grinned as he surveyed the group spread around the conservatory. "Well, this is quite the reception." He nodded at Olivia. "Good to see you, Liv. So you're involved in this, too?"

She laughed. "Wild horses couldn't keep me away."

Harlan made the introductions, and the Nephilim all shook his hand, but Shadow stayed put, greeting him from her seat. She enjoyed watching the exchange. Jackson was clearly very comfortable with himself, completed unfazed by Gabe, Nahum, and Niel, and he sat at the table looking composed.

Although Olivia seemed relaxed, no one else did, and Gabe was still brooding. He'd fought more aggressively than she'd ever experienced from him, which was fine, but bruising. Their sparring had required her full concentration, and by the time they'd finished, all three of them were out of breath. At least it had banished thoughts of the trinity from her head for a while.

"So," Harlan started, "what brings you here, Jackson?"

"I know you're looking for The Temple of the Trinity—I saw you at the auction. I also suspect that you have the map, and that Nicoli has the path. That auction theft has his sticky fingerprints all over it. I have the key."

"Really? Because it's been missing a long time," Harlan said sceptically.

"So was The Path of the Seeker." Jackson frowned. "I wouldn't come here, otherwise...I haven't got time to make empty promises."

"Show it to us, then," Gabe said from where he was seated on a long bench beneath the window.

Jackson smiled as he looked across to him. "I haven't brought it with me. I'm not a fool. But I will bring it with me when you find the entrance."

"And what do you want in return?" Harlan asked.

"I want to come with you when you enter the temple."

Harlan gave a short laugh. "You're presuming we'll find it, then."

Jackson shrugged. "It's only a matter of time. You're here now and have been for days, and so is Nicoli. I have the feeling neither of you will stop until it's been found. Eventually, all things reveal their secrets, and this one is due." He tapped the table impatiently, and his eyes narrowed. "This is the first time in hundreds of years when all three items are present at the same time. We can't let this opportunity pass!"

"Who are you working with?" Olivia asked.

"No one. At the end of a job many years ago, I found something that led me to The Key of the Seeker. " He rubbed his chin with his hand. "It was tricky to get, but I managed it, and I've been sitting on it ever since."

"Why didn't you sell it?" Harlan asked, still suspicious.

"I didn't know where the other two parts were, and without them it seemed pointless. Besides, there was something about the whole thing that attracted me. It seemed too interesting to sell." Strange looked around them all, assessing their interest.

Shadow had only one question. "Why didn't you go to Nicoli with this?"

"Because he's an untrustworthy bastard, and he's working with Erskine." He looked puzzled for a moment, and then his expression cleared. "You were at the auction the other night! I thought I recognised you. You left just as I arrived."

She nodded, and decided to keep it vague. "I had other business."

Jackson smirked. "I bet you did. Maybe Nicoli wasn't the one who stole the path after all."

"It wasn't me," she assured him.

"That's a shame, in many respects," Jackson said, "because from what I've read, you need the original manuscript to access the Inner Temple."

"Where did you read that?" Harlan asked.

"Same place I found clues to getting the key. It didn't spell it out as such, but it was suggested in the layers of meaning. I can't remember the exact wording right now." The tension in the room thickened as everyone shuffled and cast worried glances at each other, and Jackson finally said, "Yeah, I didn't think you had it." He stood up. "Look, I don't expect you to answer me right now. Talk it over. You have my number, Harlan. But you won't enter the temple without the key, and you won't get that unless I come with you. Besides," he stared at Harlan, "you have no reason to doubt me. I may operate alone most of the time, but you know you can trust me. I'll see myself out."

He turned and left, and despite his assurance, Niel followed him.

"Bollocks!" Gabe said, standing and pacing in the thickening gloom. "That's just what we didn't need."

"It's what I expected," Olivia said, watching him. "I had a gut instinct."

"I didn't want anyone else involved!" Gabe stopped suddenly and clenched his fists. "I have a very bad feeling about this temple."

There was one lamp on in the corner, and it cast Gabe's features into harsh relief. There was no sign of his teasing manner from earlier that afternoon, and Shadow could feel her arm aching from where they'd clashed swords. They all needed to know why he was so rattled. "Gabe, I think you need to tell us what you know about Raziel."

He glared at her. "I think that would be a bad idea."

A flare of anger raced through her and she stood up, hands on her hips. "Herne's hairy balls! We are all in this together, and we are all going into that temple! The more we know, the better. Two people in this room have no paranormal skills, and will be vulnerable to whatever may happen in there. I'd suggest they stay here, but I know that won't happen!"

"Absolutely not!" Olivia said, looking horrified.

"And in case you've forgotten, Gabe, this is not your show. It's JD's," Harlan said forcefully.

"He's right," Nahum agreed in his usual reasonable tone. "And so is Shadow. They don't need details, Gabe, but they need something."

Niel arrived back in the doorway and leaned against the frame, an expression of resignation on his face. "I know what you blame yourself for, Gabe, but you weren't responsible."

Gabe was silent, a myriad of emotions sweeping across his face, and Shadow wanted to reassure him in some way, but now wasn't the time. He eventually came to a decision, sitting heavily on the window seat again. "Before we even existed, Raziel gave away The Book of Knowledge. We called it *Sefer Raziel HaMalakh*. The book was given to Adam and Eve—well that's your name for them, not ours. But it was seen as a great betrayal. The book has been called the first grimoire. It contains powerful magic about life, elemental magic, words that commanded the rain, the sun, the earth, the seas—the basic matter of life. I'm not talking about The Creation, as you call it," he warned, looking particularly at Harlan and Olivia, who watched him with fierce concentration. "Life *evolved*—it was not created. But the book did contain powerful, raw magic, base spells from which all others derive."

"Why the hell would you give away something so powerful?" Harlan asked, finally finding his voice.

"That's the big question," Nahum said softly. "It was supposedly an act of charity. And a reward to the couple who questioned their existence."

"Anyway," Gabe continued, "the book was stolen back by a couple of angels who decided humans were not worthy of such information. They cast it into the sea, but the old God wanted it back. It was too important to lose. He rescued it and hid it, forgiving Raziel for his betrayal, because after all, he was his favourite. But it didn't end there. Raziel quarrelled with the old one, stole the book again, and war broke out in the Otherworld—Heaven, as you call it. It raged. And that's when angels started to fall to Earth. They left the Otherworld by the thousands, fleeing to this realm, and eventually we were created."

Olivia exhaled heavily. "Wow. And the book?"

"Still missing. Along with Raziel. The magic that was in

that book found its way everywhere—and we're not entirely sure how. By Adam and Eve, though they had it only for a short time? By Raziel himself? By another human who deciphered it and shared it? By the book itself?" He shrugged. "Regardless of the means, pockets of knowledge sprang up, elemental magic took flight, and man began to take control of his destiny."

"And women?" Olivia asked, tongue in cheek.

Shadow laughed as Gabe smiled. "And women."

"Are you serious?" Harlan asked, looking around as if someone would announce it was a huge joke. "This is amazing! Alex and El should have heard this! You're talking about the first witches!"

"I'm glad they're not here," Gabe said. "I'm happy to share this with them, but I don't want them inside the temple—if we ever get there."

"Why not?" Shadow asked, annoyed on their behalf. "They could be useful. They wield magic better than any of us. I can't manipulate it like they do."

"No," Gabe said, shaking his head firmly. "This isn't about fighting magic with magic. This is about dealing with Raziel and whatever is in there. And there are too many people involved already."

Although the room was now very dim, Shadow could see enough to know that Gabe was adamant, his face set in stone, and Shadow wasn't entirely sure he'd made the right decision. Two powerful witches had just walked out the door when the group might need them most. "But that can't be all," she said, watching Gabe. "There's something else, isn't there?"

He stared at her, his dark eyes full of sorrow and guilt. "Yes, there's more. The Book of Knowledge caused many problems long before we were born, and long after. Many of us believe that one of the reasons we were created was to control the effects that The Book of Knowledge had on humanity. Eventually, I was tasked with finding it. I failed." He sighed. "And I believe that my failure caused the flood."

"I disagree," Niel said forcefully. He was still standing in the doorway, barely visible in the gloom. "The flood would have happened anyway. Our God was vengeful, and angry about many things—humanity's independence, the loss of the book, Raziel's betrayal—and whatever else was pissing him off at the time!"

"Agreed," Nahum said. "You should not blame yourself. Even if you *had* found the book, the flood would have happened. They had determined to start anew."

"But essentially the flood failed, didn't it?" Shadow said, feeling a stir of pleasure at the Gods being thwarted. "Magic survived."

Olivia stared at her. "You think the flood was about destroying magic?"

"Maybe." Shadow laughed suddenly at the idea. "What a ridiculous notion. Magic is everywhere! My race wields it naturally, to varying degrees. To think you could erase it…"

"Not erase it entirely," Gabe told her, "just remove it from man's ability. Well, that's one theory, anyway."

Harlan stirred. "This doesn't answer what we're going to do about Jackson. I think we need to accept his help."

Gabe stood up. "I guess we do, but first I want to see the entrance to the temple myself." He glanced outside. "Rain is coming, and it's dark enough now. With luck, we won't run into The Order of Lilith."

"And if we do?" Nahum asked.

"We make sure they don't follow us," Gabe said firmly.

19

*G*abe followed Nahum and Shadow as they led the group through the dark ravine to the entrance of the temple, and he was grateful they were both so adept at working at night.

For the Nephilim and Shadow, the going was straightforward, but Harlan and Olivia struggled, stumbling on the uneven path, even with their head torches in place to keep their hands free. Gabe had tried to persuade them not to come, but his pleas were useless. He had been tempted to fly to the entrance, but in the end decided that accompanying the humans on foot was probably the safest option.

Gabe had asked Niel to hang behind to make sure they weren't being followed, and he had lost sight of him some time back. Niel could hide himself easily despite his size.

"There," Nahum said, suddenly stopping and pointing halfway up a steep, rocky hillside covered in trees and bushes. "It's hidden behind the scrub."

"Bloody hell," Olivia exclaimed. "I'm not a mountain goat!"

"I did warn you," Gabe said, annoyed.

Olivia just glared at him, although it was hard to see her expression with the torch on her forehead. "Don't worry. I can make it. It was a joke!"

Nahum said, "I can help you if you struggle. And so can Gabe, when he stops worrying." He shot him a look that warned him to play nice, and Gabe acknowledged it with an almost imperceptible nod.

He knew he was being unreasonably grumpy, but with every step that brought them closer to the temple, he felt the weight of those expectations years ago, and he'd decided that it didn't matter how much JD wanted this book, he was going to find a way to destroy it. There was no way he was letting it loose in the world. Maybe he was being as judgemental as the old God, but he had first-hand experience of cataclysmic vengeance, and could do without experiencing it again. But he hadn't even voiced that to Nahum or Niel yet.

Shadow was already scrambling up the slope, sure-footed and nimble, barely needing the stunted bushes to pull herself up, and Harlan scrambled after her. "Shadow, wait at the entrance," Gabe instructed. "Don't say or do anything!"

As he'd grown to expect, she completely failed to answer him, and he bit back his annoyance.

Olivia set off too, Nahum following, but Gabe waited, wondering if Niel was close. He listened for a moment, but only the scrape of sliding rock disturbed the silence, and Gabe ground his teeth, wishing Harlan could be quieter. Then he felt a rush of air, and in seconds Niel landed next to him, furling his wings behind him.

"Anything out there?" Gabe asked.

"Nothing. We're all alone—not surprisingly. It's going to rain." He looked up the slope. "The entrance is up there, then?"

"Yep. Can you keep watch?"

"Sure. I'll settle on the ledge above. I should be able to see most of the ravine from there."

"I'll get Nahum to relieve you later. I want your opinion of what we've found so far."

Niel nodded, and in seconds had soared above, and Gabe saw Olivia gasp and look around before focusing on the climb again. Satisfied with Niel's report, Gabe headed up too, and within a few minutes they were all precariously balanced outside the long, narrow crack in the rock face.

"I'll lead the way," Shadow said, already sliding through the gap. "It's single file, but the anteroom is big enough for all of us."

They all filed in, shuffling awkwardly along the narrow passage, the press of rock tight on either side, but any discomfort fled as soon as Gabe reached the first chamber. The smooth, polished walls were like glass, and Harlan and Olivia's torches bounced off them, the walls acting like a mirror.

"Holy shit!" Harlan exclaimed, turning slowly. "It's impossible to make rock this smooth without machinery."

"Not if you're an angel," Gabe said, overawed despite his reservations.

"If this is what the antechamber's like, the inside should be unbelievable," Harlan continued. He walked over to the door set in the rock, and examined the inscription, careful not to touch it.

Gabe headed to Harlan's side, a deep dread filling the pit of his stomach. "That's the language of fire. The language of angels. " He stared at the script faultlessly etched into the surface, elegant and powerful.

Olivia looked at Nahum and Gabe. "You understand it?"

Despite their unusual situation, Nahum looked calm and self-assured; when he answered, his voice was filled with wonder, and something else. Regret, perhaps. "We do. I have not seen it for many years."

Gabe read the inscription carefully, the words translating easily, just like breathing to him. "'Welcome, Seeker. Say the words and the worthy will enter. Be sure of your intent, for all knowledge lies here. Life lies here. Death lies here. The path to glory awaits.' He turned to Nahum. "Your translation is the same?"

Nahum nodded.

Harlan had his phone in his hand. "I need to take pictures to show JD. But it seems obvious to me—you need to say the line in that language to make it open."

"It seems the most likely suggestion," Gabe agreed. He looked up at the domed roof, and then examined the floor below. The room was immaculately constructed, with no sign of tool marks. "I haven't seen work like this for years."

Shadow frowned. She had been quiet, pacing around with her sword in her hand, but now she asked, "When was that?"

"Our father used to see me occasionally in one of these chambers. He carved it in seconds out of hillsides, just like this, but on the edge of the desert. It was like scooping water from a bowl." His tone grew impatient. "It was meant to impress me. Remind me of my place. I guess it worked."

Nahum nodded. "I had almost forgotten that. He did it so effortlessly."

"Remind us we were nothing compared to him?"

Nahum gave a short laugh. "I meant the cave, but I guess both applied."

"In fact, it was in a place like this when I was tasked with finding the book," Gabe said dryly. "How apt I am so close now." Gabe had been honoured with the request at the time. It felt like a vindication of his worth; it was only later it had felt like a death sentence. It had come at a time when he hadn't seen his father for years, a time when the Nephilim had shaken off their fathers' commands, so this request was memorable in many ways. He was annoyed with himself for even accepting it.

Who was he kidding? He had no choice.

Nahum took another look around and then said, "I'll get Niel."

While they waited, Olivia took photos too, snapping the entrance and antechamber from every angle. Gabe eyed the doorway suspiciously. This felt more like a tomb than a temple. They could all die in here. There was one thing he was sure of. This temple would become far more convoluted and complicated before it gave up The Book of Knowledge.

Harlan needed to see JD. Talking on the phone wasn't an option. JD was evasive and easily side-tracked, and while that was understandable considering the task at hand, it was still frustrating.

He announced his plan at breakfast the next day, and nobody argued with him. There was nothing for Harlan to do at the house, and Olivia had been happy enough to stay. And everyone was as tense as he was, too. Standing in the antechamber of the temple last night, Harlan had thought how tempting it was to walk straight in. It may be that the Nephilim's knowledge would be great enough they didn't need JD, but they weren't sure. And besides, JD wanted to be there.

Part of Harlan's intention today was to bring JD back with him. If Nicoli found the entrance too, they might not have the luxury of waiting for much longer. And then there was the added worry that they might need the original Path of the Seeker upon entrance.

By the time Harlan knocked on JD's door, it was late morning, and Anna answered, surprised to see him.

"You didn't ring," she said by way of welcome. Harlan wondered exactly what she did as JD's assistant. He assumed she helped to research and catalogue his library, and maybe searched for new acquisitions, but maybe not.

"I didn't see the point," he said as he brushed past her into the hall. "I have some things to show him." Harlan frowned at her expression. "I presumed it would be fine."

She shrugged, her face impassive. "He tends not to like unexpected guests, but I guess under the circumstances..."

She turned and led him up the main stairs to a room at the back of the house. *Actually*, Harlan estimated, *it was the only room at the back of the house.* It encompassed half a dozen windows that were shrouded in thick curtains; the rest of the walls were lined with shelves, all packed with books. This was JD's library. Harlan presumed the curtains were to protect his collection from sunlight. It felt stuffy, even more so considering the muggy day that hadn't been alleviated by the overnight rainfall.

JD was seated at an enormous table in the middle of the room. Overhead lights on long chains hung over it, low and intimate, and books were spread across its surface. JD was busy making notes, and it was only when Anna coughed gently that he looked up, surprised. "Anna, I told you not to disturb—" He faltered. "Harlan? What are you doing here?"

"I'm sorry to come unannounced," Harlan said, striding in, "but I have photos of the temple's antechamber. I decided to show you in person."

Harlan had stopped on the journey to print the photos so they could be studied in a reasonable size, and he pulled them out of the envelope and handed them over, sitting next to JD as he did so. It was only when he was so close that he realised how exhausted JD looked. "JD, are you all right?"

"Tired. I have only had about three hours sleep a night since I started deciphering the path."

"If that," Anne said disapprovingly, as she picked up an empty plate from next to JD's elbow. "He's eating all his meals in here." She looked at Harlan accusingly, and he wondered what the hell he should say. It wasn't his fault JD was up all night. But she marched off, calling, "I'll bring coffee," before shutting the door behind her.

"Don't mind her," JD said, flicking through the photos. "She worries, and frankly I'd starve without her." His eyebrows rose expressively as he examined them one by one. "The language of fire! I have never seen it outside of my own library."

Harlan was shocked. "You've seen it before! How?"

JD looked impatient. "The angels taught me it!"

Harlan felt like a fool. He'd assumed JD's conversations with angels were useless ramblings. "Can you read it?"

"I will be able to, with time. But the Nephilim have translated it, I presume?"

"Yes," Harlan said, pulling himself together. "We think saying the words out loud will open the door, but obviously we need The Path of the Seeker deciphered before you can go any further."

JD didn't speak for a moment, but when he looked up, his eyes were wide. "This place looks inhuman."

"It's carved by an angel, JD. Look, I hate to rush you, and I know you've had the document for only a few days, but are you making headway? We need to act quickly, before Nicoli does. It would take an act of violence to keep his group out of the temple, and although the Nephilim and Shadow are more than capable, we don't want things to get ugly."

"I'm close, very close, but there are still a couple of symbols that confuse me." He looked distractedly away, a frown furrowing his brow.

"Can you bring your research with you? Continue it at the house? I really can't express strongly enough the need for us to act quickly here. This is a race against time."

"It's been there for hundreds of years," JD tutted absently, frowning once again at the documents in front of him.

"But no one knew where it was! And we think this is Raziel's book. *The Book*." Harlan watched JD, half wondering if he'd fully absorbed everything he'd told him. "And Jackson Strange thinks we need the original path. Did I mention that?"

JD looked at him, annoyed. "No! No wonder I'm struggling." He searched through the jumble of texts on the desk, finally plucking a piece of paper from beneath a book. "This symbol here means 'within'—within the page, the paper?"

Harlan looked surprised. "You think Jackson is right?"

"It makes sense." JD looked at him, and it felt as if his pale brown eyes that had seen so much, and that had already deciphered the means to immortality, were looking straight through him. "Tell Gabe to take it."

Harlan's mouth dropped open. "You want him to steal it? From Nicoli and Erskine?"

"Yes."

"But there could be terrible consequences—Erskine conjures demons. He sent one two nights ago. He could send one here!"

JD rolled his eyes, a strangely teenage gesture in such an old man. "This house is well protected, and besides, I have dealt with demons before. Don't worry about that. But you're right. I need to come with you." JD's gaze swept over the table. "There are a few books I will bring, but that's all."

In seconds, JD had gone from absent-minded to very decisive, and Harlan stumbled over his words. "Er, okay. Good. And what about Strange? He says he has the key, but wants to be involved before he hands it over."

"I suppose you had better say yes, then. But I want to see that key before we go inside the temple—just to make sure. I have my own theories about The Key of the Seeker." His eyes glittered with excitement, and a fair degree of ruthlessness. "It wouldn't do to go in there with the wrong one."

*S*hadow ended a call with Harlan, a thrill of excitement already racing through her, and shouted to Gabe and Nahum, trying to stop their fight.

They were in the garden behind the house, and bored by inactivity, Nahum and Gabe were sparring with swords again. It had rained heavily overnight, and they were both wet and grass-stained from where they'd rolled on the ground. They were so absorbed in their fight that they didn't hear her, and Shadow felt the clash of metal in her bones. They grunted and shouted, and every now and then threw a taunt at the other, trying to provoke a miss-step; but they were equally good, combative, and unwilling to lose any advantage.

Shadow shouted again. "Harlan phoned! We have a job to do. Stop fighting!"

This time they heard her, and they reluctantly broke apart to stare at her.

"Did you say job?" Gabe asked, wiping his brow with the back of his hand and smearing more dirt over it in the process.

"Yes. JD wants us to steal The Path of the Seeker. It seems that Jackson might have been right about needing the original."

Nahum's chest was still heaving, and sweat gathered in a v down his t-shirt. "Now? In the daylight?"

"He just said the sooner the better. We should go watch the house, see who's in." She wrinkled her nose. "But you two need to shower first. You're sweaty!" She looked at Gabe's hand, and then up at his amused eyes. "I presume your hand is feeling better?"

He transferred the sword to his left hand and flexed his fingers, the bandage wrinkled and dirty. She noticed before that he fought using both hands, but he was naturally right-handed and consequently favoured that one. "Yep. Feels much better. Briar's balm is good."

"Good. I'll redress it as soon as you get out of the shower, and we'll make a plan for the break-in." She'd assumed charge and knew it would needle Gabe, but that was okay. It didn't work to always let him get his own way. Turning away, she led the way back to the house, Gabe and Nahum falling into step behind her. "Did you say you found a spot on the hill to watch their house, Gabe?"

"I did, on the hillside opposite. You want a lookout?"

Shadow entered the conservatory, spotting Olivia still searching through Hammond's papers. Niel was in the ravine, watching in case The Order of Lilith found the entrance. "Yes. I think Olivia should be up there."

She looked up as she heard her name. "Up where?"

"Harlan has just phoned. JD wants us to steal the original path. I think you should be our lookout."

Olivia leaned back in her chair, her hands behind her head. "Does he? JD's got more balls than I expected."

"Maybe it's because he isn't the one doing the stealing!"

Shadow pointed out. "You found anything interesting in there?" She gestured at the papers.

Olivia nodded. "These are fascinating. This poor man was clearly tormented by his visions. There was nothing beautiful or heavenly about them! It sounds like he got barely any sleep for weeks while he completed the trinity. He lost weight, argued with everyone, and became a semi-recluse. It sounds like torture! And I agree with Niel—he must have hidden the key somewhere close to where he lived."

"Why?" Nahum asked.

"Because he was too ill to have travelled far." Olivia's eyes slid across Nahum's muscular chest before she looked at his face, and she clearly tried to focus. "He lived not far from here. I don't know if that's why he was picked for receiving the vision. I mean, was the temple here for thousands of years beforehand? Or was it made at the same time as the visions? You said creating such a thing was easy for angels."

Gabe pulled a chair out and sat down. "I said a single chamber would be easy. I doubt whatever is beyond that door is so simple."

Nahum exhaled heavily. "Why here, in England? I'd have thought it would be somewhere in the Middle East, in Mesopotamia or Babylon."

"We may never know that," Gabe said, shrugging.

Shadow leaned against the table, absently picking up pieces of paper. "Maybe there are entrances all over the world. Perhaps this is just a portal?"

Gabe's head whipped around to look at her. "A *what*?"

"A portal to the place that stores the book." She stared at him, wondering why she hadn't thought of this sooner, because as soon as it popped into her head, it seemed natural.

"Stored between worlds?" Gabe voice rose, incredulous.

"Maybe. Or stored in one place in *this* world. " Shadow

immediately started to doubt herself. "I suppose it does sound odd."

Nahum groaned and stared at Gabe. "Actually, that sounds just about right. Raziel would have no idea who would have survived the flood, or where anyone would have lived, but he was determined to preserve his book. He created a place to store it in, but with multiple entrances."

"And then after the flood," Gabe said, his voice low as the suggestion's implications reverberated around them, "when civilisation was secure, he left clues to those entrances. Different clues in different countries."

"Different visions," Olivia echoed, her gaze distant. "Different visionaries."

Gabe laughed, almost maniacally. "That's one hell of a conspiracy theory."

But there was something else pricking at Shadow. "How many people can speak the language of fire? Surely no one except for you?"

"JD might. Other alchemists might. JD called it Enochian —I've never heard of that, but maybe it's the same thing?" He looked puzzled. "I thought it would be something we'd talk about, but we haven't yet."

Olivia tapped the papers in front of her. "Communicating with angels or spirits has been a thing many have claimed to be able to do, but surely few really have. What if some of those were *chosen* to be instructed in the language, like JD? What's the point of hiding a book, guarded by the language of fire, if no one can speak it or read it? The book would be truly lost."

"Either that," Shadow said, "or it was intended for Nephilim all along. Raziel hoped you'd survive, and this would be your gift."

"Or our curse," Nahum said, his voice grim. "Shower time,

and then we leave. With luck, most of The Order of Lilith are out searching for the site. Let's get this over with."

———

Shadow, Gabe, and Nahum had made sure Olivia was positioned on the hillside opposite the house, and then Gabe had parked his SUV at the side of the quiet lane, a few doors down from the house that Nicoli's team were staying in.

They were trying to look as unobtrusive as possible while they waited for Olivia's update, which was frankly ridiculous, Shadow noted. It was broad daylight. If any of The Order of Lilith walked up the lane towards them right now, they would be easily spotted.

"It doesn't matter if they see us. We say we've come to talk. Easy," Gabe said, shrugging.

"We want to steal it, not chat," Shadow said scathingly, annoyed at his *laissez-faire* attitude. "And let's face it, if we do steal it, they will know exactly who's taken it."

Nahum grinned. "So? They'll try to steal it back and fail."

Shadow scowled at him. "Never underestimate your opponent. You should know better than that."

"I don't underestimate *us*! We have advantages they don't."

"They have a demon!"

"Now, now children," Gabe said as his phone rang. "Olivia."

He turned away to take the call as Shadow said, "We need a back entrance. Many of these houses look quiet. We could jump over a few fences and get into the back garden. Well, I could, anyway," she said in response to Nahum's sceptical expression.

He just shook his head. "Not in the daytime! Our new employer should be better educated as to the best time to do break-ins."

Shadow looked up and down the lane. "This is the best time! There's no one here. It's Saturday. Many people are out on daytrips or shopping. And I bet Nicoli's team is off looking for the entrance!"

Gabe ended the call. "Olivia says there are no cars on the drive, and no sign of anyone in the house. Nahum, you sit behind the wheel. Shadow and I will head inside. Edge a bit closer in a few minutes, in case we need a quick getaway. Sound good?"

"Sounds good."

Shadow and Gabe set off down the lane as Nahum swapped seats. When they reached the end of the drive they turned straight into it, confidently walking up to the house, and then to the side gate.

Shadow scanned the windows. Nothing moved. They both turned to survey the houses around them, but again, everything was quiet, so in seconds Gabe boosted Shadow over the gate and then followed, landing softly next to her. They waited for a moment, listening carefully, and then proceeded down the path to the side door. Gabe pulled skeleton keys from his pocket and quickly manipulated the lock, but although the lock opened, the door wouldn't budge.

"Damn it," he whispered. "There must be bolts securing the door."

"We need to get through a window," Shadow suggested, stepping back and looking up. None of them were open, so she carried on around the house, checking each window as she passed. "Everything's secure."

"Up there," Gabe said, pointing up to where a window had been left ajar. "They must have thought that would be safe. I can reach it."

"Only if you fly. But it's broad daylight!" Shadow inspected the wall. "There's a drain pipe, but it's not close, and there are no hand holds."

Gabe turned his back to the building and surveyed the garden and the neighbours. "I can't see anyone or hear anyone, Shadow. That's our way in. Give me a minute, and I'll open the door."

"Someone could be sleeping in there!"

"Trust me," he said, winking.

Seconds later he had pulled his t-shirt off, revealing sculpted muscles across his whole upper body, and his wings unfolded majestically. Despite vowing to herself not to stare, Shadow couldn't help it. She had never seen Gabe's wings in daylight, and they were breathtaking. She could see the colours in the feathers properly—shades of bronze, copper, and brown, all slightly darker on the underside.

"You shouldn't have to hide them. They are too beautiful."

Gabe smiled, despite the tenseness of their situation. "No one's called them that in a long time."

She wondered who had. His wife, she presumed, and for a second she envied their intimacy. "I want to run my fingers through them." The admission was out before she could stop it.

Gabe's smile broadened in to a lazy, seductive grin. "Another time." And then he stepped away from her, flew up to the window, and unlocked it easily. In a heartbeat his wings had vanished, and he was clambering through it.

For anxious seconds she waited, hoping not to hear shouts or fighting, but all was silent, and then she heard the door unlock and it swung open. She pushed his t-shirt at him and entered the room, quickly shutting the door behind her. "Anything?" she asked quietly as he dressed.

"I've had a quick look in the upstairs rooms, but there's no one here. There are papers and books in the sitting room. That seems to be their base."

"You focus there," Shadow said, "I'll double check the house."

Leaving Gabe searching through the research material, Shadow methodically worked her way around the ground floor, checking any bags or papers she came across, and finding a few photocopies of documents with notes made on them. She headed upstairs, knowing Gabe would have given them a cursory search only. The bedrooms all showed signs of someone sleeping in them—five rooms, so at least five people. Books were in a couple of bedrooms, novels mainly, and bags were half emptied, clothes strewn across the floor and other furniture. Shadow sniffed and frowned at the smell of unwashed clothes. *At least the Nephilim were clean.*

She found Mia's room next. It had to be hers; she was the only female in the group, and then found the one she thought was Erskine's. There were a collection of books about black magic, demons, angels, and a large Bible with numerous bookmarks sticking out of it. She flicked through it idly, but she certainly hadn't got the time to read it all. She considered taking it, and then decided against it. She needed to head back to Gabe and see if he'd had any success.

———

Niel was lying flat on his stomach on the narrow ledge of rock above the entrance to the temple, hidden behind a screen of bushes, watching Nicoli's team toil up the gorge.

They had worked their way up the narrow track over the last couple of hours, investigating thoroughly, and concentrating on the right hand side of the gorge, which was logical. That was the side it was marked on the map. They nodded politely as hikers passed them, pausing their search until they were out of sight. The day was still overcast, the air close, and although so far it hadn't rained, it was still hard going. He lost sight of them on occasions, but they always reappeared a little closer.

Nicoli was leading the party, referring constantly to what Niel could only assume was the map. Erskine was easy to spot. He was short and fat and was clearly struggling with the trek, waddling more than walking, but to be fair, it hadn't stopped him. He clutched a leather bag close to his chest, and every now and again he pulled a document out of it. Niel suspected it was The Path of the Seeker, but as he couldn't be sure, he hadn't rang Gabe about it.

They finally paused below him, and Niel had a horrible, sinking feeling that they would find the entrance. They were well equipped too, carrying rope and heavy packs, and he had no doubt if they did find the entrance, they would attempt to enter the temple. There was a lot of pointing going on, and he heard raised voices. Eventually Jensen, the skinny man, started up the slope, directed by Erskine. His voice carried to Niel, high-pitched and mean, as he yelled instructions to Jensen. "No, higher. Naamah told me it was halfway up a steep slope. I feel sure we're close." *Naamah? His demon, perhaps.* Erskine shot a look of loathing at Nicoli. "I told you we should have started farther up the ravine. We've wasted hours."

Nicoli held on to his patience. "We searched here the other day and found nothing. It was logical to start at the beginning again."

Jensen's laboured breathing grew louder as he drew closer, and Niel could smell his fear; he didn't like Erskine. He was sure none of them did. Erskine stood slightly apart from the rest, only the tall Greek man willing to speak to him during their search. Mia looked mutinous but wary, and the other man, who they still had no name for, looked distinctly annoyed. They were not a happy team, and Niel was sure that could work to their advantage.

Jensen was getting closer, poking behind bushes and stunted trees, and although Niel was tempted to intervene, he knew it was pointless. To stop them discovering the entrance would mean killing them, or injuring them, and he wasn't about to do that.

Niel had discussed his options that morning with Gabe and Nahum before he left, just in case this happened, but they all felt they were on a collision course that couldn't be avoided. Fate was moving in odd ways, pushing them together in this crazy race. He knew why Gabe was worried. Raziel's book was powerful and had caused so much bloodshed and arguments in the past, it wasn't hard to imagine the destruction it might bring now. And Gabe had undoubtedly suffered at the time, having been unwillingly dragged into a search and lifestyle he had long abandoned.

A shout disturbed his thoughts. *Jensen*. He was lost to view now, but he heard him yell, "I found an opening in the rock!"

Shit.

Erskine punched the air with unconcealed greed and started his slow, laborious climb. Niel unhappily accepted the inevitable. It was time to call Gabe.

---

*W*hen Gabe received Niel's call, he responded quickly, anxious to get there as soon as possible. When he and the others reached the spot in the ravine below the entrance, they found Niel with the unconscious unknown member of The Order of Lilith. The man was lying on the slope as if he was asleep, and Niel stood over him, waiting impatiently.

"How did *that* happen?" Gabe jerked his head at the man.

"They left him watching. I decided he needed to be out of the way." Niel held his hand up. "Don't worry, he'll be fine. It was just a small punch, and I only did it when I knew you were close."

"Good. Are all the others in there?" Gabe asked.

"Yep. You made good time."

Shadow grimaced. "Even so, they've been in there for almost an hour. They must have progressed beyond the first door. We need to get in there. Now."

Gabe noted her determined expression. Shadow wasn't scared; in fact, he doubted much scared her at all, and that headstrong determination worried him. But she was right.

The drive hadn't been long, but they'd had to run up the valley, and that had taken time.

"I guess we'll soon find out, won't we," Nahum said, eager to head up the rocky slope.

"Hold on," Niel cut in, stretching out his arm to stop him. "What exactly are we going to do when we get in there?"

"If I'm honest," Gabe answered warily, "I'm not sure."

"They were well equipped," Niel told them. "And they haven't come out—I'm sure of that. Are we really prepared to go in after them?"

Nahum stepped close to Gabe, gripping his shoulder. "This is one of those times when we just follow our gut."

Gabe stared at the man he trusted above all others and knew he was right. "All right. If they've entered, we enter."

"Even without The Path of the Seeker?" Olivia asked, looking shocked. "They could be well ahead now, and without guidance, it could prove disastrous for us."

Gabe was filled with doubt about their next steps too, but he needed Olivia to understand. "Like Nahum said, this is one of those times where we have to run on instinct—unless you want them to get the book before us."

"Of course not!"

"Maybe we just snatch the path out of Erskine's grubby little hands," Shadow suggested, her violet eyes glittering.

Gabe held Shadow's gaze, staring her down. "We'll assess the situation. If the opportunity is right, then yes—but no jumping ahead and compromising our safety." He knew what she was like when she had an idea in her head, and he needed her to focus. "Besides, unless they have the key, I think they are in limbo, too. Whatever happens, we stay calm." He looked at them each in turn, and they all nodded, Shadow more reluctantly than the others. "Let's go."

Niel lifted the unconscious man like he was a sack of potatoes, flinging him over his shoulder as he scrambled up the slope, seemingly unimpeded by his burden, and the others scrambled next to him. They slowed when they reached the entrance to the temple, Shadow approaching first in her unnervingly graceful silence. She listened, nodded, and slipped inside. Gabe turned to Niel and with a wordless gesture, told him to remain outside, and then he followed the others.

To Gabe's ears, every slide of clothing or shoes along the rock seemed loud, but there were no shouts from up ahead, or any other sounds at all. When they finally stepped into the antechamber, they found it completely empty.

"Fuck it!" Gabe said, looking around. He'd been hoping they would find them here, still puzzling how to open the door. "They must have gone in."

Nahum examined the door etched into the rock. "This looks different now. Turn your light off, Liv." When it was fully dark again, Nahum pointed at the edges of the door. "There's a faint light there. See it?"

He was right. An almost imperceptible orange light seeped around the door, and the letters held remnants of the same colour.

Olivia groaned. "They really have gone through it."

"We have to follow," Shadow said, her voice filled with steely resolve. "Erskine must have mastered the language of fire."

"But he hasn't got the key," Olivia reminded them.

"Unless Jackson was lying and he made a better deal later," Nahum suggested.

"But he wasn't with them!" she pointed out.

"Maybe," Nahum countered "they stole it from him. Or maybe the demon got to him."

Gabe was debating their options as he asked, "Have you heard from Jackson today, Olivia?"

She shook her head and her eyes widened. "Shit. I hope he's okay."

"One of you two has to say the words and let us in," Shadow said, her sword in her hand.

Gabe blinked. Where the hell had that come from?

"We are wasting time," she persisted.

Nahum nodded at Gabe. "She's right. We have to follow them."

"And if they're stuck there? We could be, too—some weird angel purgatory." Gabe rubbed his eyes. "I don't want that for any of us." He looked at Olivia's worried face. "You don't have to come," he told her. "You can stay with Niel."

She squared her shoulders. "If I don't go, I'll never forgive myself."

Shadow raised her voice. "Gabe! Do it."

"Wait!" Gabe raised his hands, fearing once they entered, there was no going back. "I've studied our copy of the path and remember some of it. Does anyone else?"

Olivia nodded. "I was comparing it to the map and some of Hammond's rambling diary. I can remember bits of it, but not all, and it didn't make much sense to me."

Nahum nodded, too. "Same here. I remember parts of it."

"Shadow?" Gabe asked, starting to feel slightly more positive.

She shrugged. "A little."

He sighed. "Let's hope a little knowledge goes a long way. And more than anything, let's hope Erskine has the key. Nahum, go let Niel know. We'll wait."

Gabe stepped in front of the door, pulling El's sword from the scabbard he had strapped to him, and he was thankful for the feel of the cold steel in his hands. He silently rehearsed the words, the old language feeling odd because he hadn't spoken it for so long, and his heart thumped uncomfortably in his chest. Everything about this screamed danger, but he had to do this. To turn away now, knowing that Erskine could get the book, was impossible.

When Nahum reappeared at his side, he was carrying El's dagger. "Ready?"

"Ready."

Gabe spoke the inscribed words, feeling the power in them. They rumbled around the chamber, and the stone trembled. The script etched into the rock burst into flames, as did the entire outline of the doorway, and the doors swung wide silently.

Gabe eyes widened at the sight. A passageway lay beyond the doors. The walls along its entire length were inscribed with the language of fire. Every single word blazed with light, reflecting off the shiny black granite it was etched into. He heard Olivia's sharp intake of breath, sensed Nahum's grim determination and Shadow's eager curiosity, and swallowing his own reluctance, he gripped his sword tighter and stepped through the door.

Harlan was halfway back to Angel's Rest, with JD next to him, when his phone rang and Niel gave him the news. He nearly crashed the car.

"They've done *what?*"

He listened as Niel patiently related the events, but his calmness did nothing to alleviate his own panic. His driving slowed as he absorbed the news. "We're not ready, Niel."

"You'd better get ready. It's happening now, whether you like it or not. And call Jackson. We need the key."

When he hung up, JD was already glaring at him. "They had no right to go in. I expected better of Gabe. I trusted him."

"To be fair, they really had no choice, JD. Nicoli was

already ahead." He put his foot down, driving faster than the speeding limit, but he didn't care. "If you want a shot at this book, Gabe, Shadow, and the rest of their crew are it." He glanced at him, but JD was staring resolutely ahead, his lips set in a thin line, and Harlan lost patience, despite the fact that JD was his boss, and immortal to boot. "They are risking their lives, JD. They're in there without the path or the key. The consequences could be deadly! You should be grateful, not sulking." He felt JD's hard stare but he concentrated on driving, not giving a shit about what JD thought. "Olivia is with them. She could die. I happen to like Olivia, a lot. I like the others, too. This isn't some walk in the park they started without us."

JD was silent for a few minutes more, and then he said stiffly, "Sorry. I'm very anxious, and sleep-deprived."

"Then I suggest you sleep now, because once we get to Angel's Rest, we won't stop."

"I can't possibly sleep now!"

"Well, in that case, do something useful and finish deciphering the path!"

"I've tried."

"Try harder! I need to phone Jackson."

The conversation with Jackson was straightforward, and Harlan didn't mince words. "Meet me at the house with the key."

"Slow down," Jackson remonstrated. "I need some assurances first."

"I can *assure* you that potentially people could die imminently, and you will never see the book or get any future favours from me unless you meet me at the house. That good enough?" He ended the call abruptly.

JD looked at him, intrigued. "That was unexpected."

"Yeah, well, there's a whole lot more to me than meets the eye."

They completed the rest of the journey in silence.

The first thing Harlan did when they arrived at the house was call Niel while he paced around the conservatory. "Any change?"

Niel, normally upbeat and optimistic, had never sounded so despondent. "It's been over an hour, and there's been no movement from inside. Nicoli's team has been in for over two hours. I'm anxious to get in there, Harlan. Tell me you're close."

"I'm at the house with JD, waiting for Jackson. I'll be with you as soon as we have the key." He lowered his voice and headed to the far end of the room, out of JD's hearing. JD was rifling through paperwork, making space for his own, and Harlan could tell he was already lost within his own thoughts and unlikely to hear him anyway. "Look, JD hasn't deciphered all of the document. We're missing key information. I'm not sure if Gabe told you, but we need the original."

"Too late for that," Niel said. "The original Path of the Seeker is in there with Erskine, but it's good to hear that Jackson still has the key—I think. However, I might have someone who can help."

Harlan frowned. "Who?"

"Nicoli's unknown soldier is currently lying unconscious at my feet. I think it's time to wake him up."

Shadow was right behind Gabe when he stepped through the door, and she tried not to let her awe get in the way of concentrating on the way ahead.

The illuminated script blazed on either side, but gave off no heat, despite the curling flames that flickered relentlessly. And it was utterly silent, except for their muted footfalls. Olivia was behind her, with Nahum at the rear, and as soon as Nahum stepped beyond the threshold, the door swung shut behind them, leaving no sign of where it had been.

"How the hell do we get out again?" Olivia asked, her voice unsteady.

"With our wits and by the skin of our teeth," Gabe said, as he set off down the corridor.

The corridor was uniform, as carefully constructed as the antechamber, and the far end was in darkness. They kept close together, walking slowly and wary of traps.

"Gabe, what does the script say?" Shadow asked.

"'Prepare yourself for The Path. Only the worthy will succeed.'"

"We'll be fine, then. I was born worthy!" she declared, trying to feel as confident as she sounded. This place felt completely alien to her.

"Maybe you shouldn't test that statement just yet," he answered, shooting her an annoyed look over his shoulder.

The corridor ended with a door made of shiny black stone, this one etched with a symbol, and again there was no handle.

"The symbol for water," Shadow said, immediately recognising the upside-down triangle.

"How do we open it?" Olivia asked. "The language of fire again?"

Gabe shrugged. "Let's try," and he quickly uttered a phrase.

A seam appeared down the middle of the panel forming two doors, which promptly swung open. Immediately afterward, ice-cold spray hit them, and a fine mist filled the space ahead.

Shadow blinked, droplets of water already obscuring her vision and soaking through her clothing. She tried to discern what lay ahead, but it was impossible to see anything through the spray. Gabe glanced at them uneasily, and then walked through the door, the rest of them hard on his heels.

The door sealed shut behind them, and for a moment the mist cleared, allowing them to see that four passageways lay ahead. Their walls streamed with water that pooled on the ground, already submerging the path. The walls were so high it was impossible to see the top, and so narrow that the Nephilim couldn't extend their wings in the space.

"Is this some kind of water maze?" Olivia asked, already shivering in the cold.

"Perhaps." Nahum nodded at the floor. "Look, the water is already rising. We need to move, now."

"But to which entrance?" Gabe asked. "We pick the wrong one and we're dead."

"Wait," Shadow said, trying to think of what she'd seen on The Path of the Seeker. "The elements have orders. I think water is the second one. We need to take the second path."

"Are you sure?" Gabe asked, his shirt already drenched with spray, and he slicked his hair away from his eyes.

"Yes—the order is earth, water, air, fire. If this relates to that, then it's the second path." The others looked uncertainly at each other, and Shadow asked, "Have you got a better idea? Or any suggestions at all?"

They shook their heads, and Shadow shouldered Gabe out of the way. "After me, then."

The water was icy, and within seconds Shadow was drenched. She gritted her teeth to stop them from chattering and forged ahead, trying not to lose her footing on the slick surface. For the most part, the way was flat, but it snaked left and right, and was completely disorientating. It was impossible to see the end, and every now and then she stumbled on hidden steps and slopes. They had walked only a short distance when the water was up to their knees, and then thighs, and she still had no idea how close they were to the end when it became waist deep, the current pulling with every step.

Gabe tapped her on the shoulder, shouting to be heard above the fall of water. "Are you sure you're right?"

"Yes, but even if I'm not it's too late now!"

"Shadow!"

"It's a test—of faith in my decision, as well as knowledge. I'm right." She glanced behind Gabe and saw Nahum and Olivia white-faced and shivering, and she quickly continued.

By the time the next door appeared, the water was up to her chest, and she struggled against the current. As soon as she stepped onto the narrow platform, the others staggering after her, the water ebbed away, leaving them all trembling and exhausted.

Olivia nodded at the door, and with a shaking voice asked, "What's etched on this one?"

It wasn't a symbol; instead, it was another word in flowing script.

"'Fire,'" Nahum said grimly before attempting a smile. "At least we'll warm up."

---

*N*iel shook the man lying prone on the ground, noting the bruise already swelling on his chin. He'd hit him with a quick jab and he dropped quickly, and despite their situation, Niel smiled. He hadn't lost his touch.

"Hey, wake up!"

The man stirred, blinked, groaned, and then his eyes widened and he sat up, trying to edge away. "Who the hell are you?"

"Your new best friend. Tell me what you know about The Path of the Seeker."

The man's eyes clouded. "I don't know anything about that damned thing." He was English, from somewhere in the north of the country, Niel estimated. His hair was cut very short, he had a thick, muscular build, and he looked like he'd been in a few fights. His nose had clearly been broken and never fixed, he had a scar across his neck, and he looked belligerent.

"Don't lie," Niel said, leaning close. "You work with Nicoli and the demon conjuror. What do you know about the path?"

"I know they're going to beat you to the temple. You're with Harlan's team." His mouth twisted into a smile, revealing missing teeth. "They're in there now—with the document. You're too late."

"I know they're in there, you idiot. I watched you. Two hours later and they're not out yet. Tell me what's hidden in the document."

"No idea what you're saying." He stared at Niel, challenging him, and despite Niel's size, he could tell he was spoiling for a fight. Niel was inclined to give him one.

"You will tell me what's hidden in that document, or I will take you in there with me, and you can tell me there—when we're potentially on the verge of death. Your choice."

"I don't know anything."

Niel tried to decide if he was telling the truth, or really had no idea. He had been in the house, privy to the discussions and research, and although he looked like a thug, that didn't mean he wouldn't have heard something useful.

Niel lifted him up by his jacket and pinned him to the wall of rock next to the entrance, his arm across his throat, thankful they were screened from the ravine below. The man's eyes widened with shock at finding his feet off the floor, but he recovered quickly, squirming in his grasp.

"I don't believe you," Niel said. "I think you're a lying little shit, and if my friends die because of you, I will kill you."

"I don't give a shit about your friends!" the man ground out, struggling for breath.

He lifted his foot and kicked at Niel, striking his legs. Niel dropped him and he fell awkwardly, and Niel straddled him, pinning his flailing limbs easily. He leaned into him, inches from his face, and despite the man's belligerence, he could smell his fear now.

"I've decided you're coming in there with me."

"I am not going in there with that demonic idiot!"

209

"Tell me what's in the document."

"Screw you!"

Niel considered him for a brief moment longer and then punched him. The man's head hit the rock and he passed out again.

Bollocks. He really was going to have to carry him in there. Niel was pretty sure that if they ended up near death, he'd give up the information quick enough. And if not, then at least Niel would have the pleasure of them both dying together.

Harlan studied the key in Jackson's outstretched hand.

It was not a normal key. It was constructed from jade that had been carved into an octagon the size of his palm, and was made out of several interlocking pieces. It was ornate, decorative marks all over it, and a single sigil was etched into the centre.

"You can pick it up," Jackson said, sounding amused. "It won't bite."

"I know that!" Harlan grasped it, surprised at its weight. "Is something in the middle of it? It's heavy for its size."

Jackson shrugged. "I don't think so, but to be honest, I haven't taken it apart. It looks as if it breaks into separate pieces, but I confess that it has defeated me."

JD was standing next to Harlan, glasses perched on the end of his nose as he watched him handle it. "May I?"

He handed it to JD, who walked to the closest lamp and held it close, turning it over in his hands. He murmured to himself, and then marched over to his notes on the path, turned his back on them, and sat down.

Astonished, Harlan said, "Er, JD, we really need to go."

"Not yet. I'm not ready!" he said impatiently.

"But our team is in there—"

"Then shut up and let me concentrate!" JD shot back.

Harlan bit back his impatience and glared at Jackson, who had a wry smile on his face. "Something funny?"

Jackson immediately sobered up. "I guess not." He stuck his hands in his pockets and walked to the conservatory windows, looking out at the deepening gloom before turning back to Harlan. "What happened?"

Harlan sighed and joined him, keeping his voice low. "Nicoli's team found the entrance and Gabe followed them in, leaving Niel outside. I asked Niel to check the antechamber, and it's empty. They must have crossed the threshold and the door has shut behind them. That was nearly three hours ago."

"Shit. That's a long time. Who was with him?"

"Shadow, Olivia, and Nahum."

"Niel's the big blond man, right?"

"Right." Harlan looked out the window, but he wasn't focusing on the view. "I'm worried sick. Anything could be happening in there. They could be injured, or even dead."

"You say Liv is in there?"

"Yes, and although I don't know the others well, I'd say she's in good hands."

"Olivia is pretty capable herself," Jackson reminded him.

"This is something else though, isn't it?" Harlan said, not looking forward to having to go after them.

A rumble of thunder carried across the hills and Jackson groaned. "Shit. We don't need a storm now, as well as everything else."

"You're still planning on coming?"

Jackson sighed. "Are we really going to do this?"

Harlan shook his head. "No. I just wanted to see if you really wanted to go. I wouldn't if I didn't have to."

"You're nuts, then. This could be one of the biggest finds

ever! Angels, Old Testament stuff, all in those hills! You'd want to miss that?"

"Actually, yes. I'm not a believer. That alone will make me 'unworthy.'"

"Just think, you might *become* a believer after this."

"I wouldn't count on it. Don't get me wrong—I believe in the old Gods and supernatural stuff. How could I not in this job? But it doesn't make me want to worship them."

JD broke into their conversation. "This isn't the key."

Both men spun around to face him, ready to protest.

"I've had that for years, JD," Jackson said, marching over to the table. "The documents I found talked about this being The Key of Angels, and it referred to Raziel. That's what this is about, isn't it? Raziel's Book of Knowledge."

Harlan looked at him, surprised. "You know that?"

"I suspected as much."

"Shut up, both of you. Yes it's *a* key, but not the key we want," JD remonstrated. "Where did you find it?"

"In a small church in Rome dedicated to St Thomas, hidden within the stonework. It took some getting out, too."

JD banged his hand on the table. "Bloody Rome! Use your brain, you lumpish, onion-eyed pumpion!"

"What did you just call me?" Jackson asked, more bewildered than annoyed, and Harlan realised he'd just witnessed a Shakespearean insult.

"For God's sake!" JD continued. "This is an *English* series of clues given to an *English* visionary right here in Angel's Rest! What on Earth made you think that *this* key would fit *this* trinity?"

"The clues in the paper I found all referred to The Key of the Trinity! This is it!"

"This is *one* of them, you yeasty clotpole!" JD clutched his hair and paced the room, incensed.

Harlan ignored the ripe insults that were now coming

thick and fast, and that he had no idea JD would ever be the type of man to utter, and instead asked, "What do you mean, *one* of them?"

JD marched over to the table, picked his notes up, and shook them under Harlan's nose. "This is one of many trinities spread across the world! This is the key to a different entrance, you blazing nincompoop!"

Harlan's hand shot out and grasped JD's arm, hard, shocking him into silence. "There are *multiple* trinities?"

"Yes!"

"Why didn't you tell me?"

"You didn't need to know. We found *this* one!"

"Had you told me this, I would have questioned Jackson, not assumed. Didn't that strike you as important?"

"You know, I'm still standing here," Jackson pointed out. He picked his key up, examining it with fresh eyes. "Other trinities? Wow. So where is the key to this one?"

JD wrested his arm from Harlan's grasp. "I have no idea."

"Holy shit," Harlan said, his mind spinning in a million different directions. "They are in there alone, they don't have the path, and now we haven't got the key. This is a disaster! They could all die!"

"You don't know that!" JD said, annoyed. "If anything, it means Erskine *does* have the key! What is clear is that we won't get The Book of Knowledge."

Harlan was seething. "My friends are worth more than this bloody book!" And it was suddenly very clear to him that despite his short acquaintance with Shadow, Gabe, and the others, that he did consider them friends and he liked them a lot. "And can I remind you that Gabe was someone you wanted very much to meet." He didn't want to say Nephilim with Jackson there, but hoped the reminder would jolt JD to his senses.

"He's not the only one, is he?" JD said churlishly, turning away quickly and refusing to look at Harlan.

"You are unbelievable!" If Harlan was quick-witted enough to think of a Shakespearean insult he would hurl one, but right now he needed to find the key. "What made you realise Jackson's key is wrong?"

"At the end of the document—The Path of the Seeker—there is a reference to angelic music leading to glory. I think the key is something musical."

Harlan looked at him, stunned. "And that's it? That's completely vague!"

"That's all I have!" JD said crossly.

"Damn it!" Harlan said loudly, making JD flinch. "I need to speak to Niel."

He turned his back on Jackson and JD, phoned Niel, and walked to the window, seeing a flicker of lightning in the distance. As soon as Niel answered he updated him with the situation, and he could almost feel Niel's fury radiating down the phone.

"Harlan, my brothers and insane sister are in there!"

"I know. Listen, I was in London this morning, but Olivia said she was going to read Hammond's dairies again. Did she find anything of interest? Anything at all?"

The line went silent, and Harlan heard thunder rumble again in the distance.

Niel finally responded. "Nahum updated me on the latest before he went in. He said Olivia had pointed out that Hammond was too ill to travel too far to hide the key anywhere, and suggested that it had been hidden here, somewhere in Angel's Rest. I guess she presumed, like all of us, that it had been found years ago, and that's how Jackson obtained it. Anyway, in the diaries he talks about St Thomas's Church and how it was near completion. He knew some of the craftsmen who were working on it, and spoke of visiting it. It could be there, or it could be where he lived."

"Which is where?"

"I'm not entirely sure, but I think it's on Crofter's Lane—one of the cottages." Harlan could hear the frustration in Niel's voice. "I'm so annoyed with myself for not thinking about the key more. I got side-tracked when I heard Jackson had it!"

"We all did. Don't be too hard on yourself. Look, if you had to choose between the two options—house or church—which would you pick?"

"Church. Home seems too obvious, too close. And the church has more places to hide it."

"It would be somewhere very permanent, surely. Something stone, walls, carvings…" Harlan thought of where Jackson had found his key. "Okay, I'm going to head there now and start looking, although this feels like insanity."

"Thanks, Harlan. And hey, there's one thing I do recall about the key."

"Yes?"

"Hammond said it would deliver the voice of the angels—I assumed he meant the words in the book, but it might not be that."

"Voice? That's sounds similar to something JD has just said. Okay, gotta go."

"Keep me informed."

"I will—and sit tight. Shelter inside if you have to because it's going to rain, just don't go in. I promise I'll be there as soon as possible!"

He ended the call and turned to find the others watching him. "Jackson, you're coming with me. JD, work on the document, because I'm going to find this damn key and then we're going in."

23

*G*abe surveyed the chamber that lay before them, unable to stop his mouth from dropping open in surprise.

This chamber was vastly different to the one before. For a start it was hot, and for that he was thankful. The icy cold water seemed to have penetrated his bones, and his muscles ached in a way that they hadn't for centuries. Poor Olivia was blue, and she was currently jumping up and down trying to thaw out. Shadow had fared better, and she was already assessing the landscape before them.

They stood on the edge of a desert, the rolling red sand dunes stretching to a wall of sandstone in the distance, illuminated by an unknown light. It was beautiful, in an unearthly, unexpected kind of way.

"How the hell can a desert be underground?" Shadow asked.

Gabe grunted. "How the hell is any of this here? By Raziel's crazy idea of a challenge. Son of a bitch." Then he grinned, already peeling his wet t-shirt and jacket off. "On the plus side, we can fly."

Olivia's eyes widened with surprise, and probably some admiration, he noted. "Fly? Oh, wow!"

He unfurled his wings, as did Nahum, and Gabe felt his strength return. His wings always enhanced his abilities—his senses were keener, he was quicker, stronger, and more agile, even if he wasn't flying. As his wings lifted and rustled, heat flooded through him, and he assessed the way ahead.

"There's got to be a catch," Nahum said, his dagger already drawn. "That sand could hide anything. What did you say the Realm of Fire had in your world, Shadow?"

"Djinn."

"As in, Aladdin?" Olivia asked, looking out expectantly, as if one would suddenly appear.

"I have no idea what Aladdin is," Shadow confessed. "But deserts also have dragons."

"Dragons!"

"And they are mean!" She wielded her sword. "This sword is pure dragonium, made from their flesh."

Gabe wondered if she was pulling his leg. "How can you make a sword from dragons?"

"In my world, dragons are part gems and priceless metals, and when they die their body transforms. It's quite an industry—if you can kill one."

Gabe stared at the desert again. "Let's get this over with, Shadow." He beckoned to her, and she stepped within his arms. Nahum did the same with Olivia. Within seconds, they were all travelling over the hot sand.

Thermal air caressed his skin, carrying them for a short distance, and for a while Gabe thought they'd be fine. And then with an ear-splitting screech, a dragon rose from the desert below, intercepting them, and in his haste to swerve and pull his sword free, Shadow wriggled from his grasp and plummeted to the sand below.

The rumbling of thunder was growing ever closer by the time Harlan arrived at the church with Jackson.

The main door was locked and they sheltered under the porch, Harlan grateful for the failing light and impending storm that had kept pedestrians off the lane. He patted his pockets looking for the lock picks he had taken from his car, but Jackson already had his in hand and was working the lock.

It was now close to five o'clock, and Harlan was wired on adrenalin, which was fortunate because driving to London and back in such a short span of time was tiring. He'd grabbed a simple sandwich before leaving, aware he was starving. He watched Jackson's quick, sure movements and said, "Thanks for coming. You didn't have to help me with this."

Jackson concentrated on the lock, but he said, "Two of us will be quicker. I like Liv too, and hate to think I might never see her again."

Harlan wondered how true that was, and couldn't resist adding, "And of course, there's the added bonus of finding the book."

Jackson shot him an amused look. "Now is not the time to doubt my reasons for helping."

"It's the perfect time! We are essentially rivals in this."

Jackson stopped and straightened, his shaggy hair falling over his brow. "Do I need to worry about *my* safety now? Because I can assure you, I have no intention of killing you to get this thing!"

"I'm not a killer," Harlan said evenly. "I'm just like you— an occult collector. Just want to make sure you don't leave me high and dry in there."

"I won't. I think we both need to worry about Nicoli more than each other. Can I trust *your* team?"

"Yes. Although, JD is worrying me right now." JD's ominous comment about Gabe still rattled him. The last thing he needed was to find out JD was a ruthless bastard.

"The comment about there being more of them? Yeah, sounded disturbing. What does that mean?"

Harlan shook his head. "I can't say, but let's agree to keep an eye on JD, too."

Jackson resumed picking the lock. "It concerns me that you don't trust your boss. I've not heard much about him. He keeps a low profile for a bigwig."

"Yeah. Turns out his ego isn't all that low profile."

The lock clicked and Jackson slipped inside, and with one final look at the lane, Harlan followed him, passing through the small entrance hall to the nave. The church's interior was cold, gloomy, and utterly silent. The smell of polish and dust hung in the air, and Harlan wondered where to start.

As well as the stained glass windows at the end, there were three narrow windows on either side of the nave, and Harlan imagined that on a sunny day the light would flood over the rows of pews that ran to the altar.

Jackson had already started to examine the walls and floor on his left. "Didn't you say Gabe ran into Nicoli in here?"

"Yes, and noticed Mia leaving it a few days ago."

"Are you sure they haven't already found the key?" Jackson asked, repeating the question he had raised in the car. "They wouldn't have gone into the temple otherwise!"

"I honestly don't know! My initial thoughts were that they went in, like Gabe did, not knowing if they'd be stuck in there, and just wanted to explore what they could. And of course I assumed *you* had the key. But now—" he raised his shoulders in a shrug, "I don't know. If we presume they have it, then we're wasting time here. But if they haven't got it yet then they are stuck in there, and we have to find it to stand any kind of chance of getting all of them out!"

Jackson straightened up and scanned the room. "Nothing looks obviously disturbed or broken, but let's be logical. Hammond knew some of the craftsmen. He could have asked them to help him hide the key in the pews, the decorative woodwork, the altar, the pulpit, maybe even the floor. He could have hidden any part of the trinity in here. He could even have hidden them in some stone work."

"Damn it!" Harlan exclaimed as the possibilities over-whelmed him. "We've left it too late to find now. It's impossible!"

"It is with that attitude!"

Harlan needed to get his shit together, quickly. Logic was needed, not panic. He pulled the photocopies of the docu-ments covered with Niel and Olivia's notes out of his pack. Just holding them helped him focus. "JD said something about angelic music and the key being the sound of God, and Niel mentioned the voice of an angel." He marched down to the altar and scanned the papers, looking for Niel's notes in the weak light coming through the stained glass windows. "Here it is. There's some garbled reference to hearing the music of God that will reveal all knowledge. 'When angels sing, the heavens part and the radiance of God will bathe us in glory.'" He looked up at the angel in the stained glass above him. "What makes music?"

Jackson was standing at the pulpit, an ornate wooden structure, frowning as he scanned the nave. "There isn't an organ in here, there's no place for a choir, and only the parishioners would make music as they sang. "

"But look how many pews there are!" Harlan said, hoping they didn't need to examine every single one.

"It could be hidden in a place not associated with music,"

Jackson pointed out. "Hammond was hiding this forever, he hoped. Wouldn't you hide the key somewhere obscure, rather than obvious?"

"Maybe. But he was also delirious and confused. Who knows what he was thinking at that stage? And it's impossible to know what was already built at that time." Harlan strode to the middle of the aisle, turning slowly and hoping inspiration would strike. And then his gaze settled on the pulpit again, and Jackson elevated several feet above him, framed within the ornate structure—unusually so, for such a simple church. "The vicar is the voice of God in here. Well, His messenger, at least. That pulpit is fairly dramatic for a country church."

"That's true," Jackson agreed. His voice carried easily, almost booming across the nave. "But medieval pulpits could be grandiose." However, Jackson had already started to tap the wooden structure, and now he fished his flashlight out to examine it.

Harlan continued to study it from a distance, examining the area that presented itself to the parishioners. The pulpit was divided into six painted panels in a hexagonal shape, filled with detailed pictures and surrounded by carvings. The paint had faded and the images were worn in places, but the colours were bold—blue, red, and yellow, some embellished with gold. One contained the Virgin Mary, carrying the baby Jesus, and three panels referenced three different angels, dark starry skies above them radiating with light. Another depicted Noah's Ark, flailing in high seas just like on the stained glass window, and the sixth… Harlan frowned. It was hard to see from where he was standing in the middle of the aisle. It was in deep shadow, on the far side of the pulpit, and he walked towards it, hearing Jackson still tapping away.

When he reached it, he paused, and his breath caught in his throat. The image was of an open book, shrouded in smoke and darkness, the edges curling with fire. *No wonder he couldn't see it from a distance.* It was still hard to make out the image from close up. Harlan ran his fingers over the panel, feeling the imperfections beneath his fingers, and then concentrated on the intricate carvings that framed it. He tapped, prodded, pushed, and then sighed. Nothing was happening.

"What have you found?" Jackson asked.

Harlan looked up to find him peering down on him. "Nothing. You?"

"Nothing. Yet." His head receded and the tapping started again, as a rumble of thunder echoed around the church.

Harlan inwardly groaned. *If rain started, would the temple be flooded? Or would it be protected by Raziel?* He pushed the thoughts to the back of his mind and continued to explore the panels, finally hearing a hollow *thunk* when he reached the image of the flood. His heart raced, and he kept tapping, trying to narrow down the area.

Jackson shouted again. "You've found something?"

"It sounds different, can you hear it?"

In seconds Jackson was at his side, shining his light on the panel, and the old varnish reflected a dull glow. "The flood. Interesting."

"Very. According to a source I have, the flood might have been sent to destroy Raziel's book."

"Really? You know it's the same book that Solomon was reported to have had at one point?"

Harlan nodded, his face close to the panel, finally seeing the carved animals, tiny and precise, that framed the image. He applied pressure to them, hoping to feel them depress. And then he spotted a snake, curling around something. *A book.* Harlan's mouth went dry and he applied pressure, light at first and then harder, and with a satisfying *click*, the carving sank back into the frame. He heard Jackson inhale, saying, "Holy shit," but he didn't look at him, focussing instead on the wafer-thin black line that became visible along the edge of the panel.

He hardly dared to look away, but he needed something to angle into the tiny gap. Luckily, Jackson had already anticipated his need, and a small knife appeared in front of his face. He took it wordlessly and pried the panel backwards.

It opened slowly, stiff from lack of use, but inside was empty space. Harlan, unable to hide his disappointment, cried out, "No!"

"Shit," Jackson said forcefully, and he reached in, feeling around carefully. "Nothing. Maybe this was where The Path of the Trinity was initially hidden."

Harlan was silent, frustration flooding through him, and he staggered back to the front pew, looking up at the pulpit absently, his torch flashing wildly before settling on an area of carving. When Harlan eventually focussed on it, he frowned. Cherubs were carved above the panels, a whole row of them, all blowing on tiny pipes, but in this odd light, one looked slightly different. Most of them held fluted horns, but one had a normal flute that was longer than the others.

He stood up abruptly. "Jackson. Look at that cherub."

"Which one?"

"The one my torch is on, you idiot. Look at the pipe between his lips. It's different than the others!"

"So it is," Jackson said softly, already stretching up on his tip-toes, but he was inches too short to reach it. "It's too high."

They both looked around for a chair or a stool, but neither was in sight, and then tried to move the pews, but they were fixed to the floor.

"I could try to lift you," Jackson said, frowning. "But I'm not known for my gym workouts."

"I'm not sure I could lift you, either," Harlan admitted,

frowning at Jackson's long, lean build. "But, I could dangle from the pulpit, if you hold my legs."

The platform where the vicar delivered his sermon was several feet above the cherubs, and would be difficult to access from there too, but Harlan was sure he could lean over with Jackson's help.

"Let's do it," Jackson said, leading the way. In moments, Harlan was upside down, his legs on the wooden lectern as he supported himself to slide down the carved pulpit. He had discarded his jacket, and clutched the small knife in his teeth, his flashlight in his left hand. It was precarious, but Jackson's weight on his legs reassured him, and once he was eye level with the cherub, he took the knife from his mouth and studied the instrument.

"It has holes in it!" Harlan shouted. "I think it really is a working pipe." After examining it well with his light, he thrust the flashlight in his belt, hoping it wouldn't dislodge and crash to the floor, and then tried to pry the pipe free. "It's stuck. Glue, I think."

"Use the bloody knife then," Jackson said impatiently.

"I don't want to damage it!"

"It can't be destroyed, remember!"

"True," Harlan mumbled, feeling like a fool. He prodded at the pipe gently, and then when that didn't work, he became more aggressive, whittling the blade between the cherub's hands and the instrument. It was horribly awkward, the space tight, especially upside down, but eventually the pipe slid free. "Haul me up!"

With much fumbling and swearing Harlan regained his feet, both of them looking at what appeared to be an inconsequential wooden flute, unadorned except for three small holes.

Jackson laughed. "Is *that* what produces the music of the Gods?"

Harlan was just able to make out his bewildered expression in the dark church. "I don't know! Is this it? The key is a simple flute? Or have I just damaged a cherub for no reason?"

"Blow it."

Harlan just looked at him.

"I'm serious. See if it plays! If it doesn't, we're back to square one."

"What if I summon the wrath of God?"

"Then we know it works." Jackson's eyes filled with humour.

Feeling like an idiot, Harlan lifted the pipe to his lips and blew, and the clearest, sweetest tone filled the church, lifting the hairs on Harlan's arms. Ominously, as soon as the notes died away, an enormous crack of thunder sounded overhead, a flash of lightning lit the nave, the pulpit shuddered, and Jackson and Harlan both staggered as the building shook.

"There you go," Jackson said confidently. "The wrath of God. Let's rock and roll."

***

Gabe hadn't fought so hard in years.

The dragon that attacked them was huge, its wingspan three times the size of theirs, and although Gabe tried to coordinate his attack with Nahum, it was difficult when they couldn't even get close.

But it was also fun.

Shadow had landed safely, and he could see her below, a moving spot on the ground, Olivia nearby, as they made their way to a ruined building.

Gabe had no wish to kill the dragon, or even injure it; he just wanted to get past it. But the dragon had no intention of letting them, and they couldn't get close enough to inflict any kind of damage.

He shouted to Nahum, "Should we fight it on land?"

"I don't think we'd gain anything," he yelled back as he twisted gracefully to avoid a stream of fire.

The dragon turned his sharp, angular head to Gabe, fixed him with his sulphurous yellow gaze and roared fire, and any other questions Gabe had disappeared as he fought for his life.

Shadow stumbled across the burning hot sand, her clothes already dry from the furnace-like heat, finally reaching the shade of a ruined fort, half buried in the dunes.

But shade from what? She shielded her eyes, looking up to an orange sky, but there was no discernible sun, no obvious source of heat. *This place was nuts.* But it also reminded her of the Realm of Fire that she'd visited once. It was a vast expanse of desert, dunes, searing wind, an occasional oasis, and a string of volcanoes spewing lava.

The cities were hewn from red desert granite and sandstone, their streets narrow and dug deep into the earth, sheltered from the burning sun. She had hunted for a fey who had killed others and would do so again. He'd hidden in the small fey population that traded in the markets there, occasional partners with the djinn, but she'd caught him eventually.

Now, as she examined the walls, she saw script carved into the rock. A flurry of activity distracted her, and Olivia stumbled through the remnants of a doorway, breathing heavily.

"Are you okay?" Shadow asked, noting her flushed, sweating face.

"Depends what you mean by okay? I'm not freezing

anymore, and there's a bloody great dragon above us, but yeah, I'm fine."

"Good," Shadow said, not having time to chat. "These are runes. Any idea what they say? It's certainly not fey script."

Olivia studied them, running her hand across the stone to brush loose sand and dust away, coughing as she did so. "They're Futhark runes."

"They are *what?*"

"A type of writing, used across Europe and originating from old Norse." Olivia wiped her sweaty face with the back of her hand. "Not really sure why they're here, but I can have a crack at deciphering them. When you're a collector you pick up a few things."

A roar sounded overhead, closer than was comfortable, and Shadow grabbed Olivia, flattening them to the ground as a wave of flame flashed over them.

Olivia quickly regained her feet, studying the runes again. "It says something about commanding the dragon to help… no wait, to command passage."

Shadow frowned. "Is there a dragon language?"

"I have no idea! This is your world, not mine!"

Your world. That was an interesting observation. Shadow brushed the comment away, recalling a story that her friend Bloodmoon had told her once about the Wolf Mage, and with a sudden revelation she yelled, "Gabe! Nahum!"

Olivia joined in, and within a few moments that felt more like hours, Nahum dived down and landed next to them, streaked with blood and sweat, and smelling of burnt feathers. "What?"

"Dragons have a language," Shadow said quickly. "You need to command passage."

"What?"

Olivia pointed at the wall. "Command passage—*go!*"

24

By the time Harlan, JD, and Jackson met up with Niel, it was fully dark, and the storm was upon them.

Wind howled up the ravine, lightning flashed overhead, and thunder echoed around them, bouncing off the rocks and shaking the valley floor. And there was rain, torrential rain. The streams had filled, and the night seemed full of water cascading down stony gullies. Harlan half pushed and half pulled JD up the steep slope to the temple's entrance, grateful when Niel appeared and hauled them both up.

They slid through the narrow cleft like wet fish, and finally stopped in the antechamber, panting and dripping water everywhere.

"I was beginning to think you'd never make it," Niel said, worry etching lines into his face. "You have the key?"

Harlan fished it out of his pocket. "It's a pipe."

Niel took it, turning it over carefully. "You have got to be kidding me."

"No. That's it," Harlan said, still incredulous. "It plays— but don't do it here. Who knows what you'll trigger!"

"Fair enough." Niel handed it back and as Harlan tucked it safely into his pocket, Niel turned to JD, who looked distinctly grumpy for a man who desperately wanted to be here. "Are you ready?"

JD grimaced. "Not really, but I'll probably manage."

Niel could barely conceal his annoyance. "My friends went in there *hours* ago, with only a few weapons. You've got the path, the key, and plenty of other crap in those bags, so you'd better manage!"

Jackson had been silent, shaking water from his coat and watching the exchange, but hearing a groan he turned and frowned at the rumpled figure in the corner. "Is that Jimmy Wilson?"

"You know him?" Niel asked. "Not a friend, I hope."

Jackson gave a dry laugh. "No. He's a sneaky, second-rate thief. Why is he here?"

"He's with Nicoli. I figured he must have heard about what's hidden within the paper the path is written on." He glanced at JD. "We need to know that, right?"

JD nodded, "Yes, I think so."

Jackson looked at Jimmy thoughtfully. "I wouldn't trust him. Did he hit his head or something?"

"Yes. With my fist." Niel scooped him up and flung him over his shoulder. "JD, I'm going to say the words now...or do you want to? You need to speak the language of fire."

JD looked around him at the perfectly uniform room carved by Raziel's hand, appearing overwhelmed. Then he squared his shoulders, licked his lips and positioned himself in front of the door. "I'll do it."

A fierce wind blew up from a seemingly bottomless abyss in front of Shadow and the others, and not for the first time during the journey that seemed to threaten death at every turn, Shadow questioned why she was here.

"Because the Gods themselves couldn't have stopped you, you headstrong madam!" Gabe shouted over the howling gale.

"I was curious, and honestly didn't know what to expect," she shouted back.

"I did try to warn you."

"Bullshit. You didn't have a clue, either."

This was the fourth chamber they had entered, and each had been distinctly different to the one before, but this area must be the fourth and final element. They had passed through the earth element with relative ease, thanks to Shadow. So far, each chamber led to another, offering no other choices as to their route ahead. They had only had to conquer each element to pass. *Only!* She chided herself. *Like that had been easy.* Now that they were here, it seemed logical —the four elements were the basic building blocks of magic. In her world, different beings were associated with each. She was from the Realm of Earth, but water elementals lived in the Realm of Water, djinn and dragons lived in the Realm of Fire, and sylphs lived in the Realm of Air. Having Nephilim with them was a distinct advantage in every area.

"You're just going to fly us over, right?" Olivia asked, trying to secure her hair back as the wind whipped it around her face.

Shadow sheltered behind a rocky outcrop, pulling the others with her, and the wind abated, allowing her to hear more clearly. The door they had entered through had sealed shut behind them, just like all the others. This chamber, however, was more naturalistic than the proceeding ones; well, everything except for the unceasing gale. Streams of water ran down the uneven rock face that was mottled with moss, and enormous stalactites hung above them.

Nahum looked uncertain. "It's a strong wind. If we get caught in a vortex, it will be tricky."

"But how would Nicoli's team have crossed?" Gabe asked. "They can't fly!"

"Maybe Erskine used his demon in some way," Olivia suggested. "Or a spirit? He's a conjuror—he could have summoned either."

Shadow frowned at Olivia. "Something you said to me earlier makes me think these tests are tailored for us. Why would we be encountering things from my world? Dragons in a desert? Really?"

"You think each team is facing something different?" Gabe asked.

"Maybe." She shrugged. "I don't know. Perhaps in some chambers. The important thing right now is how we cross this."

"There must be a way of communicating with the element," Gabe said, "as we did with the dragon."

"I think it's just about strength," Nahum mused. "I'm going to fly high—test the wind up there." He nodded to the roof of the cavern, lost in darkness, and without waiting for comment, extended his wings and flew away.

For a short while Nahum seemed to struggle, meeting resistance at every point, until halfway along he soared across the cavern, his wings finally able to open fully. In moments he was back with them, grinning. "There's a tunnel of utter calm. But," his face fell, "there's a body down there, on a narrow shelf. It's impossible to get closer, but I think it's Jensen."

Olivia's hands flew to her mouth. "No! Poor Jensen. He was annoying as hell, but this is no place to die."

"I'm amazed no one has died before now," Gabe said. "Maybe they have and we just haven't found them. Anyway, Shadow?" He held his arms open. "Allow me."

The flight across the cavern was undeniably terrifying, but also exhilarating, and Nahum was right. Jensen's crumpled body lay on a ledge far below. As they drew closer to the end of the cave, it was clear there was no door. Instead there was an opening high in the rock and they flew through it, passing through some kind of shimmering veil, into a chamber of breathtaking magnificence.

Gabe and Nahum flew to ground level and landed on a short platform, and they looked around them, jaws dropping, as Gabe muttered, "Bollocks."

This chamber, like the antechamber, was made from polished granite of some sort. It was dark, speckled with a substance that sparkled in the unseen light source that mimicked moonlight. A series of graceful bridges soared across water, and at the far side of the vast chamber was The Temple of the Trinity—all towering columns, gilded symbols, braziers spitting fire, and an enormous statue of an angel holding an open book.

"Herne's horns. Are we in the final room?" Shadow asked, already deeply suspicious. It felt too quiet, too calm, as if something was just waiting to pounce. And there was no way out; the opening high above them had sealed.

"Seems so." Gabe gripped his blade, his eyes darting everywhere. "Where's Erskine?"

"Perhaps he's dead," Olivia whispered.

"There!" Nahum pointed to a solitary figure on a broad column that stood alone, surrounded by water. "Is that Nicoli? How the hell did he get to that?"

"Perhaps the bridges move," Olivia suggested, "and it left him stranded."

"You've been watching too many tomb-raiding games," Nahum said, laughing.

"You wait!" Olivia replied darkly.

Shadow squinted at the distant platform. "Where are Erskine and Mia?"

"Erskine's on the steps of the temple," Gabe said. His wings were still visible, and he flexed them. "I need to stop him. He's not getting that book."

"But where's Mia?" Shadow asked, feeling a weird sort of responsibility for her. Having fought with her and interrogated her in the kitchen, she was no longer a faceless enemy.

"I can't see her at all," Olivia said, worried. "I don't think that bodes well. Perhaps we should rescue Nicoli," she suggested, looking at Nahum hopefully.

He shook his head, "Sorry, not yet. He can stay exactly where he is—out of the way."

Gabe was already rising into the air, but Shadow tugged at his arm. "Wait. If he hasn't got the key, he can't get any further."

"Then what's in his hand?"

"It could be anything; we haven't got a good view. And besides, if either of you fly, they will all know what you are!"

"Too late for that," Nahum pointed out. "We flew in, and our wings are pretty obvious."

Gabe exchanged a worried glance with his brother. "We can't let Erskine get this book. It's too powerful, especially in the wrong hands."

"I doubt if you could just fly there, Gabe," Shadow said. "That's too easy—you might trigger something. And besides, we need to stick together. Harlan and Niel could be here any minute with the key."

"She's right," Nahum told him. "Let's have a good think about this before we proceed. It's been one chaotic path to get here. We don't want to mess it up now. And if Miss Headstrong advises patience, that must mean something!"

Shadow swallowed her tart reply, just grateful Nahum agreed.

Gabe finally nodded. "I'll wait...for a while."

———

Niel watched JD's fiddly preparations, deciding he was one of the most annoying men he'd ever met.

He caught Harlan's eye, and had the feeling from his tight-lipped expression that he agreed. He pressed his hand to his temple and said, "JD. Can't you do this any faster?"

"No." JD clenched his jaw and continued to lay out a collection of dried herbs, a silver dish, and a collection of jars containing liquids. "We need to conquer earth. I believe that if I concoct the right mixture, I can use to it to open our pathway ahead. Patience is a virtue. Besides," JD shot Niel and Harlan an impatient look, "you have tried and failed. And this is how I interpret the path."

Niel sighed heavily. *JD was right.* They had entered this chamber fifteen minutes ago, and found an impenetrable wall of thick, green plants blocking their way. They'd tried to push through, squeeze through, and hack through, and had failed every time, the plants impervious. And there was no way Niel could fly, either. There was no airspace at all.

He pulled Harlan and Jackson aside, leaving a now conscious Jimmy to lean sullenly against the wall. "I guess JD is right, unless you have other suggestions?"

Jackson shook his head. "I'm amazed we made it this far. Water traps and fire chambers are primitive, but effective. And JD *has* got the instructions."

"This is not what I expected," Harlan admitted. "I thought the tests would be esoteric, or mystical, and instead I feel we're in the Chrystal Maze."

Niel nodded at JD. "That looks mystical."

"Alchemical, actually," Jackson said. "I have no idea what he's doing, but let's hope it works."

"I'm beginning to wish I hadn't brought Jimmy," Niel confessed. Jimmy was conscious because Jackson said he would keep an eye on him, and so far Jimmy was compliant. But then again, he had to be, or he'd be stuck there.

"He may help us yet," Jackson said, looking at Jimmy thoughtfully.

"How do you know him?"

"I've worked in London for years doing this business. He crops up from time to time, often associated with Nicoli, but also with Occult Acquisitions, and The Grey Order."

"Who are they?" Niel asked, puzzled.

Harlan explained, "Other arcane organisations. Well, Occult Acquisitions is a shop, actually—well worth checking out."

"Dodgy, obviously," Jackson said with a wry smile, "but we all are in this business."

Niel wasn't sure what he thought of Jackson, especially after that admission. His first impression was that he was trustworthy, and he was certainly helpful, and hadn't been fazed by this insane angelic obstacle course, but as he'd thoughtfully reminded him, this was a dodgy business.

The scent of smoke drew his attention. JD was carrying his smoking bowl of herbs across the edge of the dense plants, intoning something under his breath, and with a rustle and a swirl of wind, a path opened through the greenery and JD turned to them, victorious. "Gentlemen, follow me."

25

*G*abe examined the chamber analytically, noting the complex span of bridges that crossed the large lake in a confusing web, and tentatively walked to the edge of the long platform, hoping he wouldn't trigger anything.

"This must be what The Path of the Seeker is really useful for," he suggested to the others. "There can be only one true way across, and if we pick the wrong one, we're screwed." He scratched his jaw. "I suspect that if I try to fly, I'll fail."

Nahum nodded. "I think you're right. There are seven bridges leaving this platform. We have to choose the right one."

Olivia was crouching next to the start of the bridge to Gabe's left. "This one has markings on it—a symbol etched into the stone."

"And this one," Shadow called, further along to his right. "Runes, maybe. Or alchemical symbols? I don't recognise any of them."

Nahum kneeled next to Olivia, quickly calling Gabe over. "I recognise this. Isn't this Samael's sign?"

Gabe frowned at the complex sigil etched into the rock, and his heart sank. "Yes, I think so, although it has been long since I saw it."

"Samael?" Shadow asked.

"The Angel of Death," Nahum said, already hurrying to the next bridge. "Gabriel's sigil is on this one."

Gabe groaned. *This was worse than he thought. Bloody Gabriel.* The angel who had sent Gabe on this quest in the first place.

Shadow nudged him. "The Angel of Death? There really is one?"

"Sure. He reaps souls—or used to. Not entirely sure what he gets up to now."

"You don't need help for your spirit to cross to the Otherworld," Shadow said, annoyed. "What did he do?"

"Don't ask." The Angel of Death did far worse things.

"And Gabriel?" Olivia asked.

"The Angel of Destruction—but he was also a messenger," Nahum told her bleakly.

Gabe looked at Olivia, confused. "I thought you liked all of this stuff. Shouldn't you know this?"

Olivia pushed her hair off her face, frowning. "This is Christian theology. I spend my time on other belief systems."

"Never thought of myself as a *system* before," Gabe told her, not feeling entirely sure whether he was happy about that, angry, or couldn't care less.

Olivia's startled expression told him she hadn't really considered that either, but Nahum interrupted both of them as he called out the other names. "Raphael, Sachiel, Hanael, Cassiel, and Michael. Some archangels, others not."

"What's the difference with an archangel?" Shadow asked.

"They are the more powerful than the others; the old God's princes, I suppose you could call them."

"Why these angels out of thousands?" Olivia asked.

Nahum re-joined them. "No idea. Whatever pattern these make, I don't know it."

A shout broke their concentration, and Gabe looked up, seeing Nicoli waving furiously, almost jumping up and down as he tried to attract their attention.

"What's going on?" Shadow asked, her hands moving instinctively to her blades.

"It's Erskine," Gabe said. He'd been keeping an eye on his slow progress. He'd stopped at the small fires burning across the temple, dropping something into each one before progressing, and he had now reached the feet of the statue that dwarfed him. "He's using the key. Damn it!"

A red mist of rage descended as memories of Gabe's last encounter with Gabriel clouded his thoughts, and despite everyone's warning, he flexed his wings and rose into the air, trying to fly to the temple. But it was as if he'd hit an invisible wall. A force smacked him backwards, sending him crashing into the wall and tumbling to the floor. Winded, he staggered to his feet to see Erskine twist something into a mechanism at the base of the angel.

An enormous boom echoed across the chamber and the placid water erupted in a series of geysers, blocking their view of the temple. The platform rocked, his companions stumbled, and with horror, Gabe watched as Shadow fell into the water.

By the time Harlan and the others reached the Chamber of Wind, as JD called it, he was exhausted and mentally drained.

This place was a nightmare. Despite JD being able to clear the path through the Chamber of Earth, the ground had been uneven, and every time Harlan had stumbled, the vegetation threatened to swallow him, as if the reaching fingers of the plants wanted to pull him into their depths. His skin crawled, and adrenalin was making him shake. What he needed was a big shot of bourbon. What he had was water. The good news was that they had, in general, progressed quickly.

Glancing at his companions, all sheltering from the unceasing wind behind a rocky spur, he noted that only JD and Niel looked unfazed by the entire experience. Niel watched JD with suspicion, and JD had a fanatical gleam in his eye. Jackson and Jimmy looked as over the whole thing as he did.

Jackson pulled him aside, his lips close to his ear so he could be heard over the wind. "JD looks like he's lost the plot."

"He's our only way through this. We have to trust him."

"So why don't you look more confident?"

"It's not his abilities to get us through this that I doubt. It's his intentions once we get there."

"And Niel?"

"I trust him."

Jackson looked at Niel speculatively. "He's a big guy. There's something about him. And his brothers." He stared at Harlan. "Anything I should know?"

"Er, no. They're just regular guys." Harlan tried to look as honest as he could and knew he'd failed.

"Liar." Jackson smiled.

Harlan decided to avoid this uncomfortable conversation and stepped closer to JD and Niel, who were now arguing. "Is there a problem?"

Niel looked angry. "I offered to fly. JD said it will cheat *The Path.*"

"Your secret will be out," Harlan said.

"Right now, I don't care. My brothers are through there— I hope. How else did they cross? Unless they're down there

239

somewhere, dead." He gestured to the pit before them, his face bleak.

"You think there's a way through?"

"There has to be!"

JD was scanning the document again, his fingers shaking as he traced the page. "What conquers wind?"

"Flight," Niel answered abruptly.

"No! It doesn't conquer it, it uses it!"

"Exactly, you exasperating man!"

JD's eyes blazed with fury. "In the system of magic that I designed—aided by the angels—air is the Eastern Watchtower. It is governed by the archangel Raphael, and his angel Chassan. I must summon them for our passage!"

JD rummaged in his bag producing a rolled up cloth, which he proceeded to lay on the hard, earthen ground, securing it with rocks. Once unrolled, Harlan saw the cloth had a large, complex geometric design drawn on it. JD then pulled a dagger out, engraved with magical signs, and kneeling next to it, started to chant.

Niel turned away, impatiently scanning the cave, and Harlan knew he wanted to fly.

An almighty boom rocked them all off their feet, and Harlan winced as he collided into the rock wall, smacking his head and landing in a tangled heap next to Jackson and Jimmy. JD was sprawled on his stomach, but Niel was still standing, his enormous wings now unfolded, bracing him.

Harlan ignored Jackson and Jimmy's shocked faces and instead scrambled to his feet. The howl of the wind had increased, and at the far side of the cave he saw a flash of white light.

What the hell was going on?

Shadow couldn't breathe. A vortex of water sucked her downward, and she twisted and turned in the current, struggling to break free. It was icy cold, her limbs were already numb, and she was utterly blind. It was pitch black in the water. She was dying.

Bloody determination swiftly kicked in. She was not going to die in a hole in the ground. *This is not what the Raven King had seen for her future, surely.* If that was the case, she may as well have died at the hands of the Empusa, or Kian. She was fey, powerful with earth magic, and she was going to use it. She might be surrounded by water, but beyond that was earth and rock and she instinctively felt for them. In seconds, the element responded.

Power flooded through her as she struggled against the current, and she surged towards the far, distant light. When she finally broke the surface, her lungs screaming for air, it was to find the chamber in tumult. The water was rolling across the bridges and crashing against the columns, and the platform she'd fallen from had disappeared behind the high waves. And then a surge of water lifted her, throwing her against a bridge, and she crawled onto it, gripping it fiercely.

Finally, the rising water started to abate, and she rolled onto her back, blinking at the vast expanse of starlight that glittered above her. *Herne's balls. What had happened? Where was Gabe?*

Standing on trembling legs, she finally saw Gabe, Nahum, and Olivia staring across the chamber, searching for her. She shouted, shocked at how hoarse her voice sounded, and waved, and then saw Gabe point at her, relief washing over his face. His eyes were boring into hers even from this distance. For seconds she found she couldn't look away, thinking how warm she'd be in Gabe's strong embrace, and then she blinked. *That kind of thinking wouldn't do at all.*

Shadow turned slowly, taking in her new perspective on

the cavern. Nicoli was a short distance away, clinging to the top of the column, drenched and looking terrified, but he was alive. She was closer to the temple now, too, and she examined it properly. It was far bigger than she'd realised—supersized, even—to dwarf those who tried to claim the book. Its clean lines and absolute symmetry were intimidating, alien in its Otherworldly manner, and as someone who understood the Otherworld, that was saying something. It spoke of the absolute power of the Gods—and the angel Raziel. His statue was immense, wings folded behind him but visible above his shoulders, the tips curling around his ankles. She looked up at his grave face carved in stone, and felt the weight of his pitiless regard. At his bare feet was the crumpled body of Erskine, his papers strewn around him. He'd had the wrong key, and a surge of hope rose within Shadow.

And then she realised something else. The bridge she was on was connected to the temple, admittedly by interconnecting with another two, but it was passable. *Dare she try to get there?* Gabe had been knocked back, but maybe her earth magic had brought her this far for a reason.

Shadow looked across at Gabe, who was shouting something, but he was too far away to hear clearly. *Was it encouragement, or a warning?* It didn't matter which. She was sick of being here, and she wanted to end this mad quest. She clutched her sword that she'd managed to hold on to, took a deep breath, and marched along the slippery surface that gleamed in the muted light with its remnants of water.

Niel had taken matters into his own hands. JD's rituals took time, time they hadn't got. Niel watched from above as JD stood as close to the abyss as he could get, his hands raised, appealing to the angels for help.

Niel shook his head, doubting that they would come to their rescue. Unlike JD, he had a very negative view of them, like all the Nephilim. Angels were selfish, capricious creatures, obsessed with their own immortality, and they had all learned years ago, not to place any trust in them, especially their own fathers. And perhaps, if he was honest, Niel didn't want them to appear. As he'd said to Gabe only days before, the angels didn't know of their existence, and that's the way it should remain.

Niel focussed on finding passage through the wind, but it drove him back at every point. It tugged on his wings, trying to pull him down, or force him into the rocks. But if his brothers had made it, so could he.

Then something odd happened.

A presence arrived—something powerful, but formless—and as Niel hovered on the edge of the abyss, he felt the rush of wings and smelled something he hadn't for centuries. A pungent combination of blossoms and honey, with an undercurrent of smoke. And just like that the wind dropped, leaving an eerie silence in its wake. A bridge appeared below him, gossamer thin and fragile as a cloud, and JD stepped onto it, triumphantly leading the others across the abyss.

Harlan paused to look up at him, but Niel just nodded, unable to move. He hung in the air, his wings beating gently to keep him in place, and he felt a breath across his cheek and a presence that was unmistakably angelic. Two words echoed through Niel's mind, flooding his thoughts with unbidden images of the past and his palace in the Zagros Mountains.

Welcome back.

$\mathcal{G}$abe watched helplessly as Shadow approached the temple, his heart in his mouth, and only Nahum's restraining hand stopped him from flying again.

"Whatever is happening, brother, she is meant to be there."

"It's a trick! It has to be," Gabe argued, not taking his eyes from her. So far her progress was sure but steady, as she took her time negotiating the bridges.

"There's one good thing," Olivia said, trying to smile. "At least Erskine failed."

Nahum nodded. "True. Odd, though. He must have thought he had the right key."

"Well, Shadow has *no* key," Gabe pointed out, "so what will happen to her? Erskine is in a heap on the floor, probably dead."

"She's like a cat," Nahum said, reassuring him. "She must have nine lives. She was underwater for a long time before she was spat out. Give her some credit, Gabe."

Gabe finally looked at Nahum. "It's not Shadow's abilities I doubt."

A hushed whisper carrying a breeze sounded behind them, and all three spun around, weapons raised. But to Gabe's utmost relief, JD was stepping through a shimmering white veil that filled a break in the rock, and Harlan, Jackson, Niel, and Nicoli's unknown team member were behind him.

Despite his worry about Shadow, Gabe grinned. "You made it!"

JD preened. "Of course I did, I summoned—" His voice faltered as he stared at his surroundings. "Well. We're here. The final chamber."

"And time is running out," Gabe said. "Shadow is over there, on her own, without the key. We need to get over there —now!"

JD collected himself, his glazed expression transforming into a fierce, intelligent stare. "What do we know so far?"

Nahum took over, and accompanied by Olivia, directed JD to the bridges, leaving Gabe to update the others. "What have you brought him for?" He gestured to Nicoli's teammate.

Niel grunted. "That's Jimmy. I thought he might know what was hidden within the paper the document is written on, but now I'm not so sure."

However, Jimmy, sullen, moody, and looking more like a truculent teenager than a grown man, said, "Actually, I did hear something, but it doesn't make sense to me."

"And you only thought to tell us *now*?" Jackson said, exasperated.

"You didn't need my help before, but," he swallowed, "I just want to get out of here—alive."

"Join the club," Harlan muttered. "You'd better go with JD, tell him what you know. And don't fuck up!"

Jimmy just nodded, mute, and walked across the platform to join the others.

Gabe was puzzled. They hadn't been that long in the final

chamber when the others had caught up. "Did you follow us in quickly?" he asked Niel.

He shook his head, "Not at all. We entered hours after you. Harlan had to find the key first. Why?"

"Because we only got here a short while before you did."

Niel shrugged. "It must be some weird kind of angel ability to compress time. Talking of angels," he grabbed Gabe's elbow, steering him away for privacy. "Have you felt one yet?"

"One what?" Gabe asked, confused, and still side-tracked by Shadow. He angled himself so he could continue to watch her.

"An angel, you idiot!"

"No. Should I have?"

"Well, we are in a temple designed by one—and I just did!"

That grabbed his attention, and he stared at Niel, trying to work out if he was joking. "Where?"

"In the Chamber of Wind. I felt Chassan, Raphael's right hand man. JD summoned him."

Several things rushed through Gabe's mind, not the least of which was JD's unexpected ability to summon an angel after years of claiming he hadn't spoken to one in centuries, and his own belief that he never really had. But his foremost concern was Chassan. "Did he see you?"

"Of course he bloody saw me!" Niel tapped his own head. "And spoke to me, in here. Which means Raphael will know already." Niel closed his eyes briefly, and when he opened them again his blue eyes looked resigned. "Whatever anonymity we had before is gone. Whatever life we thought we'd forged, is over."

"You don't know that."

"Gabe, who are you kidding?"

"We are few. We're no threat, and we're of no use."

But Niel's mouth was set in a stubborn line, and Gabe had a horrible feeling Niel might have been right all along. He was glad for Nahum's shout. "We're ready!"

They all clustered behind JD, who was gripping his grubby copy of The Path of the Seeker and taking deep breaths, his eyes focussed on the temple.

"What's the plan?" Gabe asked, noting Shadow was still on the final bridge.

JD snapped his head around, suddenly aware of his presence. "The angels all have correspondences—many, in fact, complex and interwoven. But these particular seven angels correspond to planets, in this instance." He gestured to the cavern roof above. "We need to navigate our way across; the temple is the sun. I will use those to guide us."

Those? Gabe realised that the sparkles he had thought were part of the finish of the cavern were actually constellations.

JD continued. "I suspect there will be more angel and planetary markings as we progress. Follow me closely." He frowned with annoyance. "There are too many of you here."

"Well, we're all coming with you, like it or not," Harlan told him as he looked around the chamber with distaste. "Let's get on with it."

Shadow finally reached the broad temple stairs and after a moment's pause, stepped onto the first, relieved that there was no earth-shattering rumble to throw her back into the water.

The steps were high, each rise reaching to her waist, making them impossible to climb easily. However, she was nimble, and she pulled herself onto them gracefully. *Seven steps*, she noted. *Seven bridges*. She wasn't sure what that meant, but she ascended to the temple proper, taking stock of her surroundings.

It was even more breathtaking close up. The columns were white, smooth and unadorned, and the floor was made of polished milky white marble that reflected the rosy glow of the fires burning within the braziers. She stepped beyond the first column, noting that the temple extended far back into the cavern, its recesses dark. She had assumed that the angel's statue was at the back of the temple, but there was so much more beyond it. Something glinted in those shadows—maybe gold? She shivered. *How long had this place stood here? It was incredible.*

Shadow was wracked with indecision. She didn't have the key, and yet she had been allowed to arrive here, and she had no idea why. *Because she was fey?* Gripping her dragonium sword in one hand and the Empusa's in the other, she headed to the base of the statue and crouched next to Erskine's inert body.

He was undoubtedly dead.

He lay on his back, staring vacantly up at the gilded roof high above them. His skin was a peculiar bluish-black colour, and his eyes were bloodshot. There was no visible sign of how he had died, and Shadow could only surmise it was because the angel had willed it. Tumbled to the side was an ornate iron key, and she tentatively picked it up. *The false key.* She tucked it into her jacket pocket and stood to examine the statue.

It towered above her; the only things on her eye level were his feet and the tips of his wings that curled around his ankles, every feather detailed, precise, and flecked with gold and silver.

Between the angel's feet, set into the sweep of his cloth-ing, was a carved panel, filled with symbols she didn't understand, and what looked like numerous keyholes of varied shapes and sizes. *Did they need more than one key?*

One more thing to worry about.

It was clear there was nothing she could do until the others arrived. Shadow turned around, looking to see where her team was, pleasantly surprised to find that they were closer than she expected — almost halfway over. The party clustered together as JD paused at the junction of several bridges.

She had time to explore the rest of the temple, so turning her back on the advancing group, Shadow headed into the temple's depths.

Harlan hated this, which surprised him. He thought he'd love exploring this temple and navigating the path, but it was not what he'd expected. This jumble of collected symbols and sigils, angels and correspondences, was esoteric and frustrating and way beyond his abilities. Give him a regular tomb, any day.

As annoying as JD was, Harlan had to admit that he was brilliant. He led them confidently across the network of bridges with their carved symbols, studying them before gazing at the constellations and planets above—not that he could see that they were planets. It was only JD who insisted they were. It was gratifying to know Harlan wasn't alone in his confusion. Every now and then JD would confer with Jimmy, and then having made his decision, advance a little further. Harlan had had his doubts about Jimmy, but he was glad to be proved wrong—at least for now.

Olivia was next to him, her normally clear brow furrowed with worry, and he lowered his voice, saying, "We're nearly there. Cheer up."

"Yeah, but what then?"

"Let's just cross one bridge at a time," Harlan said, and then grinned. "Excuse the pun. JD is doing well, though."

Olivia nodded. "We have a theory that the tests are tailored somehow to whoever the seeker is."

"That's interesting. What made you think that?"

"We faced a dragon in the Chamber of Fire. Did you?"

"No! Are you serious?"

"Yes. Shadow said they exist in her world, in the Realm of Fire. Weird, yes?"

"Very," Harlan agreed, now even more overawed with The Trinity of the Seeker.

They all shuffled forward again as JD led them onto the next bridge, finally bringing them within close range of Nicoli, whose natural swagger had vanished. He shouted over, "Check the document carefully! Erskine misread it at this juncture, and I ended up here!"

JD faced him. "Misread how?"

"I'm not sure, something about a reversed sign?" He looked frustrated. "I don't know! It was something about Venus and Mars."

"How do we know you're not trying to kill us?" Gabe asked suspiciously.

"Because you're my only way out!" Nicoli snapped. "You think I want to be stuck on this column forever?"

JD nodded and scrutinised the document, while Harlan asked, "How did you get stranded there?"

"Our misstep caused the bridge to disappear, and we ended up in the water. I managed to scramble here, Erskine made it onto the right bridge, and Mia..." He shrugged, his face bleak. "Didn't make it. I'm really hoping you can get me off here."

"We'll try," Harlan said, not wanting to leave anyone

behind, even the slippery, untrustworthy Nicoli. "Although, I have no idea how. You don't want to swim for it?"

Nicoli shook his head. "It looks calm, but there's a fierce current below the surface. I'm not risking it again. Unless, of course, I think I'll be stuck here forever. I'm not there yet."

Harlan nodded, and seeing JD about to step on the next bridge hurried to join the team, terrified he'd be stranded, too. Niel was sticking close to Jimmy, shepherding him at every turn. If Jimmy had any thoughts to betray them he was given no opportunity, although that was unlikely to happen until he was in the temple. Harlan figured all bets were off at that stage.

Shadow waited for her sight to adjust to the gloom behind the statue. There were only a couple of braziers here, but what little light they gave illuminated a collection of objects. *No, weapons.*

Swords, spears, armour, shields, helmets, daggers... All manner of them jumbled together in a heap, like in a dragon's lair. She knelt to better see them, noting their fine engravings and superior quality. They weren't quite as good as fey made weapons, but they were close. *What were they doing here?*

Leaving them, she headed to the back wall, also made of smooth, polished granite, and what appeared to be a door set into it, flush with its surroundings. *Was this their way out?* At the moment it was sealed shut. Then she noticed the strange, fluted striations in the rock on either side of the chamber, all of varying shapes and sizes that stretched far overhead. It was familiar to her, for some strange reason.

However, there was one thing she couldn't see, and that was Raziel's book. She presumed that only the key would reveal it. A clatter of footsteps behind her sent her running to the front of the temple. *The others had arrived.*

Gabe reached the top of the stairs first, and relief swept across his face when he saw her. He strode towards her, and then stopped abruptly, clenching his hands, and Shadow waited too, stopping her ridiculous urge to hug him.

"Shadow. You're okay."

"Just about, after my near death by drowning. Any mishaps on the bridge?"

"None." He glanced behind him to the others clambering up behind him. "JD knows his stuff. He summoned an angel; they know we're here."

She knew he meant the Nephilim. "That was inevitable," Shadow said softly, seeing the worry on his face. "It might mean nothing."

"It might mean everything."

"Come on you two," Nahum said as he reached Gabe's side, his tone light, but his eyes watchful. "It's key time."

27

*G*abe studied the statue of Raziel, craning to see his face far above him.

It was impressive, cold in its beauty, and Gabe wanted nothing more than to see it crumble before him. All of his rage at how they'd been betrayed, double-crossed, and used flooded back. And now that damn book—his final charge from Gabriel—was within his grasp. Shadow stood close by, and his brothers were on either side; he took strength from them all. He only wished his other brothers were here, too. Then he changed his mind. *No.* He was glad they were out of it. He just hoped he'd live to see them again.

His gaze fell to Erskine's dead body that they had moved to the side of the statue, and despite the fact that he'd sent a demon to attack them, he felt sorry that he died here. Then he watched JD, who had now put his papers away, and was instead studying the panel carved into the stone between Raziel's feet.

"What's the deal with the key?" Gabe asked. "How come Erskine had one?"

Harlan laughed, somewhat bitterly. "Turns out, JD's been

holding out on us. There are entry points to this temple across the world, and that means multiple maps, paths and keys. Erskine had the wrong one." He jerked his head at Jackson. "And so does he."

"*What?*" Gabe had thought this was his worst nightmare, but that news topped it. He glanced at Nahum, who shut his eyes at the news. "I don't understand. How does that even work?"

Niel shrugged. "We're not entirely sure. We only found out once you'd entered. Things happened pretty quickly when JD arrived and Jackson told him where he found his key."

Jackson was leaning against the closest column nonchalantly, but his eyes darted everywhere. When he heard his name, he looked sheepish. "Yeah. I found it in Rome. Stupid me. I didn't know."

Harlan added, "Thanks to Niel and Olivia, we realised our key was in St Thomas's Church. I think we found it more by dumb luck than judgement."

"Not true," Jackson corrected him. "We found it because we're smart!"

Gabe remembered the strange, shimmering veil that seemed to be between the Chamber of Wind and the temple. "That veil we passed through—does that have something to do with it?"

"I have no idea," Niel said, baffled.

Jackson shouted, "Hey, Jimmy. Don't stray so far!"

Jimmy was edging to the rear of the statue, but at Jackson's voice he froze, looking mutinous and as if he was about to argue, but seeing everyone staring at him, he crossed his arms and waited.

"Where's the key?" JD barked at Harlan.

Harlan's eyes widened. "'Please' is always polite, JD." He withdrew a simple flute from his pocket and handed it over.

"I don't think there's a place for you to stick that." His tone made Gabe think there was somewhere *specific* he wanted to stick it, and it was nowhere pleasant. "You need to play it. I'm just not sure where."

"A flute is the key?" Gabe strode over, and despite JD's sullen protest, took it from him. In the relief at seeing Niel and Harlan arrive, he hadn't thought to ask about it. "Are you serious?"

"Well, I hope so," Harlan said, "or we're screwed." He frowned at Gabe. "What?"

Gabe faltered. "I guess nothing. It's just not what I expected."

"Can I suggest we get on with it?" Jackson said. "Someone just blow the damn thing. It's clear there's nothing else to do."

JD held his hand out, and Gabe handed it back. "Go ahead, then."

JD raised it to his lips, hesitated, and then blew softly into the pipe. The sound that filled the air was pure and sweet, raising the hairs on Gabe's arm. But as the notes fell away and nothing happened, everyone looked bewildered.

"Why isn't it working?" JD demanded, searching their faces for answers, but none of them had anything to offer.

And then Jackson laughed. "Maybe we're supposed to stick it in Raziel's mouth!" His laughter died as they all stepped back to look up at Raziel's impassive face. "It was a joke. There would be a ladder up his middle, right? Or his back? Or some weird mechanism that would carry us up there?"

"There probably is, somewhere," Harlan said, scanning their surroundings.

"Or a Nephilim could fly it there," Shadow suggested, staring at Gabe. "I've just realised what I saw at the back of the temple."

"There's something behind there?" Niel asked.

"Weapons—lots of them. And weird hollow pipes in the stone walls. It's like an organ...a church organ, or something of the sort."

Unceremoniously, Niel grabbed the flute from JD's hands, thrust it at Gabe and said, "Go. I'll check the back."

Without waiting for anyone's approval, Gabe extended his wings and soared upwards, and the closer he got to Raziel's head, the more he felt as if he was in there, somewhere, lurking behind the icy facade. He passed the open book, held in outstretched hands, carved in marble, the visible pages inscribed with gilded letters, and finally hovered before Raziel's face and his blank eyes. But his lips were pursed, a small hole in the centre, and Gabe held his palm over it, feeling a rush of wind. Gabe studied the flute in his fingers. It was tiny in comparison to the lips, but the game was progressing now and he had to try. And besides, it was the only way to get out of here.

He positioned the instrument and carefully inserted it, feeling it slot into place. Immediately a soft, low tone filled the air, deeper than when JD had played it. The tone quickly changed as it resonated, becoming unearthly, haunting even, and soon it filled the air as accompanying notes rose across the chamber.

The air shifted, turbulence swirling around him, and as shouts reached his ears, he knew he had set something in motion.

———

As soon as the swell of music started, several things happened at once, and Shadow wasn't sure which way to turn first.

The panel between Raziel's feet crashed to the floor, revealing a chamber beyond, and JD, narrowly avoiding being crushed, scooted inside. At the same time, Jimmy started to scream, his hands clutched to his ears, and ran, almost drunkenly, towards the temple steps and the water below.

For an instant they all froze, and then Harlan and Olivia took off after Jimmy, and Jackson, seemingly mesmerised by the temple itself, prowled around the columns, exploring the space. Shadow, however, followed JD, Nahum right behind her.

The interior of the inner chamber was hot and dark, illuminated only by candles that flickered in the hundreds in the surprisingly large space. In the centre, on an enormous stone table, was a thick tome bound in leather. It lay open, its pages humming with power that she could feel across the room, and as Shadow drew nearer she saw that the archaic script inscribed on the pages glowed with a fiery light.

Nahum was close to her, a reassuring presence, and he lowered his lips to her ear. "The oldest grimoire."

Shadow turned to him, seeing his eyes were fixed firmly on JD, who stood before it. "Have you seen this before?"

"Never."

"Are we going to take it with us?"

"Well, that's the question, isn't it?" Nahum answered, finally meeting her eyes. "Gabe thinks not, and I agree with him. It's brought nothing but disaster."

"Not true," she countered. "It enabled mankind to master magic, and gave them freedom."

JD heard them, and spun around, furious. "Of course we're taking it with us! I haven't come all this way for nothing!" He turned his back and stepped forward, holding his hands above the book reverentially, as if scared to touch it. "Just imagine the secrets that it holds!"

Gabe's voice boomed from behind them. "Those secrets

have killed countless people. Don't touch it—it will do you no good."

If JD heard him he gave no sign of it, instead laying his hands either side of the book, and resting his fingers gently on the pages. Within seconds, he was transfixed.

"JD!" Shadow shouted, stepping to his side, alarmed. The pages of the book were moving as if flicked by an unseen hand, and JD stared with unfocussed eyes. Whatever he could see wasn't in front of him.

Gabe was beside her in seconds, and laid his hand on her arm. Shadow had never seen him look more furious—or more desolate. "Don't touch him!"

"What's going on, Gabe? Isn't this what we're here for?"

"Yes and no." He finally focussed on her. "This is our chance to destroy it forever. It's what Gabriel wanted."

"So why doesn't Gabriel destroy it himself? Why do you have to?"

"Because," Nahum said, circling the table and watching JD, "he hasn't been able to get near it. This place has protected it—shielded it from everyone."

Shadow was incredibly confused. "But they're supernatural beings! Surely he can see through this facade!"

"Not if Raziel has been hiding it!" Gabe told her. His lips tightened. "Recording the old God's magic was Raziel's life's work. He was both generous and foolish. You can't give away this kind of knowledge and not expect repercussions!"

"But you said the knowledge in this had freed people. That it enabled them to master their own destiny—shape their world. It gave us witches and an understanding of elemental magic!" Shadow stared at Gabe and Nahum, perplexed. "That's good!"

"Of course it is," Gabe replied, anguished. "I'm all for freedom and independence! But if it gets out again, there could be another disaster; another flood, or volcanic explosion, or worldwide tornados! The old God may stop at *nothing*! Do you want that on your conscience?"

Shadow reeled at his suggestions. *Could that really happen? Were the old Gods still that powerful?* "But Gods care nothing for us! We are *nothing* to them."

"We are something once our knowledge begins to rival theirs."

While they talked, JD was still transfixed by the book, its pages moving faster and faster.

"The book is filling his mind with knowledge," Nahum said. "We have to stop it—now, before we condemn him to being a hunted man. And then find a way to get out of here!"

"Did you suspect this would happen?" Shadow asked, suddenly angry. "Did you warn JD?"

"I didn't know what to expect," Gabe answered. "But yes, I warned him."

JD was shaking now, his eyes rolling back in his head, and Shadow couldn't even imagine what incredible secrets might be flooding through his brain. "Stop him!"

"How?" Nahum asked. "We could be caught in whatever is happening to him."

"Break his grip!" Shadow lunged at JD, but Gabe caught her around the waist before she could get close, pulling her back, and it was impossible to break free.

Shadow shouldn't care what happened to JD, not really, but she did. She thought of Chadwick pursuing his life's dream, and Kian killing him when he found it. She did not want that to happen this time. She had enough blood on her hands already, even though this wasn't really her fault. And then she had another thought.

Still squirming in Gabe's tight hold, she said, "Think about what you've just said—power to rival a God! What if this knowledge turns him into some kind of demi-god with a power he was never meant to wield, and he tries to kill us all?"

That got Nahum's attention, and he wrapped his powerful arms around JD, trying to wrestle him away from the book. But JD was immovable and Nahum cried out, thrown backwards by an unseen force. "Shit! Any other ideas?" he said, regaining his feet.

Gabe finally let Shadow go and she glared at him, but he was already striding around the room, eyes darting everywhere.

"What are you looking for?" she asked.

"Something to use! He must have a weakness, or the book does!"

Slightly mollified that Gabe was taking her suggestion seriously, she and Nahum joined his search. Above the table hung a gilded metal chandelier, a simple circle studded with candles that hung from the roof by chains, and she had an idea.

She jumped on to the stone table behind the book, and shouted, "Gabe, Nahum, one of you help me grab this and pull me backwards! I'm going to swing into him!"

Nahum darted behind her, lifting her higher, and she caught the light by the tips of her fingers until she had a good grip.

"Now!" she instructed.

Nahum grabbed her feet and pulled her back as far as he could, and then pushed her. The momentum wasn't enough —yet. Shadow pulled her knees up to her chest so she cleared JD's head, and then swung back and forth, again and again. When she finally had enough speed, she angled her feet towards JD, and hoped she wouldn't end up falling onto the book instead. She let go and flew forwards, ramming her feet into JD's chest, and they both crashed onto the floor, the collision knocking JD's head hard against the stone, and winding her.

"Herne's horns! Have I killed him?" she gasped, struggling to untangle herself.

Gabe crouched next to her, feeling for JD's pulse and then despite the situation, laughed. "No. He's just unconscious, but he'll have a serious headache! And maybe a few broken ribs." He pulled her to her feet and looked at her with a mixture of admiration and annoyance. "You crazy woman!"

She grinned smugly. "I know. I'm a genius!"

"Certainly one of your more interesting ideas," Nahum said. He bent down and picked JD up, throwing him over his shoulder. "Now what?"

They all swung around to look at the book. The pages were still turning as if by an unseen hand, and power was building in the chamber.

"Take JD and try to find a way out of here, and find Niel," Gabe instructed. "I'm going to find a way to destroy this. And little Miss Fey here is going to help me."

*H*arlan raced after Jimmy, Olivia right behind him, but he was a good distance ahead of them, running like he was possessed.

"What the hell's got into him?" Olivia yelled.

"Something with this damn music!" Harlan shouted, watching with horror as Jimmy jumped down the first step, and then stumbled to his knees before quickly righting himself again. His hands were still clutching his head, and his screams filled the chamber, mixing with the haunting music that resounded around the temple like a horror film.

Harlan bounded down the stairs, his knees jarring painfully. "Jimmy, stop!"But he doubted Jimmy could hear anything. Fortunately, Harlan was getting closer. Just as Jimmy reached the final step and was mere feet away from leaping into the water, Harlan tackled him from above, and they both landed heavily, Harlan feeling his knee crunch into the unyielding floor.

The adrenalin kept the pain at bay, and up close he saw that Jimmy's eyes were wild, and spit flecked his jaw. Jimmy tried to wrestle away, straining to reach the water like it gave off a Siren call, and Harlan didn't hesitate. He punched him, knocking him out cold, and then rolled to the side; his knee felt like it was on fire.

Olivia scooted next to him as he clutched his knee. "Harlan! Are you okay?"

"No. My fucking knee is killing me! Check Jimmy!"

"What's to check? He's unconscious!"

"At least he's not going to drown!" Harlan sat up, the pain in his knee ebbing slightly, and caught sight of Nicoli waving wildly. "Shit. Nicoli is still stranded."

Olivia stood and hauled Harlan to his feet. "I'll go and find Niel or Nahum. Perhaps they'll rescue him. We'll need them to carry Jimmy, too." She studied the steep rise of stairs, frowning. "There's no way I can help lift him up there."

Harlan looked around, frustrated. "This is a shitshow! What were we thinking? I can't concentrate with that god-awful music."

"Heathen! I think some would call it *uplifting*."

"Do you?"

"I might if I didn't think I was going to die here." She set off up the stairs. "Be back soon!"

Niel couldn't believe his eyes. *These were Nephilim weapons.* He bent and picked up a shield, scarred in battle. He recognised the emblem on it—*the House of Tiril*—the mark of one of the fallen. He picked up another—*the House of Baraquel*. One after another, he saw other names, Haures, Exael, Tumael, and he dropped them like they burned.

What were these doing here? Was this a warning to them? Was Raziel screwing with them? Or were they gifts?

Trying to order his chaotic mind, which wasn't easy with the increasingly powerful music vibrating in the air around him, he walked away, examining instead the back of the temple. The doorway that Shadow had mentioned was here, still impassable. But there was no writing on this one. No command to utter. However, this had to be their way out, and it must be triggered by something else. But who knows how deep they had travelled, and how long it would take to get out of there?

He paced the perimeter, looking for anything else of significance, but other than the fluted columns hollowed out of the rock and the pile of weapons, there was nothing.

A shout distracted him. It was Olivia, and she reached his side, breathless. "Can you rescue Nicoli? He's stranded on that column! And then we need help with Jimmy."

"What's he done?" Niel asked, already striding to the front of the temple.

"He went mad—tried to throw himself in the water. It's something to do with the music. Harlan knocked him out."

"Again? The guy's going to have concussion!"

"You started it!" she said. "It was the only way to stop him."

Niel winced with guilt. It was his fault Jimmy was here, but they had needed him. "Can't you and Harlan move him?"

"Harlan smashed his knee, and I can't haul them both up those steps!"

Niel nodded. "Okay. I'll get Nicoli first."

While they talked, Nahum emerged from the inner chamber, JD slung across his shoulder, and he collected Jackson en route, still pacing around the columns. Niel and Olivia intercepted him.

"What happened to JD?" Olivia asked, looking horrified.

"Shadow," Nahum replied bluntly. "It was for his own good. They're trying to decide what to do with the book now."

Jackson looked bewildered. "I think this music is getting to me. This place is surreal!"

This was worrying. The music seemed to be affecting everyone differently. "Go with Nahum," Niel said, concerned. "I think that would be safest."

"Sounds good," Nahum said, adjusting JD's weight.

Niel jerked his head to the rear of the temple. "Wait back there; I'll get the others. The exit is that way—if we can figure out a way to open the door. I'll be with you soon."

Nahum and Olivia nodded, and Niel extended his wings and flew to Nicoli.

Gabe stared at the book, hyperaware of the power flooding from it. "JD's touch must have activated it, or something of the sort."

Shadow nodded, also watching the turning pages. "It probably hasn't been handled for hundreds of years." Her face wrinkled with distaste. "We can't destroy it! It would be wrong. I don't even think we could. The Trinity of the Seeker couldn't be destroyed!"

She was right, Gabe reflected. Destroying a book written by an angel would be impossible. *But...* "We haven't even tried!" He glanced at the dragonium sword in her hand and remembering his own, pulled it from his scabbard. "I'm going to attempt it."

Shadow's violet eyes were wide as she appealed to him. "Gabe! No!"

"Shadow! The old God sent a flood and drowned everyone because he couldn't get it back! Because *I* couldn't get it back!"

He marched over to the book and without hesitation, brought the sword down with enormous force.

A white light flashed, jolted up his arm, and sent him flying back into the wall, half landing on Shadow, and she pushed him off. "Get off, you big lump! I told you so! Have you damaged the sword?"

He looked at her, disgruntled. "No. It's fine. My arm, however, feels like it's been electrified." He struggled to his feet, and pulled her with him. "I guess you're right."

"So you're saying we leave it here, then?" She looked relieved. "Good. We've got the clues to get here. We can hide them again. No one will ever know. It will be stuck here for eternity!"

Gabe folded his arms across his chest. "You're forgetting the other ways to get here! There are other trinities out there."

"How does that even work? Different countries? Different routes?"

"Raziel left opportunities to get here from all over the world! Sneaky bastard." The scale of Raziel's planning really was impressive. "You're from the Otherworld, Shadow. You understand magic. This chamber had some kind of veil over it when we first entered here. I think it's in a special portal all on its own. It's the only thing that makes sense." He suddenly knew what he had to do. "We need to destroy the temple."

She looked at him like he was nuts. "We can't even destroy the book!"

"Do me a favour. Go see what's happening out there. See if there's *something* we can do. I'll wait here."

She stepped close to him, pinning him beneath her suspicious stare. "Don't do anything stupid."

Shadow grimaced as she left the chamber between Raziel's feet. The music in the temple was louder, and everything seemed to tremble—the floor, the walls, and even the water was disturbed, ripples rolling across its surface. Power was building.

They had unleashed something.

She raced around the statue, finding the others clustered by the door set into the rock. Niel was standing over JD and Jimmy, both unconscious. *Probably for the best*, she reflected. Even unconscious, Jimmy looked tortured, his face contorted. Harlan was leaning on Olivia, wincing, Nahum was examining the door, and Nicoli and Jackson were conferring quietly. They shot Shadow a suspicious look as she approached.

"I hope you're not debating doing something stupid," she said, repeating her concern to Gabe, her hand automatically going to her blades.

"Seeing as I've just saved Nicoli's life," Niel pointed out, glaring at him, "he better not be."

"Actually," Nicoli answered, glancing nervously at Niel's wings that were still visible, "I have no intention of crossing you. I'm not insane." He lifted his chin, defiantly. "We're talking about how to open that door. We're supposed to leave with the book. That means the book triggers the exit."

Nahum groaned. "Please don't say that."

"It makes sense," Jackson reasoned, thrusting his hands in his pockets. "That is the purpose of being here, after all—to find the damn thing."

"Look at JD," Shadow said, jerking her head at him. "He laid his hands on it and it possessed him. The flood of knowledge it imparted was huge!"

"And knocked him unconscious?" Harlan asked, bewildered.

"No, that was me," she admitted sheepishly. "But it was the only way of separating him from the book."

"Wait," Jackson said thoughtfully. "JD couldn't control it?"

"It seemed not. I mean, he did for a while, and then *something* happened and he was lost."

Nahum nodded. "She's right. And I've just said a few phrases in the language of fire to try and open this door, and none of them have worked. I even tried fey, and several ancient languages."

Jackson frowned. "Hey guys, I don't know JD well, but he clearly knows his stuff. He navigated us through this madness, summoned an *angel*, and led us across the bridges. He's a *very* clever guy! If he can't handle the knowledge in the book, how can anyone else?" He stared at the Nephilim. "Just who was it that handled this book first time round?"

Nahum answered, glancing warily at Niel. "Adam and Eve. But they were human."

"Not regular humans though, right? From what you said before, they were the first to question their existence. They had longevity in life, as did their children. They must have had some Otherworldly qualities that allowed them to handle the book?"

"*No,*" Niel said, shaking his head vigorously. "They were human—that's all. But they were also chosen by Raziel. From what I heard, he gifted their entire line. Maybe he strengthened them in some way to enable them to absorb this knowledge."

Nahum nodded. "That's true. I hadn't even thought about that. It happened before our time."

"And then the magic leaked out into society," Shadow said, remembering her conversation with Gabe. "Humans learned how to manipulate it. Maybe JD tried to absorb too much, too soon."

"Well, I don't think one of us *humans* should risk it," Olivia said. Her natural buoyancy and enthusiasm had gone, and now she looked tired. "I don't want to die down here. One of *you* needs to get the book."

"We cannot return it to the world. It's too dangerous," Niel insisted. "We came here to stop this from happening, not enable it!"

Nicoli laughed bitterly. "It's too late! Events have been set in motion now! Look at this place. We have to leave!"

"And damn the consequences?" Nahum said, rounding on him angrily. "This book brought about mankind's destruction!"

"And liberated it!" Harlan said quickly. "Don't forget that."

If Nahum heard him, he didn't show it. He was still glaring at Nicoli. "No one asked you to come here! You came because someone paid you a lot of money. You didn't give a shit about the consequences then!"

Nicoli clenched his fists and shouted, "I had no idea what they were!"

"Do your fucking homework!"

Shadow had never seen Nahum look so angry.

Olivia stepped between them, pushing them apart. "*Stop it*! This is not the time for macho posturing. No one wants to die down here! Get the damn book, and open the door. Let's think about what we do with it after!"

Nahum took a deep breath and nodded at Shadow. She ran back to Gabe, finding him pacing the chamber.

"Progress?" he asked hopefully.

"None. And the atmosphere is ugly—Nahum and Nicoli nearly had a fight."

"Nahum? Not Niel?" Gabe asked, shocked.

"Yep. We think we need Raziel's book to open the door. It's the trigger, and the door is our only way out."

His face fell. "*No.*"

"Gabe," she pleaded, "see reason. We need to leave. You can't hear it in here, but the weird music is getting louder out there, and the whole place is shaking. Time is running out!

We need to leave—now!" She crossed her arms. "If you don't pick it up, I will."

Tight-lipped he turned, braced himself, and quickly slammed the cover shut and picked the book up. He went white, shaking slightly.

"Gabe, what's happening?"

"Nothing. I'm okay."

"You don't look okay."

"I can feel its power, that's all." With that, his jaw clenched, he left the chamber, with Shadow running behind him.

*a*s soon as Gabe stepped out of the inner chamber, the entire temple rocked as if a bomb had exploded beneath it, and the smooth granite walls that had emitted only starlight were suddenly covered in the blazing script of the language of fire.

"Herne's hairy bollocks!" Shadow exclaimed next to him. "What have we done?"

"Something terrible," he answered darkly.

The water was rising in the pool, waves rolling across the bridges, and in the seconds they stood there, they cracked and fell into the churning depths. The book was thrumming with power, and Gabe felt it pulsing through his arms and chest. This might be what Raziel wanted, but it wasn't good. He had cursed Gabriel at the time for asking him to find this book. He had raged, in fact, furious that his life had been dragged back to the service of angels—and not the fallen ones. At least they had an earthy humour, and a liking for humans.

But now, feeling the book and the power it held, Gabe knew he couldn't let it return to the world. He didn't even trust the witches with it. But equally, he couldn't let everyone die down here. Once again he berated himself for letting so many people come along on this mad search. If it was just himself and JD, he'd willingly die down here, and he'd be prepared to sacrifice JD, too. But that wasn't an option.

He ran to the rear of the temple, Shadow beside him, and with every step they took, the chamber shook even more, chunks of rock crashing around them. Even the statue was shaking. He did a double-take as he passed the weapons on the floor, but he kept running until he reached the others, clustered around their exit. Nahum was carrying JD, and Niel was carrying Jimmy. Everyone looked terrified.

As Gabe skidded to a halt, script appeared on the door; he looked at Nahum and Niel, taking a deep breath. "Are we sure about this?

"Yes. Do it," Nahum said, and he saw everyone's relief as he spoke.

Gabe faced the door and uttered the words of command. The door swung wide, revealing a passageway ahead, script blazing along its walls and illuminating their way. With the barest moment's pause, Nahum led the way out.

Harlan's knee was throbbing, and adrenalin was the only thing that kept him going.

He let the others go before him, worried he would hold them up, but Shadow pushed him ahead. "Go on. Gabe and I will go last."

"But I can't run properly!"

"It's fine. I'm not going to leave you behind!" She pushed him, and he limped down the long passageway.

The ground still shook, even out there, and he heard the crashing of masonry over the haunting music that continued to resound around them. And then he passed through *something*, the veil that that kept the temple suspended somewhere in time and space. The well-lit passage disappeared, and he was suddenly stumbling through darkness, the ground uneven beneath him. He fumbled for his flashlight, relieved when it switched on. He could just about see Olivia up ahead and heard her shout, "Harlan, come on!"

"I'm coming as quickly as I can!"

It was only then he realised that the ground had stopped rumbling, and the sound of the unearthly music and the destruction of the temple had disappeared, leaving an eerie silence in its wake. When he looked around, he found that Shadow and Gabe were no longer there, either.

Shadow was just about to follow Harlan through the veil that protected the temple from the world when she heard Gabe's footsteps slow.

She stopped and turned. "What are you doing?"

"I'm staying here. Go."

"*No.*" She crossed her arms, resolute.

His face was impassive, and he clutched the book to his chest. "This cannot leave here. The rest of you are safe. Go without me."

"You'll die here."

"I told you that I'm prepared to do that."

Shadow's pulse sounded in her ears and she felt dizzy. The thought of never seeing Gabe again was horrible. "I won't leave you. There's got to be another way."

"There isn't. You can see what this book can do. It had its place—once. But not now." His fingers tightened on the leather bound tome, his knuckles whitening, as if she would wrest it from him, and his dark eyes were hard.

She stepped closer to him, feeling his heat. "You don't want to do this. You've got your life back now. It's just beginning!"

"They know we're back. Our life will never be what we want it to be."

"You don't know that! You're letting Niel get to you," she said, growing angry. "And you can't leave your brothers!"

Gabe's eyes softened as he appealed to her. "By keeping the book here, I'll have earned them some freedom. We'll have paid our dues. Now go."

She started to panic. *He really meant it.* "Leave it here, in this passageway, and we'll pass through the veil—we're close enough! That would work." She stumbled as the ground shook. "Look around you. Everything is being destroyed."

"I don't know that. Leaving it here may stop the destruction. The temple may right itself." His eyes were full of regret, and her heart ached. "I can't risk that. Go. Please."

Shadow took another step towards him, tentatively, as if he might flee. "That's illogical. The same applies if you stay with it! The book will survive, but you won't! It has to cross that threshold!"

"*No.*"

"You are the most exasperating man I have ever known!"

"I'm not a man."

"You are a shit!"

He smiled and reached out a hand to stroke her cheek, and his touch was like a brand on her skin. "I'll miss you, too."

Another rumble resounded around them, and the smooth, granite surface of the walls began to crack. For a second Gabe staggered, and Shadow saw her chance. She whipped out her knife and stabbed his bandaged hand that was holding the book, and he cried out in shock, releasing it. She grabbed it, turned, and ran.

"You'd better come get it, Gabe!"

And then she plunged through the veil.

Cursing Shadow as his wounded hand throbbed, Gabe stumbled after her.

She was his friend, his partner, and he never thought she would betray him. *Never.* But now... The veil flickered, and Gabe threw himself through it, landing on the other side with a crash, and found himself in a rough-hewn stone passage. Water was pouring down the walls and along the ground, and he saw Shadow up ahead. She stopped, looked behind her, grinned, and then took off again, and with a roar, he followed.

"I am going to kill you!" he yelled.

"You've got to catch me first!"

And that was the problem. She effortlessly negotiated the way ahead, and he lost sight of her on occasion. There was no sign of the others, and he hoped they were far ahead by now. *How long was this path? How far underground where they?*

The path widened, and Gabe soon arrived at the entrance to a large cavern. It was deafening. Water roared around them, pouring down the walls and thundering into a churning lake below. The stone lip that ran around the edge was uneven and slippery, and at the far side he saw his other companions racing along a narrow ledge, disappearing into another dark passageway. The cavern narrowed at that point, and the lake plunged into a shallow cave at the base.

Shadow was moving quickly, and she had virtually caught up to Harlan at the rear. Gabe started running, and then wondered why. *He could fly. This place was big enough.* He pulled his clothes off, extended his wings, and sailed off the ledge, the spray splashing over him. It was freezing in here but he ignored it, getting ever closer to Shadow.

She paused, as if waiting for him, and for a second he couldn't work out what she was doing. She was above the highest fall of the cave, the water racing below her. Craggy rocks jutted from the slippery walls, and she started clambering down them. He swooped towards her, but just as he got close, she dropped like a stone into the churning water below.

And then something very ominous happened. The entire chamber shook, as if there was an earthquake. But he hadn't got time to question it.

He folded his wings away and dived in after her.

The water was icy, and it felt as if a hand reached into his chest and squeezed his heart. For a second he couldn't see anything, and he flailed in the current. Then he spotted her, almost crushed beneath the flow of water against the bank of the lake. She wriggled into a gap, and disappeared.

The current was insanely strong, and it took all of his strength to reach her. She had slipped inside a skinny cleft of rock, and there was no way he could follow her. The only part of her still visible was her foot, and he grabbed it and hauled her out. But she wasn't carrying the book anymore, and he was running out of air. So was she.

He pulled her in front of him, pressing her against the rock walls to prevent her from being swept away, and then gripping the rocks tightly, hauled them both to the surface, taking huge breaths of air when they finally reached it.

When he'd got his breath back, he yelled, "What the hell are you doing?"

"What does it look like, you big, winged idiot?" she asked. "I'm hiding the book!"

Gabe blinked with surprise. "What?"

"You didn't actually think I was going to let it get to the

surface, did you?" She stared at him, annoyed. Her hair was plastered to her head, and her skin looked almost blue. "No one will find it here. I wedged it in there, tight, and shoved a rock in front of it. It's gone, Gabe!"

He fell over his words. "But it might break free, or someone may find it!"

"Look around! The cavern is collapsing. Will you stop arguing with me for once? Let's get out of here."

For once? Cheeky madam. She was the one that argued, not him!

Shadow started to clamber up the slippery walls to the rocky ledge above, and for a second Gabe hesitated, looking at the icy pool and debating just how secure the book was. Then a massive chunk of rock splashed into the water, almost taking him with it, and he realised she was right.

It was time to leave.

Niel hustled the others along the path. If they didn't get out of here soon, they would drown or be trapped down here forever. Fortunately, the ground was rising steeply now, and with renewed energy everyone was running, slipping, falling, and then running again.

Fresh air streamed around him, and a patch of pale grey light appeared far ahead, as Nahum shouted, "Come on, we're nearly there!"

Jimmy was still over Niel's shoulder, groaning on occasions as he regained consciousness, but Niel had ignored him, he'd been so set on their escape. He paused and looked behind him, seeing Olivia running back to grab Harlan. She ducked under his arm, helping him limp towards their exit.

But there was still no sign of Gabe or Shadow.

"Where are they?" Niel asked, scared to hear the answer.

"They're behind us," Harlan said, "somewhere."

Niel nodded, wanting to run back, but instead he pressed on, finally emerging on a shallow hillside strewn with rocks. He put Jimmy down, noting the others were standing around, taking deep breaths and looking relieved at being alive.

It was still raining, but only a fine drizzle now, and he estimated it must be close to dawn. He sought Nahum out, and found him standing over JD, trying to rouse him.

"Nahum, I'm going back in. Gabe and Shadow are still in there."

"What?" Nahum straightened quickly. "How far back?"

"I last saw them in the cavern," Harlan explained, grimacing as he leaned heavily on Olivia. "But it was collapsing." As he spoke, the land shuddered beneath them, and the ground cracked. "What now?"

"Run!" Niel urged them. "All of you, go! This whole place is going to collapse."

Nahum paled. "JD is still out."

"Go, brother. See that they all get away." He looked beyond Nahum, seeing that Jackson supported the other side of Harlan, and was virtually frog marching him up the rise to the fields beyond. Nicoli had grabbed Jimmy and was helping him to do the same. "Take JD."

Niel had backed towards the entrance, ready to re-enter, and Nahum was about to argue, when something hit Niel from behind, knocking him off his feet, and he heard Shadow say, "Get out of the way, you big lump! Are you trying to kill me?"

He lay flat on his back, staring up at her irate expression, and then grinned as Gabe emerged behind her. "You're here!"

Shadow grinned back at him, her hands on her hips, soaked to the bone. "Of course I am! You can't get rid of me that easily."

Gabe was behind her, a wry smile on his face, and there was no sign of the book.

"Where is it?" Niel asked.

"Gone, but," Gabe said, swaying as the ground shook beneath them, "I suggest we discuss this another time."

He pulled Niel to his feet, Nahum grabbed JD, and they all ran to catch up with the others.

Harlan stood on the rise, his conspirators next to him, surveying the scene of devastation below.

A whole chunk of the hill they had emerged from had collapsed, forming a narrow ravine. In places, small openings were visible, but water poured from many of them, as underground streams found their way to the surface. Somewhere under all of that was the cavern. He wouldn't be surprised if there was another collapse eventually, but for now he was just happy to get his breath and rest his aching knee.

"So," Niel asked Gabe. "What did you do with it?"

Gabe looked at Shadow, amused. "Maybe you should ask Shadow, not me."

She shrugged, nonchalantly. "I hid it, in the cavern's pool, in a place I doubt anyone will ever find. Especially now."

"You did *what?*" JD was rousing, a mixture of fury and disbelief on his face.

Shadow looked at him, utterly unconcerned. "It's too dangerous for this world. Gabe was right. No one should ever get their hands on Raziel's book. It almost killed you."

He glared at her. "It did not!" He struggled to his feet, and Olivia helped him, but he almost brushed her off he was so cross. "I remember it…fragments, at least. It's still here." He tapped his head. "Unbelievable knowledge! Like a glimpse into another world."

"Good. You got something out of it, then." Her face hardened. "Mia, Jensen, and Erskine are all dead." She jabbed him in the chest, and he winced. "And so would you be if it wasn't for us. Be grateful for what you have."

"You still work for me!" he said, squaring up to her.

Harlan tried not to cheer as Shadow's knife suddenly appeared beneath JD's chin. "Say that again, you miserable little man, and I'll show you exactly what I think of that statement. I am fey. I work for who I choose."

Wow. She was impressive. Shadow had dropped her glamour, and her Otherness was arresting. And JD had it coming. He really had been irritating. He noticed Nicoli looking at Shadow with new appreciation, and intense speculation. That didn't bode well.

Gabe, however, laid a restraining hand on her arm, and said to JD, "I wouldn't test that threat." He held his hand out, showing his blood-stained bandage. "She stabbed me—and she likes me. I'm not sure what she thinks of you. Best not to risk it."

JD's face twisted with emotion but he remained mute, and he shifted his glare from Shadow to Gabe. "She needs a leash."

Gabe leaned in close. "Watch your mouth." He stepped back and took a deep breath. "Come on guys, home time." He looked around, narrowed his eyes, and then pointed across the hills. "That way."

Olivia murmured, "Bloody Hell," as she ducked under Harlan's arm again. "Come on old man, I'll help."

"Not so old, thank you! This injury was caused by an act of bravery." He glanced over his shoulder at Jimmy. "At least Jimmy looks okay now."

Jackson had fallen into step beside them. "Yeah, what was that about? The music was odd, and really got inside my skull, but not like Jimmy." He called over to him. "Your head okay?"

Jimmy shrugged. "I've got a splitting headache...not sure if that's from the punch or the hideous noise. Either way, I'm glad to be out of there."

"Yeah, sorry about the punch," Harlan said. "It was the only way to stop you from jumping into the water."

"I'm not sorry," Niel admitted.

Jimmy shot him an annoyed look. "I was only doing my job!"

Nicoli gave his slippery smile. Despite being soaking wet and covered in mud, he still managed to look charmingly ruthless. "My instructions. It's just business. I'm sure we'll have the pleasure again."

"I can't wait!" Niel said dryly.

"I couldn't help but notice—" Nicoli pointed to Niel's shoulders. "You appear to have wings that have now somehow disappeared!"

"Ah, those! Yes, they are useful."

"Care to explain?"

"No." And grinning broadly, Niel turned away, leaving Nicoli looking perplexed.

"Is JD keeping up?" Harlan asked Olivia, worried. "Best not to lose him now."

"He's behind us, with Nahum." She lowered her voice. "Things might be tricky at work for a while. I'm hoping this won't get us fired."

"We'll be just fine. And besides, I know too much for him to get rid of me that easily." Seeing Olivia's puzzled face, Harlan realised he'd said more than he should have, so he shut up and concentrated on hobbling to the car.

3 0

*H*arlan sat in front of Mason's large antique desk, Olivia next to him, and tried not to show his annoyance.

It was early on Sunday afternoon, and Mason had called them into the office to discuss the events of the previous few hours. Harlan had showered at the house in Angel's Rest, so he was at least clean, but he was also exhausted and wanted to go to bed. He had really hoped this conversation could wait. At least Olivia had taken JD home, which was a good thing, because he was so annoyed with him, he could barely look at him. Apparently, the feeling was mutual.

Mason grimaced. "As I'm sure you know, JD is extremely unhappy about the outcome of The Trinity of the Seeker. I am annoyed for him." He glared at both of them as if he was the headmaster and they were schoolchildren. "I would like some assurances that this won't happen again."

Harlan exchanged a glance with Olivia, noting she was as furious as he was, and said, "Mason, you have *no* idea what happened in that temple. It was insanity! We're talking old school mojo, angels, the oldest grimoire known to man, and unbelievable power! We did the world a favour!"

Mason shuffled uncomfortably. "Be that as it may, JD wanted that book, and we are here to enable his acquisitions—"

Olivia broke in, cutting him off. "And damn the consequences? I don't think so, Mason." She leaned forward, gripping the table. "Half of Nicoli's team died in there! Erskine Hardcastle—the notorious necromancer—is dead! Did you want us to let JD die, too?"

Mason sat back, chastened. "Of course not."

"Then you have to trust us, your agents in the field, to make the right decisions," she said. "JD was not in the right mind to make a rational choice."

Harlan backed her up. "Nicoli and Jackson Strange also agreed—and that's saying something."

"And that's another thing," Mason said, firing up again. "Since when do we work with the opposition? Especially The Order of Lilith!"

"We weren't working *with* Nicoli," Harlan said scathingly. "He got in there first! Jackson was helping us because he had the key...or thought he did. Anyway," he shrugged, "he was very helpful in the end. I wouldn't have found the right key without him. Like Olivia said, you have to trust your field agents. We know what we're doing, Mason."

"Actually," Olivia said, weighing in, "I'm not very impressed with JD's attitude!"

"What?" Mason said, surprised. "What do you mean?"

"He seemed to suggest that Gabe was replaceable. I don't like that kind of thinking. No one is expendable here—not me, not Harlan, not Gabe, not Shadow. We are not his tools to be discarded when they no longer suit, or when better options come along." She banged the table. "As my immediate manager, I expect you to look after my interests, too—not just JD's. Do you understand?"

"I'm with her," Harlan said, wishing he'd thought to say exactly that.

Mason clenched his jaw. "You can be sure I take your safety seriously."

"Good! Remind JD of that!" Olivia stood abruptly. "Now, I am very tired and need my bed."

Harlan stood with her, deciding to capitalise on Mason's discomfort. "Yeah, this meeting is over, Mason. See you tomorrow."

And without another word, and leaving Mason fuming, they exited the office, Olivia slamming the door behind her.

Shadow had never been more grateful to be home, and she looked around at her brothers lounging in the living room with a big smile on her face. *Well, they all felt like brothers, except for Gabe. She wasn't entirely sure what he was.*

He sat next to her, his brooding presence magnetic, and she tried not to touch him. She could still feel his hand on her cheek. Every time their skin brushed she felt sparks, and she wasn't sure that was a good thing.

The farmhouse was warm and comfortable, music was playing, and for once, they were not killing each other in a simulated game; they were chatting instead. Zee and Ash had cooked, and they were eating informally, a delicious spread of Middle Eastern and Mediterranean food laid out on platters on the coffee table in front of the fire.

They had left Angel's Rest early that morning. The trek back to the cars at the bottom of the gorge had taken well over an hour, as they'd had to skirt the newly collapsed area. It was already on the news, blamed on unusual earthquake activity and something about sinkholes. They had parted ways fairly amicably with Nicoli and Jimmy, although Jimmy had barely spoken a word. Nicoli, a sly smile on his handsome face, had told her he'd be in touch, and she just nodded. He could get in touch all he wanted; he wasn't getting anything from her.

Once back at the rented manor house, Jackson had kissed Olivia and Shadow's hands with exaggerated manners, thanked them profusely for the entertainment, and quickly left. Olivia had then bandaged up Harlan's swollen knee, and both had given JD a wide berth. In fact, they all had. JD was still fuming, and Shadow couldn't decide what to make of him. Yes, he was a clever man, and a skilled alchemist. He *was* over 500 years old, after all. But, he was also annoying, fussy, and pretentious. They had packed up all of the information on The Trinity of the Seeker for JD to take back to his estate, and then left Olivia and Harlan to close up the house after promising to call them soon.

"Penny for your thoughts," Gabe said, nudging her gently.

She smiled. "Just thinking about today. It's been a weird one."

"That's one word for it," he said, watching her in a way that brought goose bumps to her skin. "You stabbed me in my already injured hand!"

"For your own good."

Barak heard her and gave his big booming laugh. "Shadow! You have some nerve."

"It's true." She turned away, glad for an excuse to break Gabe's stare. "If it wasn't for me, Gabe would still be in that temple."

She reached forward and topped up her plate, feeling the shift in mood. Underneath the relief at Gabe, Shadow, Niel, and Nahum being home again, there was worry.

Nahum was shaking his head. "I can't believe you were going to do that, Gabe."

Gabe just shrugged. "I felt it was the only option."

"Fortunately, I made him see sense," Shadow said, pleased with herself. "Even though I did nearly drown trying to hide the damn thing."

"Well," Eli said brightly, "I am very grateful for your headstrong nature and willingness to stab anything that stands in your way. Even if you are a pain in the ass most of the time."

He was sitting on the floor cushion in front of her and she smacked him across the head. "You're lucky I know that you don't mean that!"

"Yeah, right," he grumbled.

"Seriously though, guys," Zee said, "did you really feel Chassan, Niel?"

Niel nodded. "Yes. JD summoned an angel to help cross the Chamber of Wind, and he appeared... Well, was present. I didn't *see* him. And at least it wasn't Raphael."

"Who's Raphael?" Shadow asked.

"He's an archangel," Niel explained to her. "Archangels are more powerful, and highly unlikely to appear in this realm. It doesn't suit them. Chassan is a lesser angel."

"But even so," Eli said, looking horrified. "For any of them to appear is major!"

"Did he say anything?" Zee persisted.

"Just, 'welcome back.'"

The room fell silent, and Zee rubbed his face wearily. "What does that mean? *Hi, great to see you, we'll leave you to it! Enjoy your life.* Or," he lowered his voice, making it sound more ominous, "*Hi, you unimportant worm, you'll be hearing from us!*"

"I don't know!" Niel said, frustrated. "It was non-committal!"

"So, it could mean anything," Barak concluded. "And Raziel? Was he there?"

Gabe answered that. "I didn't sense him, even when I carried his book. The whole place felt like it was set on automation. But surely he'll know his book is gone?"

"I'm not convinced," Nahum said. "That temple could have existed for a very long time—since well before Hammond's time. He may have put his book there and then got distracted!"

"With what? His laundry?" Niel asked sarcastically. "This is his big project. How likely is it he'd have forgotten about it?"

"Maybe he has other stuff brewing?" Gabe suggested thoughtfully. "Or maybe we'll wake up one day and find he's set the lesser angels on us."

"Any sign of the fallen?" Ash asked quietly. He'd been sitting and watching them, as was his way, Shadow reflected, taking it all in. But he'd hit the crux of the matter. *Their fathers.*

"No," Gabe said firmly. "Other than Chassan, there were no other angels present. Not even Gabriel, who set me off on this search in the first place. If he ever finds out what happened today, I expect a pardon!"

"Hold on," Shadow said, trying to work out all of the angels and their allegiances. "If Chassan was summoned to help you cross, that means he would know about the book. Why would he want to help?"

"Because the angels took sides," Ash explained. "Some thought The Book of Knowledge should be used by those who were worthy and clever enough to deserve it. Chassan was one of them. Most did not. It caused a war, remember, the war that led to the fallen."

"So, several angels might have known about the trinity," Shadow reasoned.

"Yes." Ash nodded.

"And were the fallen for the book, or against it?"

"There was a mix of opinions," Gabe said. "The war triggered many things, and not all fell because of Raziel's book. From what I can gather, many stayed with divided opinions, too. It's…complicated."

Shadow nodded, still confused. "Seems so."

"And what about JD?" Barak asked, reaching for his beer. "Sounds like he wasn't exactly pleased?"

"He was furious," Nahum conceded. "All the way to the car he brooded and tutted. Muttering about magic that underpins the world and being denied his history." He rolled his eyes. "What a strange man."

"You could argue that it's a noble pursuit," Ash pointed out. "Men like him have furthered everyone's knowledge."

"It's not that," Nahum said. "It's *him*. He's so fussy! So exacting!"

"You don't learn the secret to immortality by being sloppy," Shadow said. "His house is fascinating. Despite his odd ways, I think I like him."

Niel laughed at that statement. "You held a knife to his throat and called him a miserable little man!"

Shadow winced, recalling her flare of annoyance. "Well, he said that he *employed* me! I really don't like that assessment of our relationship. He offers a job, and I choose whether to take it or not. That's different."

"Too right, sister!" Zee said, raising his beer in salute. "And as far as future jobs go, anything else on the horizon?"

"Not yet," Gabe answered. "Although, I'm keen to avoid tombs for a while—and angels, if at all possible."

"And what if they come to us?" Ash asked.

Gabe shrugged, an expression of grim determination on his face. "Then we deal with it, on our terms, because I'm not prepared to lose our independence. Not now. Not ever."

Shadow watched him, hoping he was right, but fearing that the future might prove more complicated than they had all hoped.

Whatever happened, she'd be with them all the way.

Thanks for reading *Shadow's Edge.* Please make an author happy and leave a review here.
This book is a spin-off of my White Haven Witches series. The first book is called *Buried Magic,* and you can buy it here.

If you enjoyed this book and would like to read more of my stories, please subscribe to my newsletter at tjgreen.nz. You will get two free short stories, *Excalibur Rises* and *Jack's Encounter,* and will also receive free character sheets of all the main White Haven witches.

By staying on my mailing list you'll receive free excerpts of my new books, as well as short stories, news of giveaways, and a chance to join my launch team. I'll also be sharing information about other books in this genre you might enjoy.

Read on for a list of my other books.

ALSO BY T J GREEN

Rise of the King Series

A Young Adult series about a teen called Tom who's summoned to wake King Arthur. It's a fun adventure about King Arthur in the Otherworld!

Call of the King #1

King Arthur is destined to return, and Tom is destined to wake him.

When sixteen-year old Tom's grandfather mysteriously disappears, Tom stops at nothing to find him, even when that means crossing to a mysterious and unknown world.

When he gets there, Tom discovers that everything he thought he knew about himself and his life was wrong. Vivian, the Lady of the Lake, has been watching over him and manipulating his life since his birth. And now she needs his help.

The Silver Tower #2

Merlin disappeared over a thousand years ago. Now they will risk everything to find him.

Vivian needs King Arthur's help. Nimue, a powerful witch and priestess who lives on Avalon, has disappeared.

King Arthur, Tom, and his friends set off across the Otherworld to find her, following Nimue's trail. Nimue seems to have a quest of her own, one she's deliberately hiding. Arthur is convinced it's about Merlin, and he's determined to find him.

The Cursed Sword #3

An ancient sword. A dark secret. A new enemy.

Tom loves his new life in the Otherworld. He lives with Arthur in New Camelot, and Arthur is hosting a tournament. Eager to test his sword-fighting skills, Tom is competing.

But while the games are being played, his friends are attacked and everything he loves is threatened. Tom has to find the intruder before anyone else gets hurt.

Tom's sword seems to be the focus of these attacks. Their investigations uncover its dark history, and a terrible betrayal that a family has kept secret for generations.

White Haven Witches Series

Witches, secrets, myth, and folklore, set on the Cornish coast!

Buried Magic #1

Love witchy fiction? Welcome to White Haven—where secrets are deadly.

Avery, a witch who lives on the Cornish coast, finds that her past holds more secrets than she ever imagined in this spellbinding mystery.

For years witches have lived in quirky White Haven, all with an age-old connection to the town's magical roots, but Avery has been reluctant to join a coven, preferring to work alone.

However, when she inherits a rune-covered box and an intriguing letter, Avery learns that their history is darker than she realised. And when the handsome Alex Bonneville tells her he's been having ominous premonitions, they know that trouble is coming.

Magic Unbound #2

Avery and the other witches are now being hunted, and they know someone is betraying them.

The question is, who?

One thing is certain.

They have to find their missing grimoires before their attackers do, and they have to strike back.

If you love urban fantasy, filled with magic and a twist of romance, you'll love *Magic Unbound.*

Magic Unleashed #3

Old magic, new enemies. The danger never stops in White Haven.

Avery and the White Haven witches have finally found their grimoires and defeated the Favershams, but their troubles are only just beginning.

Something escaped from the spirit world when they battled beneath All Souls Church, and now it wants to stay, unleashing violence across Cornwall.

On top of that, the power they released when they reclaimed their magic is attracting powerful creatures from the deep, creatures that need men to survive.

All Hallows' Magic #4

When Samhain arrives, worlds collide.

A Shifter family arrives in White Haven, one of them close to death. Avery offers them sanctuary, only to find their pursuers are close behind, intent on retribution. In an effort to help them, Avery and Alex are dragged into a fight they didn't want but must see through.

As if that weren't enough trouble, strange signs begin to appear at Old Haven Church. Avery realises that an unknown witch has wicked plans for Samhain, and is determined to breach the veils between worlds.

Avery and her friends scramble to discover who the mysterious newcomer is, all while being attacked one by one.

Undying Magic #5

Winter grips White Haven, bringing death in its wake.

It's close to the winter solstice when Newton reports that dead bodies have been found, drained of their blood.

Then people start disappearing, and Genevieve calls a coven meeting. What they hear is chilling.

This has happened before, and it's going to get worse. The witches have to face their toughest challenge yet—*vampires.*

Crossroads Magic #6

When Myths become real, danger stalks White Haven.

The Crossroads Circus has a reputation for bringing myths to life, but it also seems that where the circus goes, death follows. When the circus sets up on the castle grounds, Newton asks Avery and the witches to investigate.

This proves trickier than they imagined when an unexpected encounter finds Avery bound to a power she can't control.

Strange magic is making the myths a little too real.

Crown of Magic #7

Passions run deep at Beltane—too deep.

With the Beltane Festival approaching, the preparations in White Haven are in full swing, but when emotions soar out of control, the witches suspect more than just high spirits.

As part of the celebrations, a local theatre group is rehearsing *Tristan and Isolde*, but it seems Beltane magic is affecting the cast, and all sorts of old myths are brought to the surface.

The May Queen brings desire, fertility, and the promise of renewal, but love can also be dark and dangerous.

AUTHOR'S NOTE

Thanks for reading *Shadow's Edge*, the second book in the White Haven Hunters series. I really enjoyed writing this and developing Shadow, the Nephilim, and The Orphic Guild characters further. It was also a lot of fun inventing new occult organisations, too.

I owe a big thanks to my Facebook group, TJ's Inner Circle. I asked them for help with occult organisation names, and they were amazing! Thank you! I used several of their suggestions in this book, and more will no doubt pop up in the future. Thanks to Jeff Kelly who suggested The Order of Lilith; Terri Cormack for Seekers of the Lost; Sally Minoli for The Grey Order; Shelley Anne Lewis for The Order of the Chalice and Blade; Lynda Cunliffe for Finders of the Forgotten; Elizabeth Storch Monticue for Occult Acquisitions.

If you'd like a chance to get involved in my books and join my fabulous group, just answer the question and I'll let you in - https://www.facebook.com/groups/696140834516292

This story is set in the Mendips in England, although

Angel's Rest is fictional. It is an area that is well known for its caverns, but I have obviously taken a few liberties! The Book of Knowledge also appears in many biblical stories, but again, I have twisted the tales to suit my own purposes. There's a blog post about it on my website.

I am still planning on writing a few short story prequels —for Shadow certainly, and hopefully Harlan and Gabe, too.

If you enjoy audiobooks, *Spirit of the Fallen*, White Haven Hunters #1, is being turned into an audiobook right now, and this book will follow soon.

Thanks to my fabulous cover designer, Fiona Jayde Media, and to Missed Period Editing.

I owe a big thanks to Jason, my partner, who has been incredibly supportive throughout my career, and is a beta reader. Thanks also to Terri and my mother, my other two beta readers. You're all awesome.

Finally, thank you to my launch team, who give valuable feedback on typos and are happy to review on release. It's lovely to hear from them—you know who you are! You're amazing! I also love hearing from all of my readers, so I welcome you to get in touch.

If you'd like to read a bit more background on my stories, please head to my website—www.tjgreen.nz—where I blog about the research I've done, among other things. I have another series set in Cornwall about witches, called White Haven Witches, so if you enjoy myths and magic, you'll love that, too. It's an adult series, not YA.

If you'd like to read more of my writing, please join my mailing list. You can get a free short story called Jack's Encounter, describing how Jack met Fahey—a longer version of the prologue in the Call of the King, my YA Arthurian series—by subscribing to my newsletter. You'll also get a FREE copy of Excalibur Rises, a short story prequel to Rise of the King.

Additionally, you will receive free character sheets on all of my main characters in White Haven Witches—exclusive to my email list!

By staying on my mailing list, you'll receive free excerpts of my new books, as well as short stories and news of giveaways. I'll also be sharing information about other books in this genre you might enjoy. Finally, I welcome you to join my readers' group for even more great content, called TJ's Inner Circle, on Facebook. Please answer the questions to join! https://business.facebook.com/groups/696140834516292/

Give me my FREE short stories!

https://tjgreen.nz/

ABOUT THE AUTHOR

I write books about magic, mystery, myths, and legends, and they're action-packed!

My primary series is adult urban fantasy, called White Haven Witches. There's lots of magic, action, and a little bit of romance.

My YA series, Rise of the King, is about a teen named Tom and his discovery that he is a descendant of King Arthur. It's a fun-filled, clean read with a new twist on the Arthurian tales.

I've got loads of ideas for future books in all of my series, including spin-offs, novellas, and short stories, so if you'd like to be kept up to date, subscribe to my newsletter. You'll get free short stories, character sheets, and other fun stuff. Interested? Subscribe here.

I was born in England, in the Black Country, but moved to New Zealand 14 years ago. England is great, but I'm over the traffic! I now live near Wellington with my partner, Jase, and my cats, Sacha and Leia. When I'm not busy writing I read lots, indulge in gardening and shopping, and I love yoga.

Confession time! I'm a Star Trek geek—old and new—and love urban fantasy and detective shows. My secret passion is Columbo! My favourite Star Trek film is The Wrath of Khan, the original! Other top films for me are Predator, the original, and Aliens.

In a previous life, I was a singer in a band, and used to do some acting with a theatre company. On occasion, a few friends and I like to make short films, which begs the question, where are the book trailers? I'm thinking on it…

For more on me, check out a couple of my blog posts. I'm an old grunge queen, so you can read about my love of that here. For more random news, read this.

Why magic and mystery?

I've always loved the weird, the wonderful, and the inexplicable. My favourite stories are those of magic and mystery, set on the edges of the known, particularly tales of folklore, faerie, and legend—all the narratives that try to explain our reality.

The King Arthur stories are fascinating because they sit between reality and myth. They encompass real life concerns, but also cross boundaries with the world of faerie —or the Otherworld, as I call it. There are green knights, witches, wizards, and dragons, and that's what I find particularly fascinating. They are stories that have intrigued people for generations, and like many others, I'm adding my own interpretation.

I also love witches and magic, hence my additional series set in beautiful Cornwall. There are witches, missing grimoires, supernatural threats, and ghosts, and as the series progresses, even weirder stuff happens.

Have a poke around in my blog posts, and you'll find all sorts of articles about my series and my characters, and quite a few book reviews.

If you'd like to follow me on social media, you'll find me here:

Facebook, Twitter, Pinterest, Instagram, BookBub.

facebook.com/tjgreenauthor
twitter.com/tjay_green
instagram.com/tjgreenauthor

Printed in Great Britain
by Amazon